D1479271

THERE'S NOTHING I CAN DO *When I Think of You Late at Night*

WEATHERHEAD BOOKS ON ASIA *weatherhead east asian institute, columbia university*

WEATHERHEAD BOOKS ON ASIA

weatherhead east asian institute, columbia university

LITERATURE

David Der-wei Wang, Editor

Ye Zhaoyan, *Nanjing 1937: A Love Story*, translated by Michael Berry (2003)
Oda Makato, *The Breaking Jewel*, translated by Donald Keene (2003)
Han Shaogong, *A Dictionary of Maqiao*, translated by Julia Lovell (2003)
Takahashi Takako, *Lonely Woman*, translated by Maryellen Toman Mori (2004)
Chen Ran, *A Private Life*, translated by John Howard-Gibbon (2004)
Eileen Chang, *Written on Water*, translated by Andrew F. Jones (2004)
Writing Women in Modern China: The Revolutionary Years, 1936–1976, edited by
    Amy D. Dooling (2005)
Han Bangqing, *The Sing-song Girls of Shanghai*, first translated by Eileen Chang,
    revised and edited by Eva Hung (2005)
Loud Sparrows: Contemporary Chinese Short-Shorts, translated and edited by
    Aili Mu, Julie Chiu, Howard Goldblatt (2006)
Hiratsuka Raich, *In the Beginning, Woman Was the Sun*, translated by
    Teruko Craig (2006)
Zhu Wen, *I Love Dollars and Other Stories of China*, translated by Julia Lovell (2007)
Kim Sowol, *Azaleas: A Book of Poems*, translated by David McCann (2007)
Wang Anyi, *The Song of Everlasting Sorrow: A Novel of Shanghai*, translated by
    Michael Berry with Susan Chan Egan (2008)
Ch'oe Yun, *There a Petal Silently Falls: Three Stories by Ch'oe Yun*, translated by
    Bruce and Ju-Chan Fulton (2008)
Inoue Yasushi, *The Blue Wolf: A Novel of the Life of Chinggis Khan*, translated by
    Joshua A. Fogel (2009)
Anonymous, *Courtesans and Opium: Romantic Illusions of the Fool of Yangzhou*,
    translated by Patrick Hanan (2009)

HISTORY, SOCIETY, AND CULTURE

Carol Gluck, Editor

Takeuchi Yoshimi, *What Is Modernity? Writings of Takeuchi Yoshimi*, edited and
    translated, with an introduction, by Richard F. Calichman (2005)
Contemporary Japanese Thought, edited and translated by Richard F. Calichman
    (2005)
Overcoming Modernity, edited and translated by Richard F. Calichman (2008)
Theory of Literature and Other Critical Writings by Natsumi Soseki (2009)

CAO NAIQIAN

TRANSLATED BY JOHN BALCOM

THERE'S NOTHING I CAN DO

When I Think of You Late at Night

columbia university press NEW YORK

This publication has been supported by the Richard W. Weatherhead Publication
Fund of the Weatherhead East Asian Institute, Columbia University.

Columbia University Press
Publishers Since 1893
New York   Chichester, West Sussex

Library of Congress Cataloging-in-Publication Data
  Cao, Naiqian, 1949–
  [Dao heiyi xiang ni meibanfa. English]
  There's nothing I can do when I think of you late at night / Cao Naiqian ;
  translated by John Balcom.
     p.   cm. — (Weatherhead books on Asia)
  ISBN 978-0-231-14810-8 (alk. paper)
  I. Shanxi Sheng (China)—Social life and customs—Fiction. I. Balcom, John.
  II. Title. III. Series.
PL2932.A683D3613   2009
895.1'352—dc22
2008040954

References to Internet Web sites (URLs) were accurate at the time of writing.
Neither the author nor Columbia University Press is responsible for URLs that may
have expired or changed since the manuscript was prepared.

Designed by Chang Jae Lee & composed by Anne Landgraf/Brooklyn BookWorks

CONTENTS

INTRODUCTION *The Austere Lyricism of Cao Naiqian*

John Balcom

Cao Naiqian was born in 1949 into a farming family in rural Shanxi. He was sent to school in Datong, but often spent his summers in a rural village. From an early age he was a voracious reader, preferring China's realist classics. He also developed a great fondness for Western literature in translation. After graduating from high school in 1968, he worked in offices in a mine and later in a factory. He is an accomplished singer and can play a number of musical instruments. When it was discovered that he had some talent as a writer, he was assigned to the Public Security Bureau, where he wrote reports. Following a quarrel with his superior, he was sent out to a rural village for one year to supervise a group of urban youth who had been sent down to the countryside during the Cultural Revolution. It was an impoverished village, and the experience was a formative one for Cao as a writer. When he began to write fiction, he drew upon his memories of rural life. The story of how he came to write is interesting in itself. He began writing in 1986, at the age of thirty-seven, as the result of a bet. A friend of his, while visiting his home, commented on his extensive library but said that one book was missing from the collection. Cao asked which one. His friend replied, "Yours." The two made a bet as to whether Cao could break into print within a year. Cao won.

Despite being a fine writer for three decades, Cao has had a small following until only recently. He is not a professional writer who can devote himself exclusively to crafting fiction—he has a day job as a detective in the Public Security Bureau—and his output to date has been small and sporadic. His writing has appeared over the years in a variety of literary publications, and did attract the attention of some critics early on. He also went through a ten-year hiatus in which he wrote and published little because he was taking care of his ailing mother. The stories that make up *There's Nothing I Can Do When I Think of You Late at Night* (the title comes from a folk song) were begun in the mid-1980s and appeared irregularly over the years, most in the early 1990s after Cao received a small stipend from the Shanxi Writers Association that allowed him to write without interruption for a period of three years. The novel was published in its entirety in Taiwan only in 2005. A mainland edition was published in 2007 and was one of the ten best books of the year on one list. A good deal of interest in Cao's writing has been generated by the efforts of Goeran Malmqvist of the Swedish Academy.

Another factor that perhaps limited interest is that as a writer Cao stands clearly in the realist tradition, the mainstream for fiction in China before and throughout the twentieth century. These days, when postmodernism dominates critical discourse and literary production has moved online, Cao's work may seem more like a throwback to earlier times in that it deals with the lives of poor peasants from Shanxi province and is written in the regional dialect (perhaps yet another reason it was for a while overlooked). But such a view would be mistaken, because Cao's oeuvre represents a significant expressive advance in modern Chinese fiction, especially in the representation of peasants and rural life. But still, it is within the context of the realist tradition that his work takes on additional significance.

Literature in China, since the Yen'an Forum on Literature and the Arts in 1942, has been subservient to politics and decidedly realist. In May 1942, Chairman Mao summoned the Yen'an writers and artists to a conference to reaffirm Party authority over all spheres of life in the base areas under Communist control. The conference, which lasted twenty-three days, had been called in response to criticism of the Party. In his opening remarks, Chairman Mao set out several issues for discussion: the writer's position, attitude, audience, work, and study. In his concluding remarks, Mao laid down his views that in literature, politics comes before art for both readers and writers. Mao stated that literature is not independent from politics but is a political tool, and that proletarian literature should be the political tool for the Chinese Communist Party. On publication a year later as *Talks at the Yen'an Forum on Literature and the Arts,* the record of the conference became the official policy of the CCP for the next forty years or more.[1]

One of the most accomplished writers in post-Yen'an China was Zhao Shuli (1906–70), born in Qinshui, Shanxi. His works, largely positive accounts of the communist liberation and reform in the rural areas, were seen as the successful embodiment of Mao's dictums. Zhao's first novel, *Changes in Li Village,* concerns the fortunes of peasants in a Shanxi village, led by the CCP, as they appropriate political power from the landlords and local officials. His second novel, *Sanliwan Village,* was the product of extensive fieldwork and his experience in rural areas and details the collectivization process. In an ironic twist of history, his work came under increasing ideological criticism beginning in the early 1960s. In the heyday of revolutionary realism in later years, he was criticized because he focused too heavily on "middle characters," those whose ideological position could not be readily identified. Zhao perished during the Cultural Revolution. In another, doubly ironic twist of history, much of his work has been dismissed as propaganda since the 1980s. However, his early fiction will be remembered for its contribution to the creation of a new written language to represent peasant speech in modern Chinese fiction.[2]

Cao uses the language of rural Shanxi province in his writing, and builds upon the legacy of Zhao Shuli. The use of dialect is an important feature that gives Cao's writing much of its pungent character and veracity. Even Chinese readers will have some difficulty with the text. However, it is well nigh impossible to convey the dialect quality in English. The use of rural language, in fact, posed one of the biggest challenges in translating this book. In the process, I compiled about fifty pages of lexical items related to ecology, material culture, social culture, organizations, customs, ideas, and slang.

The Wen Clan Caves, the village depicted in the book, is based on a real village Cao where spent a year during the Cultural Revolution. He had trouble with his boss in the Public Security Bureau and was forced to lead a group of young people from the city after they were sent down to the countryside. The village, located just 3 miles from the border of Inner Mongolia, contained 30 households of approximately 200 people. Life was hard due to the poor, arid land of extreme temperatures. People survived largely through subsistence agriculture, raising beans, oats, and millet. The villagers lived in poverty and lacked education. Some of the tales are based on actual events in the village or those Cao learned about growing up, when his father was a political cadre, and after he himself went to work as a policeman. Although based on fact, Cao's Wen Clan Caves is also a fictional, imagined place, like Faulkner's Yoknapatawpha County or Garcia Marquez's Macondo. Creating this place allowed Cao to, as he has said, write these stories to tell readers a hundred or a thousand years from now that people once lived this way. It is his artistry that makes the tales more than mere reportage.

Cao is an excellent storyteller, and the economy of expression and understatement of his writing are unique in contemporary China. His style is as austere as the place he writes about, but his work is also a lyrical evocation of the lives of people who rarely, if ever rise above the realm of necessity. This same lyrical economy or austerity is also at work on the formal and structural level. Although Cao considers the book a novel, most readers will find that it actually lies somewhere between a novel proper and a collection of short stories. It consists of thirty interlocking stories depicting the lives of a group of uneducated people in a remote village of cave dwellings in Shanxi province during two years (1973–74) of the Cultural Revolution. On a structural level, *There's Nothing I Can Do When I Think of You Late at Night* provides a comprehensive view of the village through multiple perspectives. A series of well-wrought tales take the place of a single overarching plot. The order of the stories also contributes to the overall power of the work. For example, the pastoral tale of childhood innocence, "Flushing out Ground Squirrels," precedes and serves to heighten the horror and the tragedy of "Corncob." In the complementarity and cumulative strength of its parts, the book resembles Sherwood Anderson's *Winesburg, Ohio* as well as William Faulkner's *The Unvanquished* and *Go Down, Moses* and Erskine Caldwell's *Georgia Boy*.

Cao once commented that the entire book is concerned with the basic instincts for food and sex. The social nexus depicted in the novel is centered on this struggle for material production and reproduction, and can perhaps best be summed up with words from the *Book of Rites*, one of the Confucian classics: "The things which men greatly desire are comprehended in meat, drink and sexual pleasure; those which they greatly dislike are comprehended in death, exile, and suffering" (VII.2.20 Liji).[3]

The content is unique in contemporary writing because it deals with a number of taboo subjects, such as polyandrous relationships, incest, bestiality, and adultery. In China the two areas that are typically off-limits in literature are politics and sex. Cao's stories contain no graphic descriptions of sex, but small portions of some were deleted by editors when they were published in the PRC. As in much of modern Chinese fiction, politics is present. However, Cao's stories have not been censored in this regard, presumably because they critique the political excesses of the Cultural Revolution and not the current powers.

A good example of this is found in the story "Dog." The main character is a humble, uneducated peasant who knows only the honor and dignity of work. Like the other characters in the book, Dog is often preoccupied with food and sex, but he is also selfless and hardworking. There are a couple of telling passages that come toward the end of the story. Dog is on his way to the commune to run some errands for the village. Hail begins to fall and he takes shelter in a pile of hay. The hailstones grow larger. Dog notices that the hail is damaging mud bricks made by the commune members. He braves the hailstones and covers the bricks with straw, thereby saving them from destruction. Naturally, his selfless deed is reported—and embellished—as it is pushed up the political ladder.

When reporters eventually arrive in the village to interview Dog about why he risked his life to save public property, he responds that he doesn't know anything about male and female property. With the simple play on one word ("public" and "male" are homophonous in Chinese), Cao is able to fully bring out Dog's simplicity and naïveté. His point of reference is male and female, not public and private. As a poor peasant, he has always worked for whoever holds power. In fact, when the reporters continue to question Dog, he proudly informs them of how the Japanese had praised his work. Everyone else in the village is smart enough not to mention anything of the sort, and they berate Dog for saying such things. But he is more interested in letting people know that he works hard. Cao's depiction of the simple peasant is truthful as well as humorous and ironic, another feature of his writing style.

This sort of irony would have been ideologically unacceptable for most of the history of the PRC. Indeed, the very "backwardness" of his peasant characters is an indicator of how things have changed in China. Liu Shaoqi (1898–1969), vice chairman of the CCP and president of the PRC, was the most senior victim of the Cultural Revolution. In an article titled "The Class Character of Man," written in 1941, he had criticized the backwardness of China's peasants. His comments were repudiated during the Cultural Revolution as vilifications of the masses of workers and peasants. Writers were supposed to depict peasants as heroes of ideological purity who were leading the country toward a communist paradise. Cao's character, fixated as he is on food and sex and totally lacking in correct ideology, would have been unimaginable just decades ago. The story can also be read as a commentary in the sense that the peasants are as old as the land itself; they adapt to the political situation and survive, usually outliving whatever government or political system may be in place—a position that once could have been fatal for an author.

Throughout the book, the Party and its representatives are depicted as bullying, selfish, largely ineffectual, and reluctant to get involved in anything unless it concerns their own interests. Old Zhao, the cadre sent down to the countryside, has a good heart but expects sexual favors in return for his assistance to the village women when it comes, say, to finding a good job for a child. The Brigade Leader and the Accountant are both depicted as bullies, forcing people to participate in political activities and struggle sessions. However, in cases where their authority is actually needed, they tend to disappear from the scene and request assistance from a Party committee with a police function. But even such a committee will shy away from any situation that could be perceived as dangerous. When justice is meted out, it is usually an unnamed, grizzled old man, a village elder, who does the dirty work. One gets the impression that that is how things have been done since the beginning of time, and that's the way things will be handled in the future. There is a certain sense of timelessness about the village and its ways.

Cao Naiqian is a talented, if not natural-born writer, greatly sympathetic with the fate of the most downtrodden of his compatriots. As he himself has said, he is concerned about the poverty-stricken peasants of China because he himself is of peasant stock. This sympathy for his fellow man and the unflinching way he portrays the tragic lives of those whom many would consider disposable give power and authority to his work. His art is in his ability to raise it all to the level of poetry through his austere lyricism, and he has created one of the finest and most memorable books to come out of China in recent years.   Monterey/Dallas/Paris, 2009

ACKNOWLEDGMENTS

Translating Cao Naiqian's masterly novel has been an immensely rewarding experience, though also difficult at times. This translation would not have been possible without the help of a number of people. First I would like to thank my friend Goeran Malmqvist, sinologist, member of the Swedish Academy, and the Swedish translator of Cao Naiqian's work, for encouraging me to undertake this project in the first place. Cao Naiqian patiently answered my numerous queries and explained his work with the detail and clarity of a fine teacher. A tip of the hat to Howard Goldblatt, friend and mentor, for his Uncle Pothook. I am grateful to Leslie Kriesel, my editor at Columbia, for her sensitive editing and attention to detail. Last, but not least, I also thank my wife, Yingtsih, a translator herself, for having the patience to read through the many drafts as the book took shape over the last year and for her incisive comments, which have made this a far better and more accurate translation than it might otherwise have been.

Portions of this introduction appeared in a slightly different form in my "Bridging the Gap: Translating Contemporary Chinese Literature from a Translator's Perspective," which was published in *Wasafiri* 55 (2008): 19–23. I thank *Wasafiri* for allowing me to quote from that article.

NOTES

1. This paragraph on the Yen'an Forum is drawn from *The Literature of China in the Twentieth Century* by Bonnie S. McDougall and Kam Louie (New York: Columbia University Press, 1997), 194–195.
2. The information on and evaluation of Zhao Shuli are summarized from ibid., 220–224.
3. James Legge, trans., *Li Chi, the Book of Rites* (Hyde Park, N.Y.: University Books, 1967), 380.

THERE'S NOTHING I CAN DO *When I Think of You Late at Night*

The In-law

The early morning silence was broken by the braying of a donkey outside the courtyard.

Blackie said, "That fucking In-law is here for you."

The woman said, "Don't let him in. Wait till I put on my pants."

Blackie said, "Shit, what difference does it make?"

Blushing, the woman said, "Why don't you just tell him I'm sick? It is that time of the month, anyway."

"How can I do that?" asked Blackie. "We Chinese always keep our word."

Blackie went out to meet the In-law.

The In-law straightened the frame of the courtyard gate, tied the donkey to the frame, and then straightened it once more.

Blackie shouted back to the cave: "Go fetch a chicken for our In-law. I'll go borrow a bottle of wine from Uncle Pothook."

"In-law," said Blackie's In-law to him, "I've brought a bottle. I always drink yours."

Blackie said, "Shit, what's with this 'mine' and 'yours'?"

Head lowered without looking at anyone, Blackie's woman set off to get a chicken from the coop.

"No, no, no, don't bother. A village cow fell and died last night," shouted the In-law to Blackie's woman. "I went to the Brigade Leader's house to borrow a donkey and the whole fucking place was filled with the smell of cooking beef."

The In-law untied a bag from the neck of the donkey and said, "Here. If it's tough, cook it some more."

Head lowered without looking at anyone, Blackie's woman took the bag and went into the cave.

Drinking some wine, Blackie said to his In-law, "Her period started two days ago. Maybe you'll want to come back when her period's done."

His In-law said, "Fine with me."

Blackie said, "The Brigade Leader will surely deduct work points for using the Brigade's donkey, so you two had better leave today. Anyway, you have to wait till her period's done before you do it."

The In-law replied, "Fine with me."

Blackie said, "Bring her back next month, because I can't borrow a donkey here."

The In-law replied, "Fine with me."

Without glancing at them, Blackie's woman sat on the ground inside the cave and busied herself while listening to the two men talk.

After the men finished drinking, Blackie said to the woman, "Put on your clean clothes so the village doesn't laugh at you."

The In-law said, "No, no, no, don't bother. I can stop at the commune and buy her some cotton pants."

Blackie said, "I can't let my In-law go to that expense."

The In-law said, "That's fucking nonsense."

Blackie saw off his woman with his In-law, over one ridge after another and down one gully after another.

The In-law said, "You head back; I'll continue up the mountain."

Blackie said, "You continue up the mountain; I'll head back."

Blackie turned back with hesitation. The In-law raised his large hand and slapped the donkey on the rump. The donkey perked up, brayed, and trotted off.

Shit, off with you. By taking a thousand less, they really gave you the woman. Shit, off with you. Anyway, it's only for one month a year. We Chinese always keep our word, thought Blackie as he walked back.

He turned around for another look.

Blackie saw his woman's feet swinging back and forth like two turnips down around the donkey's belly.

Blackie's heart was swinging back and forth, like those two feet that looked like turnips.

Women

Wen Hai finally took a wife. The whole village was pretty happy about
it. But people listening outside the bridal chamber said that Wen Hai's
woman wouldn't let him do it. She tied her red sash in a knot that
couldn't be undone. She cried and cried all night long.

Later it was said that Wen Hai's woman not only refused to take off
her pants for him, she also refused to work in the fields. When Wen
Hai returned from working in the fields, she refused to cook for him
too. She cried and cried all day long.

Later the whole village was in an uproar because, while they could
forgive her for not taking off her pants at night, they couldn't forgive
her for not working in the fields and cooking during the day.

"In all the generations of the Wen Clan Caves, this has never happened," people said to Wen Hai.

"What should I do?"

"You think she'll obey without a beating?"

"How can I do that?"

"Ask your mom," said the old man whose face looked like a mountainside field that had been plowed but not harrowed and whose
beard resembled the stubble left on graves grazed by sheep.

Wen Hai asked his mom. His mom replied, "A tree's branches must
be knocked off if it is to grow straight. It's the same with a woman."

After listening to his mom, Wen Hai went home and beat the living
daylights out of his woman. He beat her black and blue.

The people listening outside the bridal chamber said it worked. He
got on top of her and did it. All he kept saying was, "Fuck your mother,
your old man is going to give it to you. Your old man had to plunk
down two thousand for you. Fuck your mother, your old man is going

to give it to you. Your old man had to plunk down over two thousand for you."

"Wen Hai's dad disciplined his mom in exactly the same way," someone said.

Later, Wen Hai's woman cooked for him.

After that, Wen Hai's woman would follow him at a distance, shovel on her shoulder, out to the fields.

"Tsk, tsk, black and blue."

"Tsk, tsk, black and blue."

So spoke the women working in the fields, pursing their lips in contempt as they winked and shook their heads.

Leng Er's Madness

Nobody knew why Leng Er went mad; and nobody knew why his madness went away.

Leng Er's dad had asthma on account of his unsavory past. Licorice shoots had no effect, so he decided to go up to the mine and see Leng Da for some ephedrine. Leng Er's mom said, "Go! We haven't seen a cent from him in six months. While you're at it, get some cement bags from him." Leng Er's dad trembled and shook as he climbed up on the night-soil cart going to the mine.

Leng Er went mad the day after his dad left, crazy as the time before—from morning till night, he did nothing but shout "Kill, kill" and strike the *kang*.

Leng Er lay on the *kang* looking up. He stretched out his large black palms and struck the *kang* as if he were swinging a flail at the threshing ground. When he got tired of slapping the *kang*, he would press his head to the *kang*, raise his body, and shout, "Kill, kill." When he got tired of shouting, he'd return to striking the *kang*.

Leng Er's mom kept watch over him and never left his side.

If he really kills someone, it's over; if he really kills someone, it'll be the devil to pay, Leng Er's mom thought as she sat by the cooking platform, her eyes wide open. She would think for a while, then lift the lapel of her coat and wipe her eyes, then think some more and then lift the lapel of her coat and wipe her eyes.

Leng Er often said, "We're so fucking poor we can't even afford steamed bread made of pure oat flour. It's always potatoes." Leng Er's mom would reply, "We want to save some money for you." Leng Er would say, "Shit. Think of how many fucking years it'll take to save two thousand just by not eating steamed oat bread."

This time, Leng Er's mom made some steamed oat bread for him, but he refused to eat it. He just remained stretched out and shouted, "Kill, kill" and slapped the *kang*. He struck it so hard that he tore the cement bags covering the *kang*, exposing its mud surface.

The villagers all said that if the barefoot doctor was of no use in such a case, the local shaman ought to be consulted. Leng Er's mom shook her head. She knew it was all of no use. She knew from the last time that it wasn't the barefoot doctor or the shaman who cured him.

If he really kills someone, it'll be over; if he really kills someone, it'll be the devil to pay, thought Leng Er's mom.

But the people in the village had no idea which morning of what day it was that they no longer heard Leng Er shouting "Kill" and slapping the *kang*.

Leng Er lay curled up, snoring on the *kang*.

"Has he eaten?" someone asked Leng Er's mom as she was carrying water.

"Yes."

"Is he all right?"

"Yes."

"What made him well?"

"Yes." Leng Er's mom hurried away.

Leng Er's dad came back on the night-soil cart. Leng Er's dad said that Leng Da's wife decided not to give them any money, just some ephedrine. He also brought back some cement bags.

Like the time before, Leng Er's mom told his father nothing about Leng Er's bout of madness. Leng Er's dad didn't bother himself about how badly shredded the *kang* cover was last time, nor did he trouble himself this time. The only thing Leng Er's dad troubled himself about was getting ephedrine. As long as he had the ephedrine pills to chew, he was okay. He claimed that chewing a fucking pill was enough to make him feel real good.

Leng Er's mom took apart the cement bags, removing the brown paper and boiling it till it was soft, and then mashed some boiled potatoes into a paste. With the potato paste, Leng Er attached the soft brown paper to the shredded *kang* cover.

It's better than killing someone; it's better than having to pay the devil, thought Leng Er's mom.

Leng Er's mom sat by the cooking platform watching Leng Er paper the *kang*. She thought for a while, then lifted the lapel of her coat and wiped her eyes, then thought some more before lifting the lapel of her coat to wipe her eyes.

In a Nest of Oat Straw

Everything was quiet and the threshing ground shone white by the light of the moon. He and she made a nest for themselves in the side of a pile of oat straw facing the moon.

"You climb in."

"You climb in."

"Let's climb in together then."

The two of them burrowed into the nest, making it collapse. The oat straw gently fell from the rack, burying them.

Opening his thick arms, he raised up the straw.

"Never mind. This is pretty nice, isn't it?" she said, snuggling against him.

"Yeah."

"You probably hate me, don't you, Brother Chou?"

"No. Heizi from the coal pit has more money than I do."

"I don't spend his money. I'll save it so you can get married."

"I don't want it."

"I want to save it."

"I don't want it."

"You have to have it."

Hearing her on the verge of tears, he shut up.

"Brother Chou," she said after a long while.

"Huh?"

"Brother Chou, give me a kiss."

"Don't be that way."

"I want to."

"I don't feel like it today."

"I want to."

She sounded like she was on the verge of tears, so he lowered his head and gave her a peck, ever so gently and softly.

"Not there, here," she said, puckering her lips.

He kissed her on the lips, ever so cool and moist.

"What do you taste?"

"What do you mean, what do I taste?"

"On my lips."

"Oat flour."

"Wrong. Try again," she said, pulling down his head.

He kissed her again and said, "Still oat flour."

"Nonsense. I just ate some rock candy. Try again." She pulled his head down again.

"Rock candy, rock candy," he hurriedly said.

They were both silent for a long while.

"Brother Chou."

"..."

"Brother Chou."

"Huh?"

"Well, let's do it first tonight."

"No! No! The moon is out tonight. It's forbidden for the girls of our Wen Clan Caves to do that."

"Well, later then. When I get back from the mine."

"..."

Again they were both silent for a long while. They could hear the moon moving and breathing outside.

"Brother Chou."

"What?"

"That's fate."

"..."

"We both have bad fates."

"Mine's bad; yours is okay."

"No it's not."

"Yours is okay."

"No it's not."

"Sure it is."

"It's bad and that's all there is to it. . . ."

When he heard her crying, he wept as well. *Pit-pat* fell his warm tears onto her face.

Uncle Pothook

Uncle Pothook had to be carried back again from the wild, overgrown graveyard.

Pothook was an outsider from a different province. He had no relatives in the village, but everyone called him Uncle Pothook. When he got drunk, he made no distinction between age and seniority and wanted to be everyone's uncle. The villagers, regardless of age, all referred to him as uncle.

In the village of the Wen Clan Caves, he was one who wanted to drink every day and was able to do so. Uncle Pothook's younger brother, Penkou, was a provincial official. Every month without fail he sent him twenty or thirty *yuan*, and just as surely he'd spend it all on drink.

Uncle Pothook would drink without eating, and he warmed his wine. His way of heating wine was different from the way used by other people. He had a pocket in the crotch of his pants into which he would insert the bottle of wine. He'd take a couple of swigs and then replace it. Then he'd take another couple of swigs and replace it.

Uncle Pothook would let other people partake of his wine.

"Come on, have a fucking sip of my wine," he'd say, inhaling to make room in his wrinkled belly. He'd reach down to his crotch and pull out the bottle of wine, which would be nice and warm. In addition to the aroma of the wine, there'd be another smell.

Some declined to drink; others didn't and lifted the bottle like a bugle and drank it down.

His eyes narrowing in a smile, Uncle Pothook would tilt his head and watch the others drink. His mouth would move as if he were pouring the drink down his own gullet.

Whenever Uncle Pothook had had plenty to drink, he'd head to the graveyard with the same two lines from the beggar's song on his lips:

During the day, I climb your wall when I think of you
Late at night, there's nothing I can do when I think of you.

Upon arriving at the graveyard, he'd collapse spread-eagled atop a large blue boulder and sleep. If it was warm, he'd strip completely naked and the ants and beetles would crawl up and down all over him.

"Go on! Go down to the graveyard and carry Uncle Pothook back before he catches cold," the older people would say to one of the younger people, who'd then call several of the other young people together to go after him.

If he was sobering up when they found him, they'd tease him. "Uncle Pothook, jump like a tiger for us."

"I'm too old now," he'd reply.

"You're not old," they'd say as they pulled up grass and began braiding it into rope. Uncle Pothook would hoist up his rear, stick the rope in the crack of his ass, and crawl around on all fours.

"Jump! Jump!" they'd all shout.

Uncle Pothook would open his mouth and roar. After roaring, he would fix his eyes on one of the men and charge. The grass rope would stay fixed in the crack of his ass, swinging back and forth with that little thing hanging between his legs. This went on until everyone was doubled over with laughter.

They carried Uncle Pothook back from the graveyard, but on this occasion he only spat out a few words and never regained consciousness.

He said, "Bury me with Widow San."

All the villagers were caught off guard by his words. All they could do was to stare at one another.

Men

Old Zhuzhu sat cross-legged in front of the oil lamp, his eyes fixed on the movements of two fluttering moths. The sudden beating of their clumsy wings drove them against the lamp. The lamp flame flickered under their wings, throwing the cave into moments of darkness.

Old Zhuzhu couldn't stand watching the two moths being burned alive, so he flung them away.

He pricked up his ears trying to hear what was being said in the western room—his woman and his younger brother Young Zhu were still talking.

Half the night spent talking, and they were still at it. It should take no time to determine if something is round or square, but they were still talking. Young Zhu liked nothing better than talking with his sister-in-law. This didn't escape Old Zhuzhu's notice.

"Sister-in-law, Sister-in-law, I remember you were fourteen when you had your firstborn. Could you really have a baby when you were only fourteen?"

"Sister-in-law, Sister-in-law, some of the people who have been sent down to our countryside think that you and I are together and that my older brother is your father-in-law. Isn't that funny?"

"Sister-in-law, people say that your second child looks like me. They say that I help my brother in all things. What kind of talk is that?"

Young Zhu dared to say such things even in the presence of his brother Old Zhuzhu.

Old Zhuzhu always figured he said even worse behind his back. Old Zhuzhu believed his brother had a fucking thing for his sister-in-law. At first, whenever he had such thoughts, he would grow anxious;

later he was never troubled by such thoughts. At first he hoped that Young Zhu would hurry up and get married and live his own life elsewhere; later such thoughts and hopes never crossed his mind.

Things will be determined this very night, thought Old Zhuzhu.

Old Zhuzhu looked at the *kang*. Two young men with close-cropped heads were sleeping there. Normally they slept in the western room with their uncle, but their mother had to reach an agreement with their uncle that very night. After dinner, Old Zhuzhu had the two boys stay in the room with him.

Ai—twenty-four or twenty-five years old is twenty-four or twenty-five; and twenty-eight or twenty-nine years old is twenty-eight or twenty-nine. Why didn't I have a daughter? A daughter would have been nice. I could have traded a daughter for a daughter-in-law, thought Old Zhuzhu.

Young Zhu was nearly forty and still unmarried. Over the years, he had saved enough money for a wife, but there was no woman for him—this was wrong or that was wrong. A few days earlier, someone had mentioned a widow from Inner Mongolia. The problem was that she had three sons who would come with the marriage. Young Zhu said, "What should I do? If I don't get this one, I'll never get one."

"You can't do it. Can't you see it would be the pit of hell? You can't do it. Once you were married, there would be no going back," said Old Zhuzhu.

The two moths returned. First one flew against the lamp, then the other one, then both together. They struck the flame, and the cave flickered between light and dark.

Zi! Half a wing of one of the moths was burned away; smoking, it fluttered off into the darkness. The other moth kept fluttering around the flame.

"See. That's good, just don't touch the flame," said Old Zhuzhu, looking at the moth with the burnt wing.

It had flown into the darkness and couldn't be seen. Old Zhuzhu turned to look at the other moth. It was still striking the lamp, but growing more frenzied. It was as if it were in a fight to the death with the lamp.

What's the obsession? Why the need to fly at the flame without regard for life? wondered Old Zhuzhu.

What's the obsession? They have to fly at it, they have to fly at it, thought Old Zhuzhu.

Ai—I've got it. In this world, men have no future, just like these moths. Women are like the lamps that drive men to their deaths. Men hurl themselves at the women, but in the end, isn't it still a disaster? thought Old Zhuzhu.

That's just the way it is, isn't it? That's just the way it is, thought Old Zhuzhu.

Old Zhuzhu pricked up his ears. The talking in the western room seemed to have ceased.

Resolved—had it been resolved? Old Zhuzhu felt both startled and happy. He slid off the *kang* and slipped over to the door. He raised his backside and thrust his head forward to listen. The talking of moments ago had ceased, replaced by a different sound. Old Zhuzhu wasn't sure if he really heard something or if he was imaging it.

Resolved. Old Zhuzhu's heart trembled. He hurriedly looked at the close-cropped heads of the two young men sleeping on the *kang*.

What should he do? *Twenty-four or twenty-five years old is twenty-four or twenty-five; twenty-eight or twenty-nine years old is twenty-eight or twenty-nine,* thought Old Zhuzhu.

He thought about having a look. That sound, real or imagined, was again coming from the western room, but louder and clearer, making Old Zhuzhu's head spin. He quickly looked at the two youngsters sleeping on the *kang*. Only then did that sound diminish and fade away.

The moth with the burnt wing returned unsteadily to flutter around the lamp flame again. It was not steady on its wings, but all the same it wanted to fly at the flame.

But Old Zhuzhu couldn't have cared less now. Watching it fly toward a fiery death, he couldn't care less. He knew there was nothing he could do about it. He could do something this time, but not next time; he could do something today, but maybe not tomorrow. He knew that the moth was something that hurled itself at the flames. It lived to hurl itself at the flames. It was that simple.

Zi! The other wing of the moth began to smolder. It flapped the stump several times before falling on the lamp stand. Belly up, legs flailing in the air, it sought to right itself, but couldn't. Its efforts to right itself were ever more futile.

Plop! The other moth fell on the lamp stand, its legs unmoving. It had been burned alive.

See, and so it dies, thought Old Zhuzhu.

Ai—taking a wife has its own worries, just as not taking a wife does. Anyway, they're all worries. Ai—men, men are people with troubles, thought Old Zhuzhu.

Old Zhuzhu heard the door to the western room open. He hurriedly slipped back to his place in front of the lamp.

Young Zhu came in, his face neither happy nor upset. He handed Old Zhuzhu a red cloth bag.

"Brother, as you wish."

Old Zhuzhu took the bag without uttering a sound.

"Take this money first and dig out a third room for the boys."

Old Zhuzhu clutched the bag without uttering a sound.

"We'll take turns—two weeks in this room and two weeks in that room."

Old Zhuzhu stared at the bag without uttering a sound.

After speaking, Young Zhu went back to the western room.

Old Zhuzhu looked at the red cloth bag, looked at the close-cropped heads of the two young men, and then looked at the lamp in front of him. Two more moths had flown over and with a burst of strength hurled themselves at the lamp.

Thieves

It was really dark.

It was so dark you couldn't see the low caves; it was so dark you couldn't see your hands or your feet.

It was so dark you couldn't see a thing, but Bannu could see her way.

The road was glowing.

Dragging one leg, Bannu hobbled along carrying three baked wheat-flour buns.

Milk Brother's cave was at the other end of the road.

Bannu hadn't been to his cave in two years. Even if she'd gone, she couldn't've gotten in, because the cave had been sealed for two whole years.

⁓

Milk Brother had been nursed by her mother. She and Milk Brother were very close. When they were little, she wanted to be Milk Brother's wife and he would let her. When they were a little older, she said to Milk Brother, "Milk Brother, Milk Brother, do you really want me for your wife?" Milk Brother replied, "Sure I do."

It was for Milk Brother's sake that she hadn't hanged herself or thrown herself down a well fifteen years before, when she married an idiot in Milk Brother's village. During the day the idiot had spells of lucidity, but by nightfall he was completely dead to the world. As soon as his head hit the *kang*, he'd sleep like a dead hog.

Bannu would wait until he slept like a dead hog and the night grew so dark you couldn't see a thing before she'd slip over to Milk Brother's place.

"I finally made it."

"Always have to wait till our girls are asleep."

They didn't say anything else. Everything else was pointless. They stripped naked and went at it. He was skinny; she was fleshy. Perched on her body, he resembled a locust on a toad.

When they were finished, he would not climb off her. She wouldn't let him. She would tell him to sleep that way. He listened to her and drifted off to sleep. She was his mat and he was her cover.

Every time, she woke him.

"Hey, have something to eat."

She would give him something to eat. She would bring him whatever she had at home to eat—steamed oat bread, potato cakes, or bitter vegetable dumplings. When the cupboard was bare, she'd go out into the fields and steal some ears of corn or dig up a few potatoes and put them in her trousers and then boil them for him to eat.

She watched him eat.

"You have some too."

"I'm not hungry."

"I'll eat it all."

"You're so thin."

Sometimes, she'd have him eat sitting atop her belly. Listening to him chewing and swallowing his food made her belly move up and down and she was very happy. Nothing made her happier.

This time, she had nothing to bring him.

"Ai—so poor," she sighed as she shook him awake.

"I had picked some black soybean pods to boil for you, but the guy watching the field took them away," she said.

"At home all we had was some thin porridge, so I didn't have anything to bring you today," she said.

"I'm not hungry."

"You're so thin."

"What about our girls?"

"Don't worry about them. I can usually pilfer a few things from the fields. But today, I ran into the guy from the commune who was watching the fields. The fucker insisted upon searching me," she said.

"I don't have anything for you either."

"A half catty of grain a day isn't enough for you."

"Why don't I make a steaming pot of oat porridge?"

"Ai—so poor."

"I can throw some dry wild garlic flowers into the pot. That would be good, but a little oil would make it heavenly."

"Ai—so poor."

He climbed off the *kang* to start a fire.

"The fire is going," she said, "but don't you make the porridge."

He looked at her.

"I'm going out and will be back soon."

He looked at her.

"This afternoon, I saw the fucking Accountant going to the western room to get some white flour."

"Don't get into trouble—he has relatives at the commune."

"I'm not afraid of him. Only those fuckers get any flour to eat."

"Then I'll go."

"No way, not with your class background."

She pushed him back onto the *kang*.

He anxiously awaited her return.

She threw the sack of white flour that she carried on her shoulder onto the *kang*. Squatting, she said, "The fuckers. They're the only ones who get any of this."

They ate their fill of hard skillet bread.

"It's delicious. The more you chew the better it tastes. It tastes so good I don't even want to swallow it."

"Eat it all up. I put away a sack under a pile of oat straw on the threshing ground."

"A little wine and I'd be living like an emperor."

They filled up on skillet bread and water. She took off her clothes again and said, "Come on. This is the only happiness for rich and poor alike."

After they finished, he said his head was spinning.

"Are you really dizzy? That must mean you've had your wine too."

They both laughed. Living the good life of an emperor made them laugh, but laughing, they forgot that a certain matter might be awaiting them the following day.

He was given two years by the court.

Her idiot husband beat her and broke one of her legs.

⁓

It was really dark.

It was so dark you couldn't see a thing. But Bannu could see her way.

The road was glowing.

She hobbled along, dragging one leg; she picked up her pace.

At the end of the road, her Milk Brother was waiting for her.

Widow San

I want to die. . . . I want to die soon. . . .

Widow San had not eaten or had anything to drink in ten days. She was cruelly set upon dying. She hoped to die soon, very, very soon.

I want to die . . . I want to die soon. . . . Otherwise . . . I will bring disaster down on the children. . . .

Widow San had had a hard life, she had endured a lifetime, she had held out for a lifetime. Near the end, she had fallen ill and couldn't get up.

It was jaundice, said the barefoot doctor.

It was fate, thought Widow San.

When no one was around, she got up and felt her way to the wood-shed. She'd tightly grasp a stick of firewood and hit anyone who showed up. She'd hit her son or her grandkids. She hit her son and the doctor wearing shoes brought in by the commune. She also struck the bowls of food and water brought by her son.

Widow San decided that before she breathed her last, she would never come out of the woodshed.

That year, Caicai's dad had done the same.

⁓

In her youth, Widow San had spent some time in a brothel on Sandao Barracks Lane in Datong City. At first she was in charge of chopping firewood, carrying coal, and other such simple chores. She was also in charge of making sure that there was always hot water for tea. Later, the madam forced her to sleep with the customers. She even taught her how to writhe, pant, and moan when she was doing it with the customers. In a word, the more debauched, the better. But she was incapable of doing any of what the madam taught her. For this reason, the madam let her go hungry so that she would remember what she was taught. But it was no use, she just couldn't do it.

She was homely, tall, and of large build—the type that only low-class customers would want. They would say, "Who cares? Blow out the light and they're all the fucking same, only she's cheaper." They wanted to get their money's worth and would keep her awake all night long. They'd do it once and want to do it again and again.

She couldn't sleep nights, and during the day she had her regular chores to attend to.

Widow San couldn't take it any longer, so when the opportunity presented itself, she ran away with a pair of fire tongs. She wanted to go beyond the pass. She had heard that after her father had sold her to the brothel, he had gone to Hetao in Inner Mongolia. She wanted to find her father. She didn't hate him, even after he sold her to the brothel. She knew he had no other choice. Otherwise her mother would have had no coffin—they would have had to wrap her in a mat and bury her. She didn't hate her dad. She wanted to find him.

~

I want to die . . . I want to die soon. . . . Otherwise I'll bring disaster down on the children. . . .

She covered herself with her tattered leather coat. She faced upward, and tears welled from her tightly closed eyes that resembled dried apricots.

A large, coarse hand, rough as a corncob, wiped away the two streaks of tears. At eighteen or nineteen, she couldn't think of anyone, save herself, who had ever wiped her tears away.

After taking hold of his hand, she threw her arms around his neck.

~

She headed north after running away from Datong. She had no idea how far away Hetao was, but she knew it was to the northwest. Walking and walking, she discovered that five wolves, their ears erect, were following her. She knew they weren't following her just to follow her, nor had they come to accompany her in her loneliness. They were going to devour her. She didn't scream or shout. When her mother was alive, she said you couldn't scream when you saw a wolf, because the moment you uttered a sound, it would pounce on you. Holding the tongs, she walked steadily and slowly. The wolves followed her for five *li* without making a move. Instead of the person she hoped to see, she saw an isolated melon hut. As she entered the melon hut, she stood blocking the door with her tongs.

She forgot how she had fought with the wolves. All she could remember was how someone outside had cleared them away and how his dog had savagely bitten them. She'd passed out and couldn't remember anything else.

"You're pretty tough. You stabbed three wolves to death—you ripped open the belly of one and tore open the throats of two others," he said. "One of them bit you," he said.

It was only then that she realized her thigh ached and learned that a wolf had bitten off a chunk of her flesh. Listening to him, she realized that three days had already passed and that she was lying on a *kang* in a dark little cave.

She wept, but she wept in silence. Her tears flowed, flowed down. That large, coarse hand, rough as a corncob, wiped away the two streaks of tears. At eighteen or nineteen, she couldn't think of anyone, save herself, who had ever wiped away her tears. First she seized hold of his hand, and then she threw her arms around his neck. From then on, they spent their days together. When they did it, no one needed to teach her how to writhe, pant, and moan. She never told him that she had run away from the brothel on Sandao Barracks Lane; she simply said that she wanted to go beyond the pass in search of her father.

⁓

I want to die . . . I want to die soon. . . . Why go on living? . . . I'll just bring disaster down on the children. . . .

She stroked the tattered leather coat that he'd made from the pelts of those three wolves. He said when it was hot she should use it as a mat; when it was cold she should use it as a cover; and when it was cloudy or rainy she should wear it with the fur out. The skins had not been well cured, so they weren't very soft; at first the coat made a sound when she put it on, but later the sound stopped.

She always kept that wolfskin coat. When it was hot she used it as a mat; when it was cold she used it as a cover; and when it was cloudy or rainy she wore it with the fur out. But it had long since lost its fur and become bare, bare like his back.

⁓

"Mom, force yourself to eat something." She heard a voice speaking to her.

She opened her eyes that resembled dried apricots. It was her son Caicai with some food for her. He knelt before her bed, holding a bowl in two hands.

"No. . . . I want to die. . . . I want . . . to die. . . ." Her lips moved as she spoke. She no longer had the strength to lift the club to strike anyone.

"Mom, the doctor says that they can cure jaundice at the county seat," said Caicai.

"No. . . . I want to die. . . ."

"Mom, Uncle Pothook says he has gone to borrow money for it."

"No. . . . I want to die. . . ."

She stuck out her tongue to lick away the tears that had flowed to her lips. She swallowed them.

"Mom, drink some water. Drink."

"No. . . . I want to die. . . ."

⁓

She closed her eyes and her tears rolled down in two streaks. That large, coarse hand wiped them away again. She threw her arms tightly around his neck.

"Hurry and get up. Don't cry. There's no point in crying. Nearly the whole village has died from the jaundice, and now I have it. My time has come. I have to die too," he said.

"If you die, I'll die too," she said.

"Hurry and get up. Get going. Go find your dad in Hetao; otherwise you'll catch it from me," he said.

"I'm not afraid, not afraid," she said.

"That won't do. You have to be afraid; otherwise it might harm the baby in your belly," he said.

"Let's call the baby Caicai," he said.

"Okay," she said.

When she wasn't around, he'd climb into the woodshed and not come out. He'd grasp a stick of firewood and not let her approach. He knocked over all the food and water she brought to him. Seven days later, he was dead.

Her big belly sticking out, she threw the wolfskin coat over her shoulders and set off to the northwest, to Hetao to find her father. But she got no farther than the Wen Clan Caves. She gave birth to Caicai beside a pile of oat straw on the threshing ground. She stayed at the Wen Clan Caves and never left.

People asked her name. She told them San Ban. Nobody called her San Ban, they all called her Widow San. That's what they called her for as long as she lived.

⁓

"Mom, Mom, Mom, you can stay at the county hospital. Uncle Pothook borrowed the money from the province," said Caicai.

Widow San was silent.

Widow San didn't even say "No. . . . I want to die. . . ."

She was no longer worried because she knew that she really was dead.

Dog

"You've really gone and done it now."

"What did I do?"

"Are you nuts?"

"What did I do?"

Everyone was scolding Dog, but he couldn't figure out what was wrong or why they thought he was nuts.

Although he was old, he could still work. He worked for anybody who wanted him. He worked hard and was honest. Everyone said he was like a good beast of burden—he'd do the dirty jobs and never eat.

"Dog, go down to the commune and buy us five plowshares. The plowshares at the supply and marketing cooperative last," said the Brigade Leader.

"Okay," said Dog.

"Dog, get me four bolts of hemp. There isn't any hemp for shoe soles."

"Dog, get me a box of matches, the ones with white tips."

"Dog, get me a chamber pot. The mouth of this one is broken and I nearly cut myself on it."

"Dog, get me a thimble—the cat was playing with it and now I can't find it."

"Okay, okay, okay." Dog always said "Okay." He would set off from the village and head for Nanchao Commune.

The damn sun is scorching hot. I'm covered with sweat from head to toe. Dog cursed the sun as he walked.

The damn road is hot. Are you trying to roast my feet? Dog cursed the road as he walked.

Dog checked both sides of the road, looking for some grass to walk on because grass wouldn't be hot on his feet. But there was no grass on either side; there was nothing but rock or sand. Dog had no choice but to keep to the dirt road. The dirt of the road was so fine and dry that it resembled sifted potato flour. His bare feet threw up puffs of dust.

If only it were potato flour, thought Dog. *If it really were potato flour, no one would die from hunger and my adopted sister wouldn't have had to go away and marry in Inner Mongolia.*

Who is that on the ridge of the embankment?
It is my adopted sister whom I love to death.

The poplars on the cliff are all of differing heights
My adopted sister is the best in all the world.

You're on the embankment ridge, I'm in the ditch
Unable to exchange a kiss, we can only wave.

Every time Dog thought of his adopted sister, he would sing this song. He would sing whenever he thought of her, regardless of the hour. Once around midnight she'd come to mind and he'd begun singing at the top of his lungs. He never worried about waking anyone. He'd sing and sing, verse after verse, until his tears fell. But this time Dog sang three verses and stopped. It wasn't because his mouth was parched or his tongue dry. It was because Dog's sister, Dog Girl, came to mind. He hadn't thought about her in ages, but for some reason he did this time. Whenever he thought of Dog Girl, he was in no mood to sing. He would quickly try to think of something else in order to forget his sister.

What should I do? A man must always have something to do. Idlers get into trouble. Everyone must have something to do. Dog suddenly thought of something. He thought of Widow San. Thinking of Widow San made Dog happy. Dog was always happy whenever he thought of Widow San.

Plop!

As Dog was thinking about Widow San, a huge drop of rain fell from the sky, leaving a depression in the flourlike dust of the road, as if the sky had cast down a large bronze coin.

Plop! fell another.

Plop! fell another.

Plop, plop, plop, plop. The big raindrops immediately pocked the road's surface. The fragrant smell of damp earth he had smelled his whole life rose at once. Dog inhaled deeply through his nose several times.

It smelled good. As he inhaled several more times through his nose, Dog wondered why it smelled so good.

Damned Old Man in Heaven changes without a moment's notice, which is good 'cause it'll cool things off and I won't sweat so much.

Dog looked up and saw a bright-edged black cloud approaching. Close behind it spread a huge stretch of dark clouds.

Looks bad! When people get mad, they make trouble; when Heaven gets mad, it hurls hail. Dog stepped up his pace.

In the distance, Dog saw a threshing ground and on it a pile of oat straw shaped like steamed bread. Dog increased his pace again.

By the time Dog reached the threshing ground, the cold hail was falling. Some of the hailstones were the size of beans, some the size of eggs. Dog hoisted his ass and burrowed into his dog den of straw, hiding within.

Fuck it. He had to go hungry too. Curled up inside his dog's den of straw, he could see the hailstones bouncing on the threshing ground. Fuck it. He had to go hungry too.

It was then that Dog thought of Widow San again.

He recalled that time. He was always recalling that time. He couldn't remember how many years ago it had been. But Dog remembered that time was like this time, with hailstones bouncing all around. It wasn't on a threshing ground that time, but in the wild, overgrown graveyard.

Dog had no wild garlic flowers at home. He could do without many things, but not wild garlic flowers. Wild garlic flowers were a must for thin salty potato gruel, dough fish, cold potato strips, and seasoning bitter herbs. Wild garlic flowers were the poor man's seasoning.

Dog had heard that the wild garlic flowers in the wild, overgrown graveyard were good, so he set off to pick some in the afternoon when they were in full bloom. At first the sun was bright red and hot and he was soon covered with sweat. As he neared the wild, overgrown graveyard, the wind had picked up and the Old Man in Heaven was casting down raindrops the size of bronze coins.

Dog saw a big tree and ran over to take shelter beneath it. Squatting under the tree, he watched the rain fall.

A couple of people came running through the wild, overgrown graveyard. Dog was just about to shout for them to come over when they turned to a place under the cliff. It was then that Dog saw that the man was Uncle Pothook and the woman Widow San. It was then that the hail started to fall.

"Look at how the hail is bouncing." Dog could make out the voice of Widow San.

"Who cares?" That was Uncle Pothook's voice.

What were they doing together? What were they doing in the grave-yard? Were they also picking wild garlic flowers? wondered Dog.

Later the hail stopped, but the rain fell harder and began coming through the tree leaves, getting Dog wet. Dog thought of the place below the cliff and how the rain didn't reach there.

Covering his head with his arms, he ran from beneath the tree, turned, but stopped dead in his tracks. Uncle Pothook and Widow San were stark naked. Uncle Pothook was bent over, spreading their clothes on the ground. Widow San stood there watching him. From her gestures you could tell that she was having him spread them again closer to the cliff wall. Uncle Pothook listened to her and spread them again. Widow San stood facing Dog. She didn't see him, but he saw every inch of her. After Uncle Pothook had spread the clothes on the ground, Widow San lay down on her back. Dog watched as she spread her white legs like a pair of shears for Uncle Pothook. It was at that moment the hail started falling, *beng, beng, beng*. Dog covered his head again and ran back beneath the big tree.

Black clouds rolled overhead. A cloudburst passed; a hailstorm passed. Dog came out from under the tree again to watch the hanky-panky, but Uncle Pothook and Widow San were already gone.

Dog never told anyone about what he had seen.

He could never forget that day. He always thought about how miserably he had been drenched under that tree. After that, whenever Dog saw Widow San, he wanted to smile.

This time, he smiled and smiled, and when he laughed, he realized he was inside his dog den of oat straw watching the hailstones bouncing on the threshing ground.

What's that?

Dog looked out at the threshing ground and saw row after row of mud bricks being pounded into mush.

Fuck it! The hail would certainly ruin all the bricks.

Dog climbed out of his dog den of oat straw, hurriedly bent over, and grabbed some straw. He'd grab some straw and then run over and cover the bricks with it. He did this again and again as hailstones the size of beans and eggs fell around his head.

Fuck your mother, Old Man in Heaven. If you can't kill me with your hail, you aren't worth much. Fuck your mother, Dog. If you can't cover the bricks, you aren't worth much.

Dog cursed the Old Man in Heaven and himself as he ran to cover the bricks with oat straw. By the time the egg-sized hail stopped and only bean-sized hail was falling, the people summoned by the commune came running with bamboo scoops and baskets. From a distance, Dog thought they looked like mushrooms that had grown arms. One of them took a tumble and rolled a couple of times. He managed to stop but fell again. Dog couldn't understand why the others all ran past him without paying the least attention and why they kept letting him fall. When they reached the threshing ground, they discovered that Dog had already covered the bricks. But Dog's head was covered with bumps from the hail.

The commune reported the incident to the county. The county reported it to the prefectural commissioner's office. The prefectural commissioner's office dispatched newspaper and radio reporters to the Wen Clan Caves to locate Dog and ask him why he was willing to risk bowl-sized hailstones to save public property from destruction.

"Fuck. The hailstones were the size of eggs, not bowls. If they had been the size of bowls, I'd be dead," said Dog.

"Fuck, I don't know anything about male or female property," said Dog. (The words for "public" and "male" are homophonous in Chinese.)

Hearing this, the people from the newspaper and the radio shook their heads. When they finished shaking their heads, they asked him about his motives and his goals. They spent a lot of time asking him questions and trying to explain their questions, but Dog couldn't figure out what the city people were talking about.

Finally, one reporter said, "Okay, in your own words, just tell us why you were willing to suffer."

"Fuck. I'm an old man. When I was young, the Japanese Imperial Army had me build a gun turret, which was a lot harder. The Imperial Army praised me, saying, '*Yoshi, yoshi.*' That's Japanese for 'good, good.'"

The newspaper and radio people didn't shake their heads. They turned and left together.

"You've really gone and done it now."

"What did I do?"

"Are you nuts?"

"What did I do?"

Everyone was scolding Dog, but he couldn't figure out what was wrong or why they thought he was nuts.

Party

Every month or two, the not-so-young unmarried men would get together and stuff themselves with an ample meal.

"How about it? We haven't had a party in a long time. Why don't
we have a fucking party?"

"What about tonight?"

"If you say tonight, let's make it tonight."

It was settled. Now they just had to wait to see who would bring
what.

No need to ask. There was no wine, and meat never appeared even
in their wildest dreams.

"Leng Er, you bring a *sheng* of oat flour."

"You always tell me to bring oat flour."

"There's no point in asking you for sesame oil; you don't have any
at home."

"My mom sold all the oil we were allocated."

"Onions, garlic, hot pepper?"

"We don't have any. All we have is wild garlic flowers."

"See, see. Maybe you shouldn't join us this time."

"Okay, I'll get some flour."

Leng Er went home and said to his mother, "The guys are having
a party so I need some oat flour." Leng Er's mother replied, "We don't
have anything to eat these days. The pot is empty." Leng Er said, "Are
you going to give me some or not?" Leng Er's mom dared not argue
with him for fear he would go crazy again. If he did, Leng Er's mother
would get no sleep at night, which was too much for her.

Although it was supposed to be a party for the younger unmarried
men, there were two older guys who were always included. One was
Zits Wu and the other was Grunt.

Years ago Grunt had served as a mess cook in the army of Fu Zuoyi. He knew that onions must be cut in thin diagonal slices and not in rings. He also knew that in cooking, oil had to be added at the very last; otherwise you'd never know it was there. If you had white flour, meat, and seasoning, he could make dumplings. He was the cook for the unmarried men.

Zits Wu, in addition to living in a three-room cave, had a big pot for pig slop. For a party, a big pot was a necessity. Zits Wu's place served as the dining room for the unmarried men.

The unmarried men did their best to swipe whatever they could from home.

"Leng Er, how many of us are there?"

"Testing me again to see if I can count," said Leng Er, extending his finger to count aloud the heads of those present. When he finished counting, he said, "Nine heads."

"Wrong. There are ten."

Leng Er counted heads again—one, two, three—and said, "There are nine."

"Leng Er, what's that growing on top of your neck?"

"Ai, ai, I forgot to count my own filthy, stupid noggin," said Leng Er, tapping his head.

Everyone laughed. They needed a good laugh before they ate to dispel their fatigue.

Grunt said they had only three *sheng* of flour for ten people, which wasn't enough for steamed oat bread, so they'd have to eat dough fish. So saying, he mixed the flour. Everyone stood around him and watched.

Grunt distributed a small amount of dough to each one of them with which to clean their hands before shaping the dough fish. He went to boil the water for the soup. They managed to turn their tiny bits of grayish dough black, making them look like pellets of Chinese medicine.

Their hands clean now, they began to shape the dough. They each pulled a chunk of dough from the mixture and rolled it out in a thick cylindrical shape like a radish, then pinched off a piece and, using thumb and forefinger, rolled it until it resembled the cigarettes smoked by Old Zhao, the cadre who had been sent to their countryside. They then pinched off a small piece and flattened it between their palms. Patting it several times, they transformed the dough into a "fish." Grunt told them that they had to shape the dough into small elongated shapes with pointed ends. But they couldn't manage it. Some were large, some small, some fat, some thin—none was just right.

Leng Er didn't make fish; he couldn't shape them if he tried. Instead, he gathered together the black bits and mashed them together and said he was going to mold a puppy. But whatever he did, it didn't turn out right. Then he said he was going to make a piglet but was no more successful. He finally pulled the black mass into a longish shape, and dangling it from his crotch said, "Does this look like Corncob's?" When Corncob heard him, he jumped up and knocked him down. Leng Er was quick to say, "It's not yours, it's not yours, it's mine."

Only then did Corncob lay off him and go back to shaping dough fish. Leng Er looked at the black thing and said, "Mine's not that big. It must be one of Old Guiju's donkey ones." All the unmarried men roared with laughter.

Leng Er was the liveliest of the bunch; without him it wouldn't have been as much fun.

The water began to boil in the pot. The potatoes were boiled as soup and then the dough fish, large and small, were added. Pieces of red hot pepper and the sliced green onion rose and sank with the dough fish, fat and thin, large and small, in the boiling water, making everyone swallow their saliva.

When the pot was lifted off the fire, the fish settled down. No one laughed or said a thing: all eyes were fixed on Grunt as he ladled out a big bowl for each person. Some squatted, leaning against clay urns; those on the *kang* didn't sit but squatted with their backs to the wall. Heads down, they vigorously slurped up the contents of their bowls.

Slurp, slurp. Slurp, slurp.

All that could be heard in the room was the sound of slurping. If you didn't know what they were doing, you would have assumed they were all sobbing.

After three bowls each, they looked at the slop pot. It was still half full. Only then did they relax and slow down.

"You said they had eight bowls and eight plates in the commune film. Now that must have been a real feast."

"You bet."

"You said it must have been a party."

"You bet."

"You said the men and women kissing were really kissing."

"You bet."

"You said the actors playing the man and wife were really doing it."

"You bet."

"Shut up! Let's hear how big your fucking dicks are," swore Leng Er, standing up suddenly and tapping his bowl with his chopsticks. After cursing this way, he walked over to the pig-slop pot and scooped out another bowl.

"Fuck you," swore Leng Er furiously. After swearing this way, he went and squatted in the corner by an urn and began slurping his food.

After that bout of swearing, no one said a thing. It wasn't that they were afraid of Leng Er, they just didn't say anything or joke after his rant. They all lowered their heads and began slurping up the contents of their bowls. They slurped until sweat was running down their noses. Maybe the sweat was mixed with the tears of the unmarried men.

Slurp, slurp.

Slurp, slurp.

The room was filled with the sound of slurping.

Slurp, slurp.

Slurp, slurp.

The whole cave was filled with a slurping sound that resembled sobbing.

Leng Er, Leng Er

"Give me fifty *yuan*," said Leng Er as he entered.

Leng Er's mother washed the oatmeal pot and said nothing.

"I said give me fifty *yuan*," said Leng Er.

"Are you nuts?" said Leng Er's mother.

Leng Er's mother looked at the head of the *kang,* on which sat a terra-cotta dish half filled with oatmeal that had been set aside for Leng Er, who had been outside walking around and had not eaten.

"Did you hear me? I want fifty *yuan*," said Leng Er.

Leng Er's mother was using a bunch of millet leaves to scrape out the pot into a bowl for chicken feed. She poured a ladle of water into the pot without paying any attention to Leng Er.

"I don't want anyone to come and get engaged to Golden Orchid," said Leng Er.

Leng Er's mother turned and looked at Leng Er. No lamp had been lit in the room, so she couldn't make out his face. He was like a door— a black silhouette blocking the doorway.

"Are you nuts?" said Leng Er's mother.

"I stopped Silver Orchid at the well step and told her I didn't want anyone to become a match for Golden Orchid. She asked me if I had any money," said Leng Er.

"I think you're completely nuts."

Leng Er's mother went back to washing the pot. All that could be heard in the pitch-dark room was the scouring of the millet leaves against the metal pot and the splashing of water.

Leng Er threw open the door and departed.

There was a stoop-backed shadow at the rear of the *kang* chewing something. It was Leng Er's dad. His dad didn't care about anything except eating his porridge followed by an ephedrine pill. He concerned himself with nothing else: if the bottle of oil fell over, he wouldn't even pick it up. In order to chew on the ephedrine as long as possible, he would dry the steamed oat bread on the *kang* and then break it up into nail-sized pieces. When he chewed on the ephedrine, he'd place two pieces of steamed oat bread in his mouth and chew it with the ephedrine pill.

Crunch, crunch. Crunch, crunch.

At the rear of the *kang*, that stoop-backed shadow continued to chew.

～

Golden Orchid sat cross-legged at the head of the *kang* pulling apart the old cotton. Behind her, the *kang* was piled high with old cotton.

Cheng-cheng-cheng. Cheng-cheng-cheng, she pulled apart the old cotton.

Golden Orchid spent days pulling apart the old cotton; as soon as she returned from the fields she would pull apart the cotton.

Cheng-cheng-cheng. Cheng-cheng-cheng, she pulled apart the old cotton.

"Hurry up and dump it here. Don't just pull it apart," said Silver Orchid.

"Pulling the cotton apart doesn't bother you, but watching you annoys me," said Silver Orchid.

～

By midnight, Leng Er had still been unable to obtain the fifty *yuan*, so he decided to go up to the mine and get it from his older brother Leng Da.

Leng Er got dressed in the dark.

"Where are you going?" asked Leng Er's mother.

"None of your business," said Leng Er.

The mine was eighty *li* from the village. Leng Er had been to the mine several times while hauling night soil. He rode the night-soil cart each time. He would spread a layer of dry straw on top of the night-soil tank, where he would sit comfortably. Sitting up, he could watch the men and women laboring on either side of the road; lying down, he could gaze up at the white or black clouds floating leisurely up in the sky. Sure, it smelled bad at first, but after a while he no longer noticed it. Everything was that way—once you were accustomed to something, you no longer noticed it. Fragrant or smelly, sweet or bitter, it was all the same. But there was one exception: not having a woman. That was something that nobody could ever get used to, unless one was castrated. That's what Grunt said. Fuck it, he wouldn't be castrated for anything.

But this time he didn't have the night-soil cart to ride on and had to walk. Outside the village, Leng Er picked up his pace and headed south.

Crossing the second ridge, Leng Er could see the sun just breaking the horizon in the east. It appeared gradually before suddenly shooting up. The mountain ridge prevented the sunlight from penetrating all quarters: where the sun shone it was yellow; where it failed to reach, it remained black.

The shadows of the rocks on the road, whether large or small, stretched to the west. The road was hatched with short and long shadows of the rocks. Leng Er thought the road looked like a long ladder with the shadows forming the rungs. He thought he could climb the ladder into Heaven.

Such thoughts made Leng Er happy, so he began to shout.

"Ah-ou!"

That's the way Leng Er was. When he was happy he would suddenly raise his voice and shout. "Ah-ou." One sound. At home it was the same. When he shouted, the dry dirt would shake down from the cave ceiling and sometimes a whole clod of earth with it.

Leng Er suddenly thought he ought to shout out Golden Orchid's name. When he was young, he would shout "Golden Orchid." If he hadn't seen her for a spell, he'd walk around the village shouting her name. Sometimes she would hide on purpose or follow along behind him out of sight, just to hear him shout her name. When she got older and began working, she no longer allowed him to shout her name. She told him that if he kept it up, she would be annoyed. He no longer dared shout her name.

Leng Er turned and looked back toward the Wen Clan Caves, but the sight of the village was blocked by the layered ridges.

"Golden Orchid, Golden Orchid, Golden . . . Orchid."

Leng Er took a deep breath and shouted her name. Shouting, he felt invigorated; his stride increased.

Sometimes Leng Er would ignore the twists and turns in the road and walk straight. This meant that he had to descend gullies and clamber up slopes, wasting a lot of energy. But that's the way he was—full of energy.

Leng Er watched his shadow cross ditches and slopes. By the time his shadow shrank to half his size, Leng Er felt tired and in need of rest.

A willow tree stood by the road. Grazing animals had gnawed off the bark on the lower half. Leng Er felt the tree looked like a bare-assed human being standing there. He stretched out beneath the bare-assed tree. He kicked off his shoes and flexed his toes as if they were fingers. There was a time when Leng Er couldn't flex his toes. But that afternoon when he was listening outside Wen Hai's bridal chamber, he peeked through a hole in the window and watched Wen Hai doing it and began to flex his toes. Ever since then, he could flex his toes.

Leng Er felt better after flexing his toes. Feeling more relaxed, he felt like singing a couple of lines from a beggar's song. In the past he'd always sung whatever first came to mind; now, whenever he felt like singing, he had to think about it first.

He thought and thought before he came up with the lines: "Hang a copper ladle, hang an iron ladle, hang a water jug / but don't say anything to lose heart till death."

Yes, that was it.

But the moment he opened his mouth to sing a small gadfly flew in. Just as he was taking a deep breath to sing, the small gadfly flew into his mouth. He spat and spat. After spitting, he was no longer in the mood to sing. That's the way it was sometimes: anxious to do something initially, but later dropping the matter in an instant.

"Fuck your mother to death," said Leng Er.

A cow pie lay by the roadside, around which a swarm of gadflies buzzed. A group of dung beetles rolled around in the shit. One dung beetle rolled a ball of dung out of the pile with its front legs. It pushed for a while, then turned around and rolled the dung ball with its hind legs while constantly checking to see if it was still headed in the right direction. It was trying to put the dung ball in its nest to pass the winter. Another dung beetle came over to assist it.

It must be its wife, thought Leng Er.

"Fuck your mother to death."

After cursing, Leng Er swept the beetles and the dung into the ditch with his foot.

Leng Er felt as if he were getting even.

He stretched out his foot to retrieve his two cooling shoes. He inserted his hands into his shoes and banged then together, dumped out the dirt and sand, and put them on.

Usually he didn't wear shoes, but he had to put them on to go to the mine. His sister-in-law was a pharmacist at the mine hospital and was a stickler for cleanliness. If he showed up without shoes on, she wouldn't let him in the door. She didn't like fucking dirt.

⁓

Golden Orchid sat cross-legged at the head of the *kang* pulling apart old cotton, which had come from a padded coat that had been worn all winter long. Once the cotton was removed from the padded coat and pants, the clothes became unpadded garments to be worn in spring and autumn. Golden Orchid's father had just gone to see his sister in such clothes from which the cotton padding had been removed.

Golden Orchid's father had gone to his sister's place to see a prospective son-in-law, one who worked in the county well-digging team. If he liked, the young man said he would hand over fifty *yuan* to meet with Golden Orchid.

Cheng-cheng-cheng. Cheng-cheng-cheng, Golden Orchid pulled apart the cotton.

In her free time, Golden Orchid always pulled apart cotton.

"You're still pulling apart the cotton. I'll be damned if I don't throw it away after you go to sleep," said Silver Orchid.

Cheng-cheng-cheng. Cheng-cheng-cheng, Golden Orchid pulled apart the cotton.

⁓

It wasn't that hot, but the streets were quiet.

Everyone rested in the afternoon. Resting was good. Resting was good for the spirit, and by sleeping one could forget and accomplish many things. The people of the Wen Clan Caves all rested in the afternoon. It was the way of their ancestors.

Leng Er returned from the mine.

He looked up to ascertain the position of the sun. He wondered if everyone would be finished resting. But he couldn't find the sun.

"It's dead," said Leng Er.

Leng Er scooped up some water with his hands to drink from a mortar on the well step. When the water calmed, Leng Er stooped over the mortar to use it as a mirror to look at his face. He couldn't remember his family ever owning a mirror; whenever he needed one, he'd use water. Looking at his reflection, he thought he looked okay. He wore the new work clothes Leng Da had secretly slipped to him.

The work clothes were made of sailcloth. They were first rate, though the collar of the coat was a bit stiff. Wearing the work clothes, he felt the collar was like a knife at his throat. For this reason he kept his neck stiff and straight so as not to touch the collar.

On the left pocket of the coat was printed: GRASP REVOLUTION, PROMOTE PRODUCTION. Four words—one, two, three, four. Four words. Four red words—one, two, three, four. Although Leng Er didn't know what the words said, he thought they looked sharp. But more important, the pocket with the words on it contained fifty *yuan*: five ten-*yuan* notes, crisp, new notes.

The money provided Leng Er with hope. Leng Er hoped for nothing else but that Golden Orchid would not become engaged to someone else. That way, he could see her every fucking day. He'd be satisfied just seeing her. He hoped for nothing else, but he knew his hopes were pointless.

⁓

Golden Orchid sat cross-legged on the *kang* pulling apart old cotton.

Cheng-cheng-cheng. Cheng-cheng-cheng, she pulled apart the cotton.

The old cotton resembled chicken shit, but Golden Orchid did not throw it away.

Golden Orchid pulled the cotton apart into little bits, small, downy bits that looked like elm seed. She laid the bits on the mat and pulled them apart again. Pressing them with her hand, she made them adhere together in pieces the size of two elm seeds.

Adhering together, the elm seed-sized bits would grow larger and larger, becoming the size of a palm. When the cotton mass had reached the size of a table, she would roll it up in a sheet of hemp paper. With the arrival of autumn, she would unroll the cotton and stuff the un-padded coats and pants with it, hemp paper and all. This is how the coats and pants were padded—everyone in the Wen Clan Caves did it this way.

The cotton was pulled apart and sitting on urn lids on top of the *kang.* Golden Orchid was waiting for her father to return with hemp paper so that she could roll the cotton up in it. There was still a large pile behind her waiting to be pulled apart. Golden Orchid was still pulling apart the old cotton.

Cheng-cheng-cheng. Cheng-cheng-cheng, she pulled apart the cotton.

"You have to pull apart the cotton. The well-digger will certainly give you whatever you want," said Silver Orchid.

Cheng-cheng-cheng. Cheng-cheng-cheng, she pulled apart the cotton.

"Your fate is a harsh one," said Silver Orchid.

Leng Er didn't go home; instead he went to Golden Orchid's place. Like a thief, he opened the door and stepped into the cave.

"You're pulling apart cotton," said Leng Er to Golden Orchid.

When Golden Orchid saw Leng Er dressed in his new work clothes and his neck stiff and straight, she thought he looked terribly funny. She suppressed a laugh and nodded.

"See, one glance and I know you're pulling apart cotton," said Leng Er.

Golden Orchid continued to pull apart her cotton without saying a word.

"You pull the cotton apart in such a pretty way; I really like watching you pull apart cotton," said Leng Er.

"You know, Golden Orchid, I really like looking at your bare feet. You know, your bare feet are really pretty. Look, you covered them up," said Leng Er.

"When you were little, I really liked looking at the soles of your feet. Your five toes were like five beans. Have you forgotten?" said Leng Er.

"You don't remember how Old Zhuzhu's rooster pecked you. I was pissed. I caught him and chopped his head off with a machete. But he fucking clawed the back of my hand till it bled. See, I still have the scars. One, two, three, three gouges," said Leng Er.

"There is some cotton stuck to your eyebrows, Golden Orchid. It looks like it's going to fall off, but it doesn't," said Leng Er.

"What are you doing here?" asked Golden Orchid.

"Nothing. I just got back from the mine. Nothing," said Leng Er.

"If you don't have any business here, then leave," said Golden Orchid.

"Nothing in particular. I'm just talking with you. Oh, yeah, look—I have a job," said Leng Er.

"At the mine. If you don't believe me, look at my work clothes. Look at the words—four words," said Leng Er.

"My sister-in-law always ignored me. But this time I told her my mom wanted fifty *yuan*. She got me a job," said Leng Er.

"You're shaking your head. I'm working in sister-in-law's clinic. I made fifty *yuan* my first time," said Leng Er.

"This is for you!" said Leng Er.

"Get out," Silver Orchid said, jumping up off the *kang*. "Get out!"

"I thought you were asleep, Silver Orchid. You weren't asleep," said Leng Er.

"Get out!" shouted Silver Orchid.

"I'm like you. Sometimes I feel like sleeping but can't because I start thinking about all sorts of things," said Leng Er.

"Are you going to leave or not?" asked Silver Orchid, picking up a ruler.

"Silver Orchid!" Golden Orchid scolded her sister.

Silver Orchid lay down facing the wall.

"I know you don't believe me. But if you don't believe me, just look at my arm," said Leng Er.

Leng Er rolled up his sleeve, but dared not step forward and remained standing in the doorway.

He stretched out his arm. There at the bend of his arm was a bruise. It looked like a fly had landed there.

"My sister-In-law said my blood is real good—nothing wrong with it. She said I could come back in two weeks," said Leng Er.

Golden Orchid stopped pulling apart the cotton and looked directly at Leng Er. Leng Er didn't know which way to turn his eyes. Finally he looked at the money in his hand.

"This is for you. In two months, I'll have more for you," said Leng Er.

Leng Er threw the roll of money on the *kang*.

Silver Orchid sat up, grabbed the money, and threw it in Leng Er's face.

Leng Er was momentarily stunned; he then turned and ran out.

Leng Er ran home, threw himself on the *kang*, and began shouting, "Kill, kill!" as he slapped the *kang* with his huge dark hands. The shouting "Kill, kill" and the slapping went on for two days.

Leng Er went crazy like that.

⁓

Golden Orchid no longer pulled apart old cotton.

Cha-cha-cha-cha, she messed up all the cotton she had pulled apart over the last few days.

Golden Orchid climbed on top of the cotton and wept.

Silver Orchid watched as Golden Orchid wept.

Lucky Ox

After Leng Er recovered from his madness, fucking Lucky Ox went crazy.

Lucky Ox went crazy after he returned from the county opera troupe.

Lucky Ox's madness was different from Leng Er's. Leng Er went crazy in his own house and never left the *kang*. Lucky Ox was different: he went crazy wherever there were a lot of people, that's where he went mad. Nor did he shout "Kill, kill" like Leng Er, but rather sang opera. He couldn't sing, but he sang all the same. There was no doubt he was a bad singer, but he wanted people to praise him. If anyone said he sang badly, he'd become angry.

"Who is that man there before you? / Oat flour is cooked but it isn't / It's been eight years / Don't mention him / He ... he ... he's a big onion." That's how he'd sing.

But those were not the lyrics as they were originally composed. The original lyrics were: "Who is that man there before you? / The face looks familiar, but then it doesn't / He ... he ... he ... he's Big Chun." This was part of an aria from the model opera *The White-Haired Girl*.

The lines "It's been eight years / Don't mention him" came from the model opera *Taking Tiger Mountain by Strategy*.

He would mix up the lines and sing them that way.

Not only did he sing, but he also insisted on performing. His movements consisted of three types: the flying dung-beetle kick, the cat turns a somersault, and one big step forward and two small steps back, a move he'd learned from the rice-planting dance. He would alternate these three movements without stopping.

At first no one thought he was crazy, but they did think he was making an ass of himself on purpose after he had been back from the opera troupe for half a month. People surrounded him to watch the show. The people of the Wen Clan Caves, who never saw a dog fight, surrounded him to watch because they found his singing and performing pretty interesting. But after watching for a while they realized he sang the same few lines and made the same three movements. Some people said, "That's no good, do something else." Others shouted, "Do something different, that's no good."

Hearing people shout, Lucky Ox stopped singing and gesturing. Panting, his face filled with suffering, he looked like he was on the verge of tears.

"Do something different, that's no good," shouted several people.

Lucky Ox turned to look at the people around him. His appearance shifted from looking as if he were on the verge of tears to looking violent. He bared his yellow teeth as if he were a mad dog ready to bite. Continuing to bare his teeth, he raised his two huge hands, extending his fingers and then curling them until his hands looked like two rakes.

But Lucky Ox didn't hit anyone; he clawed at his own face.

"Say I'm no good again," he said, scratching his own face.

"Say I'm no good again," he said, scratching his own face.

He spoke and clawed his face without stopping.

Everyone was stunned. Finally someone thought to say, "Good."

"Good! Good, good."

"Good . . . .good . . . ."

They all shouted "good" in unison.

Only then did Lucky Ox stop scratching himself, his violent look becoming one of suffering and then the look of suffering giving way to a smile. Streaks of blood mingled with the tears that rolled down his smiling face.

It was then that people realized Lucky Ox was crazy.

～

Two months before, the county opera troupe had gone from commune to commune performing. The troupe was going to put on five shows for their commune. That way the commune members from the thirteen villages would all have a chance to see a performance. Originally, the Wen Clan Caves were scheduled to see the third show. But on the first afternoon, while the sun was high overhead, Lucky Ox had hurried off to the commune.

A large stage was set up facing the commune gate.

The actors were busy moving things to the stage. Afraid that someone might get mad, Lucky Ox didn't dare get too close. He squatted by the commune gate and watched from a distance. Then he heard the actors practicing their singing in the commune courtyard behind him.

"Yi. Yi. Yi. Yi. Yi."

"Ya. Ya. Ya. Ya. Ya."

"Ao. Ao. Ao. Ao. Ao."

"Ah. Ah. Ah. Ah. Ah."

He thought it sounded like a female wolf howling.

Two actors carried a long wooden box shaped like a coffin through the commune gate and made their way slowly toward the stage. They hadn't taken more than a few steps when the one in back began shouting that it was no good and his legs began to give way. It looked like he was going to sit down on the ground.

Lucky Ox stood up and ran over. He took the box around its middle, under his arm, and asked them where they wanted it. After the actors looked at each other in disbelief, they led Lucky Ox to the rear of the stage.

"Man, you sure are strong," said the one with big eyes, who a moment ago had said it was no good, as he clapped Lucky Ox on the back. He looked like a carter patting his draught animal.

"Anything else to move?" asked Lucky Ox.

"Come with us," said the actors, leading him into the commune courtyard.

A crate that normally required two actors to carry was nothing for Lucky Ox. He picked it up under one arm and headed off with it. He would also carry something else in his free hand.

He helped them carry everything that had to be moved to the rear of the stage.

"Anything else to move?" asked Lucky Ox.

"Here. Come along."

Under their direction, Lucky Ox helped them hang some big metal boxes the size of a bellows as well as some thick, downy pieces of cloth larger than a house, and other things. He helped them until there was nothing left to do. The guy with the big eyes spoke with the fat guy and sat Lucky Ox down in the left wing of the stage to watch the performance.

During the performance, a number of people were talking noisily behind and below the stage. The guy with the big eyes bound a red band around Lucky Ox's upper arm and told him to take care of the noise makers. He also told him that he should apprehend the trouble-maker and bring him to them.

Lucky Ox didn't apprehend anyone, he just gave them all a shove. Once he made contact, he sent them all tumbling in a wave ten deep.

The actors changed, but the show was always the same. After the performance, Lucky Ox helped them move everything that had to be moved back to the large courtyard of the commune. Looking up at the sky and seeing the three stars of Orion's belt, he knew that it was nearly midnight.

"What else needs to be done?" asked Lucky Ox.

"Come with me."

The guy with big eyes led Lucky Ox into a room that was brighter than the light of day. He thought the room was pretty good-sized, big enough to hold three pens of village livestock. More than a dozen lights hung from the ceiling like more than a dozen suns shining in the sky.

Suddenly Lucky Ox felt something was wrong with his nose. He smelled something, something good. He blinked his eyes before he realized that under each sun was a table covered with dishes of food. That's what he had smelled.

Fucking Lucky Ox was scared out of his wits and turned and bolted. In a single breath, he was outside the village. He looked back and when he saw no one was coming after him, he relaxed and slowed his pace.

At midnight, he returned to the Wen Clan Caves in pitch dark. He returned to his own pitch-dark cave. He felt tired and hungry. Thinking about it, he realized he had nothing to eat in his cave. He felt his way in the dark and scooped half a ladle of water from the urn. The water smelled like steaming hot urine, but he gulped it down as if it were sweet and fragrant.

"First thing tomorrow morning I'll have some sticky cakes made of pure oat flour," said Lucky Ox.

He wondered what was on those fucking tables. It smelled real good.

That fucking Xi'er was pretty. Real pretty. How could her ma have produced such a pretty thing?

Lucky Ox fell asleep thinking about what was on the tables and lovely Xi'er.

The following day, Lucky Ox set off early for the commune to help the actors.

The following day he did the same. That day it was the turn of his village to watch the show.

Lucky Ox sat on the left wing of the stage and did his best to be seen by his fellow villagers. When some of the people in the audience recognized fucking Lucky Ox and pointed at him, he immediately shrank back like a snail, his heart thumping. After he calmed down a bit, he peeked out again. When people pointed at him, he withdrew again.

Five days passed.

The opera troupe was going to another commune to perform. Lucky Ox showed up the morning they were going to leave to help them load the truck.

Ai, he would no longer be able to see Xi'er, that fucking little Xi'er who was so pretty. So Lucky Ox thought as he helped to load the truck.

After loading the trucks, poor Lucky Ox stepped far to the rear and watched as the actors climbed into the covered truck one by one.

The guy with big eyes and the fat one approached him and asked if he wanted to come with them. One *yuan* a day and he would return to his village when they were done performing in the countryside.

"I can't sing; I can't even jump. All I can do is dance the rice-planting dance, and I can't do that very well," said Lucky Ox.

The guy with big eyes laughed until he almost choked.

"You can do the odd jobs," said the fat one. When he saw that he still didn't understand, he said, "You can do what you've been doing for the last two days."

The guy with big eyes told Lucky Ox to get in the freight truck. He had never ridden in a truck before, so didn't know how to get in. He clung to the back of the truck, his two legs flailing in midair, but he couldn't climb into the truck. Giving it their all, the people in the truck hoisted him in like a dead donkey. Working the last few days, Lucky Ox had never broken a sweat, but this time he was sweating. He was embarrassed and glanced over at the truck carrying the actors to see if Xi'er was watching him. The truck bucked and set off, nearly sending him spilling out the back end. He immediately grabbed onto a rope.

Lucky ox, lucky ox, I really am a lucky ox, thought Lucky Ox.

Had anyone in the Wen Clan Caves ever ridden in a truck? Had they ever sped by in such a way? The fucking Brigade Leader hadn't, nor had the fucking Accountant. If anyone had, it was Wen Bao. He might have when he was in prison. *He said prison had everything,* thought Lucky Ox.

Lucky ox, lucky ox, I really am a lucky ox, thought Lucky Ox.

But the opera troupe hadn't finished performing in the countryside when Lucky Ox was fired. He was fired without even being paid.

It happened because once, after the actors got him drunk, he made an ass of himself.

Lucky Ox had one problem—he couldn't control himself when he got drunk. He insisted upon chasing Xi'er to touch her hands; he even chased Tie Mei to touch her. If he did nothing else with them, he wanted to sniff their jacket sleeves. The actresses were so frightened by him that when they saw him coming it was as if a bunch of little hens had seen a big yellow rat—they screamed and scattered in all directions.

The actors who played Huang Shiren, Da Chun, Li Yu, and Jiu Shan beat Lucky Ox to a pulp.

Fucking Lucky Ox returned to the village and went crazy.

$\sim$

Knowing that he was crazy, the villagers avoided him. Seeing him coming, they would make a "Quick, quick" motion to one another. If they couldn't get away, they'd just run into the nearest courtyard and close the gate behind them. If they were still slower, they'd shout "Good, good" and wait for the first chance to get away.

The word "good" was heard all over the village in those days. It could be heard at any time all over the village.

After two days, Lucky Ox's madness grew worse. If things didn't go well, he'd vigorously claw at his face even if no one had said he was bad.

It seemed as if he no longer wanted his face.

In another two days, he didn't return home. Wen Hai's woman took food over to his place and left it on the *kang*, but he didn't have enough sense to go home and eat.

No one heard him sing; no one saw him gesture. He would just stop people on the road. People seeing him on the road knew he was crazy and would take to their heels and run.

When he couldn't stop anyone, he'd sing to the chickens and the goats. Singing a few lines was okay, but not gesturing. The chickens and the goats would run away in fright too. Toward the end, he sang to the trees and gestured to the trees. The poor trees wanted to run away, but they had to listen to him and watch him.

Just when he was singing and gesturing, a gust of wind blew from the south.

Huala, huala, the tree leaves rustled.

Lucky Ox stopped singing.

Huala, huala, the tree leaves rustled.

Lucky Ox stopped gesturing.

"Fuck your mothers. You're all saying I'm no good. You're all saying I'm no good."

Lucky Ox bared his yellow teeth and his angry face turned blood red. Shouting, he lifted a huge rock unsteadily overhead.

"Say I'm no good one more time!"

Huala, huala, the tree leaves rustled.

As soon as Lucky Ox heard the leaves saying he was no good, he struck his head with the huge rock.

Without feeling, the trees looked at Lucky Ox, who resembled a bundle of millet stalks fallen on the ground; their leaves went on rustling, *huala, huala*.

Eating Cakes

"The lights are on. Go call them to come and eat," said the Brigade Leader.

"They have been waiting outside for ages," said the Accountant.

"The fuckers. No need to worry about them."

"That's for sure."

The Accountant stuck his head out and shouted. They doddered along and squeezed into the commune room and made their way to two wicker baskets of deep-fried cakes, where everyone filled both hands. They began eating right away.

The commune room was partitioned out of the livestock pen. A wall down the middle with a door divided the room—one side for the livestock and the other side for Old Guiju, who fed the livestock and herded them.

The women sat cross-legged on Old Guiju's *kang*, while the men squatted by the wall. *Bacha, bacha*, the sound of their eating drowned out the sound of livestock eating on the other side of the door.

"Leng Er, don't choke, just eat your fill," said Caicai.

Everyone looked at Leng Er as he rubbed his extended neck with the back of his hand.

"I, I know, but the fucking deep-fried cakes scratched my throat," said Leng Er.

Seeing his tear-filled eyes, everyone laughed.

"Brigade Leader, what's next after we finish building the high irrigation station?" asked Danwa.

"Fuck, you're all eating one thing and craving something else," said the Accountant.

"You know our Brigade Leader is taking risks. His superiors want the irrigation works built entirely out of bricks. Our Brigade Leader told me that we'd just surface it with bricks and use earth for the inside. With the money we saved, everyone could have a meal," said the Accountant.

"The job is done. Frankly, it wasn't much work. Why do you think each household was asked to supply one laborer? So that you could all have something to eat," said the Brigade Leader.

Everyone nodded as they ate.

"We're telling you this up front. You can't let any of this out. If you do, we'll see you at the end of the year," said the Accountant.

"They won't get any flour or oil and won't have any deep-fried cakes," added Zits Wu.

"If someone gets married, they'll be able to have deep-fried cakes," said Leng Er.

"Who can get married on seven cents a day for labor?" asked someone.

"Only Wen Hai has been married here in the last five years," said another.

"That's right," said another.

Everyone sighed. After sighing, they continued eating.

"Leng Er, how many have you eaten?" asked one of the women on the *kang*, teasing him.

"Eight," replied Leng Er as he counted on his fingers.

"You must have swallowed them whole without chewing."

"That's not true. Ah . . ." Leng Er opened his mouth and rushed toward the *kang* to show the women the chewed cake in his mouth.

"You didn't swallow them whole. Do they taste good?"

"Do you have to ask? Everyone knows deep-fried cakes and pussy are good things."

"Animal!"

"Animal!"

The women all cursed Leng Er.

"It's true. If you don't believe me, just ask Grunt," said Leng Er.

"That's right. Aren't those the two things everyone wants out of life?" said Guan Guan.

"Aren't those the two things that even chickens and dogs get in life?" said Grunt.

Everyone nodded. The women stopped cursing.

"Except poor unmarried men," said the Brigade Leader.

"You said it," said someone.

"Brigade Leader, since you feel sorry for the unmarried men, why don't you let us taste what you got from the mine?" said Zits Wu.

"Why not? Can you drink? Those that can drink, come with me. Come on, let's go, Leng Er," said the Brigade Leader.

Called by the Brigade Leader, Leng Er set off with him.

Leng Er returned shortly with three bottles and some green onions under his arm.

"The Brigade Leader said the wine is strong, so he added water to make three bottles," said Leng Er.

Grunt had Zits Wu go fetch some bowls while he shooed the women off the *kang* to divvy the wine up among the unmarried men. He poured a little extra for himself and Zits Wu. He then gave one green onion to each man and the leftovers were taken by the women.

Grunt took an oat stalk from the *kang* mat and lit it at the coal oil lamp. He tossed the burning stalk into Leng Er's bowl. With a *whoosh*, a blue flame shot up and flickered over Leng Er's bowl of wine.

"Good wine, good wine," they all shouted.

"Fuck your mother. Why didn't you light your own?" said Leng Er.

Leng Er bent over and blew on his bowl, but the blue flame flared up with an audible *hu-hu*.

"Fuck! It singed my hair and eyebrows," complained Leng Er as he rubbed his head and eyebrows, sending down singed hair.

Everyone had a good laugh.

Grunt removed his hat and covered Leng Er's bowl with it. When he lifted his hat, the flame had been extinguished.

"Fuck, that's great," said Leng Er.

Leng Er admired Grunt; all the unmarried men did. Grunt was the leader of the unmarried men.

"Drink!" said Grunt as he lifted his bowl.

"Drink!" said the unmarried men, lifting their bowls.

"Bottoms up!" said Grunt.

"Bottoms up! echoed Zits Wu.

"May those who can't drain their bowl be unmarried in their next life," said Leng Er.

"May his dad, granddad, sons, and grandsons all be unmarried," said the half-wit, standing outside the door.

"Get lost," said Bannu, the half-wit's wife, as she tossed a fried cake at him. Laughing, he caught it and took off.

The unmarried men banged their bowls together and proceeded to swill the watered-down wine.

"Good wine. Good wine."

"It's stronger than Uncle Pothook's wine."

After praising the wine, they began eating the green onions, which were so hot they had to inhale to try to cool their mouths. Some of them took off their hats and rubbed their eyes.

They resumed eating deep-fried cakes, but before they had eaten two, they all felt dizzy. They felt the room was spinning; the door to the livestock pen was spinning; the women on the floor below the baskets of deep-fried cakes on the *kang* were spinning.

"Fucking good wine."

"Good fucking wine."

Grunt swayed and threw an arm around Zits Wu's neck. The two of them toppled onto the *kang*.

"Hey, I'm not your woman. What are you doing grabbing me?"

"You are my woman."

"It's you who is my woman."

"I'm going to do you."

"I'm going to do you."

Amid the explosion of laughter, Grunt and Zits Wu rolled around on the *kang*, each trying to get on top of the other. Old Guiju's rotten blanket got pushed aside. They ended up mouth to mouth. Each being afraid to lose, they kept a tight hold on each other as they kissed.

"Look at what asses they are making of themselves."

"How low."

"How disgusting."

The women cursed; the men laughed. The livestock on the other side of the door all squeezed together, watching them to see what was happening.

The whole commune room was in an uproar.

"What the hell is going on?" the Brigade Leader asked as he entered. "You've all had your fill and you're still here."

Only then did they all quiet down and look at the two large wicker baskets, which still contained quite a few deep-fried cakes.

"Okay," said the Brigade Leader to the Accountant, "give everyone a few cakes to take home for their families to eat."

Everyone left off watching Grunt and Zits Wu and squeezed tightly around the Accountant and the baskets of deep-fried cakes.

Grunt and Zits Wu were no longer wrestling nor kissing. They each had a hold of the other's head and cried.

"Ow, ow."

"Ow, ow."

They both cried out like a mother who had lost her baby.

Old Guiju

The round, blood-red sun was about to hit the mountain range, and Old Guiju still had not led the animals back to the village. He sat with his back to the field embankment without moving, without moving.

He was afraid to go back to the village.

Old Zhao, the cadre who had been sent down to the countryside, had told him that he'd have to speak tonight.

This afternoon he had driven his companions, which included three young donkeys, four goats, and one mule, to the ridge, where he had tethered each one to a tree so that they could graze only on the grass around them and not wander off. He squatted with his back to the embankment all afternoon without moving.

He was afraid to go back to the village.

He spent the entire afternoon thinking back over the events of his sad and happy life. Sometimes while thinking he would shake his head, sometimes he would sigh, sometimes he wanted to cry, and sometimes he wanted to laugh.

This time he squinted and smiled and went to the west side of the field embankment where he had been cutting oats.

The sun was scorching hot and seemed to breathe fire on him. Old Guiju straightened his back and looked toward the village. There was no sign of the landlord's wife bringing him his lunch.

There wasn't a cool, shady place around. He made a wall of oat stalks, but the ground was too hot to sleep on, so he placed a layer of stalks on the ground to serve as a *kang* on which he could lie comfortably.

Dazed with sleep, Old Guiju seemed to hear a voice sweetly singing:

Two white hankies face to face
Our hearts are as one.

A red rooster sits atop a stone roller
Singing what cannot be said.

Old Guiju thought he was dreaming. He rolled over without opening his eyes and fell asleep again.

Sleeping, he again heard a sweet voice shout:

"Hello . . . where are you?"

"Hello . . . is there anyone waiting to eat?"

"Here. I'm over here," said Old Guiju, clambering to his feet.

The landlord's wife was standing right in front of him, smiling sweetly. She had shouted on purpose.

"Well, you look pretty comfortable here," said the landlord's wife.

"Why so late? Are you trying to starve me to death."

"Not me. If you were to die, who would cut the oats?" she said as she sat down on his makeshift *kang* and handed him two black porcelain dishes.

"Steamed oat bread again," he said.

"Listen, it's steamed oat bread and that's what it'll be."

"Always the same."

"What would you like to eat?"

"Uh, I like . . ."

"What? What is it you like?"

"You don't give a person a chance to speak. Softer cakes with more meat, and the landlord's wife would be sweeter still."

"You want too much. That's a pipe dream."

"I was dreaming a little while ago."

He lifted the bowl to his mouth, and with his eyes fixed on her, he gave her a suggestive look. She sat up straight and said, "What do you want? You."

"You tell me."

"If I have to tell you, you won't be able to even touch me with the tip of your little finger."

". . ."

"That's right."

Her eyes were fixed on him with a suggestive look. Eyes fixed on him, she saw his Adam's apple bob several times; then he lowered his head, like a dry pumpkin hanging on a vine.

"See, I guessed right."

He remained silent.

He lowered his head and kept shoving food into his mouth.

"Hey, why are you swallowing without chewing?" she asked.

"Hey, why don't you finish everything?" she asked.

He remained silent.

"It's so hot out, why don't you at least have some green bean soup?" she asked. "Otherwise you'll get heatstroke."

He plunked down the dish, took up his scythe, and set off. In the field, he began mowing down swaths of oats—*swish, swish, swish*—leaving the fallen stalks behind him.

"Hey, are you crazy, or what?" she asked.

He remained silent.

He bent and cut mid-stalk without the level sweep he employed before. He proceeded vigorously ahead. He cut a passage through to the other side of the field. He plopped down on the field embankment, panting.

"Crazy, completely crazy," she said.

The following day, beside the wall of oat stalks, she once again handed him his lunch.

"Ah, chicken in corn cakes."

"Don't forget to have some green bean soup."

She fanned herself with a white hankie as she watched him eat.

The aroma that wafted over his meal from the hankie wasn't of chicken or corn.

When he finished eating, she asked, "Were the cakes soft?"

"Yeah."

"Was there enough meat?"

"Yeah...."

"Isn't the landlord's wife sweet?"

"..."

His Adam's apple rose and fell.

"Hey, I'm asking you a question."

"Huh?"

"Isn't the landlord's wife sweet?"

He remained silent.

He suddenly pounced and pressed her beneath him beside the wall of oat stalks.

Three months later in the mill, she said to him in a flattering tone of voice, "Brother Guiju, I'm pregnant. It's your child."

One day three years later as she was coming back from her parents' place, she said to him in a flattering tone of voice, "Brother Guiju, the little bastard has your walk. He walks like he is pushing an invisible wheelbarrow."

The lowing of the cow called Old Guiju back to the present, decades after the event.

"Moo," answered a calf in reply to its mother.

Old Guiju looked up at the sky and saw that it was almost dark. Yellow smoke rose from every chimney of every cave in the village at the foot of the hillock. Lights could be seen in each cave. There was only one cave from which no smoke rose—that was the commune room, where he lived with the livestock. There was an opening in the wall through which he could feed the animals at night. It also served as a door. The village had neither temple nor school, so his place was where the commune members held meetings. Tonight they were going to hold a big meeting, and he was supposed to speak. Last night, Old Zhao, the cadre who had been sent to the countryside, had ordered him to speak this evening. Old Zhao had said, "Uncle Guiju, you will lead off tomorrow, after which the Accountant will give you ten work points."

Thinking of this made Old Guiju so worried and put him in such a panic that he had no desire to return home.

He pulled a wormwood cord from his waist, struck a match, and lit the cord. Squinting, he blew on it.

He always had a wormwood cord tucked into his belt in back. Everyone said he looked like a member of the commune's Committee of the Dictatorship of the Masses who always had a rope ready with which to tie up someone.

Old Guiju didn't light the wormwood cord to keep the mosquitoes away. His skin was like tree bark; if a mosquito landed and tried to bite him, it would fly away because his skin was too thick. He lit the wormwood because he liked its smell. Once, the landlord's wife rubbed his chest and said, "Brother Guiju, you always smell like wormwood, bitter and fragrant." In the decades since then, he would light the wormwood as soon as night fell. Looking at the burning tip, he never felt alone. Hearing the wormwood seeds pop, he felt as if someone were talking to him. Later, day or night, he would light the wormwood. He found it calming and he could think things through.

He had to think now about what he was going to say after it got dark.

The livestock were growing restless. Seeing the whip in his hand, they bleated, brayed, and mooed, pressing him. It was already dark, and they wondered why they had not returned home.

"Let's go."

Leaning on the embankment, Old Guiju stood up and cracked his whip, the sound of which resounded in the darkness toward the desolate ridge.

When they returned, their home was full.

A wooden plank, a meter and half in length, was set up in front of the center opening in the pen to serve as a table. Sitting behind the table, Old Zhao, the cadre who had been sent to the countryside, motioned to him with his finger and smiled. Old Guiju acted as if he had not seen him and squeezed through the crowd to sit on his own small *kang*.

Old Zhao nudged the Brigade Leader with his elbow; the Brigade Leader walked toward Old Guiju.

"Have you thought about it thoroughly?" asked the Brigade Leader.

"Yes," replied Old Guiju.

The Brigade Leader turned to Old Zhao and said, "All right." Old Zhao said to the Accountant, "Start the meeting." The Accountant took the flashlight that he always carried with him from his belt, stood up, held it with both hands in the air, and flashed it. After pressing several times, he said, "Okay! We will continue with the meeting now. All right! Bring in Wen Hehe of the landlord class."

Everyone fixed their eyes on the opening in the pen. Three people filed in through the opening. They lined up in front of the table facing the commune members.

Old Zhao, the cadre who had been sent to the countryside, motioned for the two people holding red-tasseled spears to stand aside. A tall, thin man around forty was left standing there. It was Wen Hehe of the landlord class whom the Accountant had summoned. The sweat on his head glistened under the gas lamp above him.

"All right," the Accountant said, "the masses will speak freely tonight. He who wishes to speak, go ahead and speak up."

As on the first night, everyone lowered their heads, afraid that the Accountant would shine his flashlight on them.

The room was silent. All that could be heard was a mule stamping its feet to relieve its fatigue and the cattle swatting with their tails at the mosquitoes to keep them from the tender flesh below their rumps, on the other side of the door.

"All right," said the Accountant, rising to his feet, "let the long-suffering old farm laborer Wen Guiju, who harbors deep hatred, be the first to accuse."

"Come up here; come up here," said Old Zhao.

Old Guiju stood up but did not step forward.

All eyes in the room were upon him.

Old Guiju blew on the smoldering wormwood a couple of times, until the red light illumined his wrinkled old face and his slightly trembling beard.

He looked around at the people filling the room and opened his mouth several times as if to speak. Finally he steeled himself and spoke: "Suffered. I've suffered my whole life. But without suffering hardship, can one really be said to have suffered?" He paused a moment before continuing, "Hatred. I've never made an enemy of anyone. And speaking of him," said Old Guiju, his eyes fixed on the younger man standing before him with his head bowed, "he, he's not from the landlord class. He's a poor peasant. He, he's my son. He's my son. If you don't believe me, ask his mother." Finished speaking, Old Guiju sat down on the edge of his *kang*.

After a long while, the room finally exploded in fevered excitement.

After that, the man by the name of Wen Hehe dared to cough and raise his eyes and look at the others.

Danwa

He didn't really need to go out for a piss, but still Danwa left his court-yard to take a leak. He undid his pants and stood by the wall for what seemed like ages before he finally squeezed out a few drops. He had intended to fill that small hole in the corner of the wall with urine, but he had such pitiful little piss. He peed weakly, sending a dribble over the ground, his pants, and the back of his hand.

"Damn it," said Danwa.

"I'm hungry," said Danwa.

After taking a leak, he did up his pants and pricked up his ears. He had merely pretended to go out for a piss; in fact, he had come out to listen. In the distance he could hear the laughter and loud talk of many people. It came in waves, first loudly and then quietly, pierc-ing his ears, piercing his flesh, piecing his bones, making him ill at ease.

"Fuck your mother, Old Zhuzhu," said Danwa.

"Fuck your ancestors, Old Zhuzhu," said Danwa.

After cursing Old Zhuzhu, he went back to the cave.

The cave was pitch black as he entered from the bright sunlight outside. It was so black it was greenish black. With a blink of his eyes, gold specks would appear and float amid the greenish blackness, where they would remain briefly before disappearing.

Pickup, his woman, was frying oats on a corner of the stove. The scorched smell of the fried oats filled the place.

Danwa sniffed as if he were trying to keep snot from running from his nose. He sniffed a couple of times.

He sniffed as he clambered onto the *kang*.

"I tell you to eat and you don't eat; I tell you to go work in the fields and you don't go," said Pickup.

"You just don't want to do anything; you just don't want to do anything," said Pickup.

"It's not because I don't want to do anything," replied Danwa.

"Then why don't you go work in the fields?" asked Pickup.

"'Cause I'm sick. I'm really sick," said Danwa.

"If you're sick you should lie down, but you won't," said Pickup.

"The sun is almost directly overhead," said Pickup.

Danwa was silent.

Danwa watched as several flies lit on the steamed corn bread. He shooed them away with his hand.

The steamed corn bread was in a willow strainer on the *kang*, next to which was a bowl of oatmeal. Although the oatmeal was on the thin side, it had developed a skin after sitting for a while. It was still watery around the edge of the bowl. Danwa felt like gulping it all down. He knew it would take no more than three bites to finish the steamed corn bread, and two gulps to finish the oatmeal. He was reluctant to do so because he'd said he was sick, very sick. He had told Pickup that he had no appetite. How could he eat after what he had said? *I have my pride. We Chinese always keep our word. If I said I wasn't going to eat, I won't eat.*

Raising his rear, Danwa peered out from a hole in the window. Seeing nothing of interest, he rolled back.

They really won't come; they really won't come for me, thought Danwa.

Danwa was waiting for someone to come and fetch him.

After Old Zhuzhu and Young Zhu started sharing the same woman, Old Zhuzhu had taken the bride money his younger brother had saved and had a third room dug out. The door and windows were going in today. Someone from each household was asked to contribute "neck work," as it was known in the Wen Clan Caves. When a donkey's neck itched and it couldn't scratch it, it would have one of its kind take care of the itch with its teeth. When two donkeys were together, they could use their teeth on each other to take care of any itch. For this reason, such mutual assistance was referred to as "neck work" in Wen Clan Caves.

Installing doors and windows didn't require much; it was a way of having people over for deep-fried cakes. This was the village custom.

If there were no deep-fried cakes, then there would be pieces of skillet cake.

Danwa had been waiting since early that morning for someone from Old Zhuzhu's to come and get him, but no one came to knock on his courtyard gate or call him from the street.

Danwa really hoped that someone would come and call him, but no one did.

The fucker forgot me, thought Danwa.

They're so fucking busy that they forgot me, thought Danwa.

About the only time to eat deep-fried cakes was at New Year's. It looked like there would be no deep-fried cakes for him today, thought Danwa.

He glanced at the steamed corn bread. Another horde of flies had alighted. He reached out and shooed them away with his right hand. But before he had lowered his hand, the brazen flies were back on the steamed corn bread. His left hand being closer, he used it to shoo them away. But they were back in the blink of an eye. He shooed them away again. It went on this way between Danwa and the flies without either side giving in. It seemed like a competition to see who had the most patience. In the end, it was Danwa who gave in. He no longer bothered to shoo them away. He let them crawl over the steamed corn bread.

Suddenly he heard the sound of voices in the courtyard. He raised his rear and glued his eye to the hole in the bottom of the window.

It was the wife of Caicai, the son of Widow San. She was standing in the courtyard, looking all around.

"Did our Fengfeng come over to your place?" asked Caicai's wife.

"Every time she wants to lay an egg, she runs off to someone else's place," said Caicai's wife.

"Haven't seen her," replied Pickup.

"We don't have a rooster here," added Pickup.

"Did Caicai go out to the fields to work?" asked Danwa.

"The Brigade Leader said he wouldn't deduct work points today if you don't go. Who'd go?" said Caicai's wife.

"Is he at home?" asked Danwa.

Caicai's wife had not caught Danwa's question before she left.

"Fuck!" said Danwa.

Danwa rolled back over on the *kang*.

There were more dark spots on the steamed corn bread—fly droppings. At first the fly droppings couldn't be seen on the bread, but gradually they turned black.

Several flies flew from the steamed corn bread to the edge of the bowl. Asses up, they drank from the bowl. They lapped up the oatmeal with their hairlike probosces.

Fuck you; your master is hungry and you keep eating and drinking, thought Danwa.

Danwa was about to shoo them away with his left hand when he changed to his right hand. He cupped his right hand and slowly but surely moved it closer to the bowl to catch one alive.

"Hey!"

With a vigorous sweep of his hand, he caught a fly. It hopped around in his hand, making his palm itch. Feeling his palm itch made the soles of his feet itch. His crotch began to itch, so he scratched his ass.

Your master is going to kill you, you fuck, thought Danwa.

Your master is not going to let you die that easily, thought Danwa.

He carefully grasped the fly in his hand by its wings. He broke off a piece of straw sticking out of the mat on the *kang*. He grasped one end with his teeth and shaved the other end into a blade with his fingernails. With the straw blade, he cut off the poor fly's head. Only then did he release it.

The headless fly buzzed off. It hit the window and fell on the window sill, then again took flight with a buzz. Danwa didn't see where it flew off to.

He cupped his hand again and moved it toward the steamed corn bread and the bowl of oatmeal where several unwitting souls ate and drank, unaware that death was so near.

Danwa decapitated several more flies in the same fashion. Soon the entire room was full of headless flies buzzing around bumping into things.

A man can't live without his head, thought Danwa.

But a fucking fly can, thought Danwa.

"Look who's playing around," said Pickup.

"What patience; what skill," said Pickup.

"Why are you called 'pickup'?" asked Danwa.

"No one is called 'pickup' except you," said Danwa.

"Leave me alone," said Pickup.

"I know why you're called 'pickup'," said Danwa.

"I heard my mom say she heard your dad say that you were picked up on the road," said Danwa.

"Your dad can really pick a name. Picked up off the road, so he calls you 'pickup.' Is your dad dumb, or what?" asked Danwa.

"Who cares if I was picked up on the road or not?" asked Pickup.

"My mom said that your dad originally didn't have a woman," said Danwa.

"You stick your nose into too many things," said Pickup.

"Your dad said my mom had to go to his place one month a year. But your dad always had to come and get my mom and bring her back again," said Danwa.

"He'd bring her back and then he'd have to come back for her; he'd bring her back and he'd have to come back for her," said Danwa.

"What business is that of yours?" asked Pickup.

"You ought to know that when your dad comes for my mom, my dad is left all alone," said Danwa.

"When your dad comes for my mom, he is no longer a poor bachelor, but my dad becomes one," said Danwa.

"So long as you're not a bachelor. Come with me and do some grinding," said Pickup.

"I'm not doing any grinding, that's women's work," said Danwa.

"I'm going to go dig potatoes at the household plot," said Danwa.

Pickup remained silent. She placed the flour sifter and the *kang* broom in a basket of toasted oats, which she hoisted onto her shoulder, and then departed.

Seeing his woman depart, Danwa grabbed the steamed corn bread and devoured it in two or three bites, following which he picked up the bowl of oatmeal and practically inhaled it. A headless fly had fallen into his bowl and he sucked it down too.

The fly heads on the *kang* all stared at him with their big eyes, but he paid no attention. He took a hoe from the courtyard gate where it was hanging and set off.

The noise and laughter in the distance pierced his ears, pierced his bones.

Shouldering his hoe, he continued walking. But he didn't go to his household plot. He headed toward Old Zhuzhu's new room.

"Sorghum, Sorghum, is the new room ready?" he asked Sorghum, Old Zhuzhu's eldest son. Sorghum was busy and didn't hear him.

"Corncob, Corncob, is the new room ready?" he asked Corncob, Old Zhuzhu's youngest son. But Corncob didn't hear him either.

"Uncle Zhuzhu, today is a happy occasion. Are the door and windows in?" he asked Old Zhuzhu. Old Zhuzhu heard him.

"You're back from the fields early," commented Old Zhuzhu.

"I heard that points were not being deducted for not working today. Who's going to work?" replied Danwa.

Danwa wanted to ask Old Zhuzhu another question, but he was called away by someone else. Danwa looked around and saw his father among those present helping out.

Fuck it. So he's here, thought Danwa.

I'm sure he gets to eat deep-fried cakes, thought Danwa.

So they invited him instead of me. But I should be counted as a separate household. We're two different families. We each have our own, but they invited him and not me, thought Danwa.

It's his fault—he gets to eat and I don't, thought Danwa.

Angry, Danwa had an idea. He wanted to play a trick on his old man. His idea made him very happy.

"Dad . . ." called Danwa.

"Dad . . ." called Danwa.

Blackie heard his son calling. He left off working and went over to him.

"Dad, Pickup's dad is here. He's brought Mom back. He looked all over for you and finally left," said Danwa.

"Really?" asked Blackie.

"Call me a donkey if I'm lying," replied Danwa.

Blackie left Danwa and ran home in hurry.

Fuck, he believed it, thought Danwa.

Fuck, he can't wait. He misses his old lady, thought Danwa.

Fuck, he ought to use his head—does he think Pickup's dad would bring my mom back before the month was over? thought Danwa.

No longer able to see his father, Danwa set off toward the outskirts of the village.

Danwa's household plot adjoined that of Old Zhuzhu. When he arrived, he tossed his hoe aside and sat down on the field embankment.

Fuck, Old Zhuzhu didn't forget me; he never intended to invite me. I stood right there in front of him and he didn't invite me. The fucker actually said I was back early from the fields, but he didn't even ask me to have some deep-fried cakes. Fuck, thought Danwa.

Fuck. When did I piss him off? wondered Danwa.

Was it that time? Danwa thought of that incident at the threshing ground.

What happened was:

The threshing ground was covered with ears of grain. Danwa led a donkey with blinders. The donkey pulled a stone roller, that one with one big end and one smaller end. Danwa led the donkey in circles, pulling the stone roller over the grain.

At the grain rack, the women cut the heads of grain from the stalks using small hand scythes.

Danwa saw Old Zhuzhu's eldest son, Sorghum, among the women, pressed close to Pickup. He saw Sorghum's thigh pressed close to Pickup's thigh. He watched as Sorghum rubbed his thigh against Pickup's each time he cut the heads of grain from the stalks.

Danwa threw down his whip and charged at Sorghum.

"Sorghum, why are you rubbing your leg against my wife's?" asked Danwa.

"I didn't," replied Sorghum.

"You didn't rub but you rubbed?" asked Danwa.

"I didn't rub," said Sorghum.

"You did."

"I didn't."

"You did."

"I didn't."

"Shame on you!" said Pickup. She spoke in a clear, resonant voice. So saying, she stood up and walked away.

"Shame on you," said Danwa.

"Shame on you," said Sorghum.

"Shame on you!"

"Shame on you!"

"Shame on you shame on you shame on you!"

"Shame on you shame on you shame on you!"

"Shame shame shame shame shame...."

"Shame shame shame shame shame...."

They went on shouting "shame, shame, shame, shame" at each other at the same time, neither one of them stopping. Finally the Brigade Leader shouted for them to stop. The Brigade Leader said if their red lips itched so much, they could go do it with the commune's male pig, Bakexia. This time neither one of them said a thing, and each returned to his work.

He can't be angry with me for that, thought Danwa. *He rubbed up against my woman and he expected me to say nothing? Besides, after work Sorghum got me by the neck and boxed my ears. I didn't hit him. It can't be on account of that, it can't be,* thought Danwa.

Well, then what was it? What did I do to offend his family? wondered Danwa.

Dong . . . ga. . . .

Pipai, pipai, pipai. . . .

"Fuck your damned firecrackers," said Danwa.

"After the firecrackers, the deep-fried cakes are eaten," said Danwa.

"Everyone's eating deep-fried cakes," said Danwa.

Danwa leaped up, picked up his hoe, and went to his household plot.

Then he entered Old Zhuzhu's household plot.

Cha! Cha! Cha! He thrust his hoe.

Cha! Cha! Cha! He wielded his hoe vigorously.

He dug until he was covered with sweat from head to toe. He was very happy.

He heard the roots of the corn shoots snapping in the earth, *gebeng, gebeng.*

Hearing that *gebeng, gebeng* of the roots of the corn shoots snapping made him very happy.

Fuck your mother for not inviting your master to have deep-fried cakes, cursed Danwa inwardly as he dug.

Fuck your mother, your master is telling you that you didn't invite him to eat deep-fried cakes. Danwa hoed and cursed in his heart.

Danwa hoed and cursed, hoed and cursed. He dug until he nearly blacked out; seeing that the sky was no longer blue, only then did he stop.

The corn plants that he had root-cut were still standing, green and upright. But Danwa knew what they'd look like by the same time the next day.

Having vented his anger, he was very happy.

Danwa sat on the field embankment resting for a time, looking at the corn. Only then did he shoulder his hoe and head home. He sang as he walked:

Deep-fried crisp millet cakes with a dish of potato strips
Little sister, there's no money for you to loosen your pants.

He sang the same two lines all the way home.

He ran into Pickup at the courtyard gate.

"Why are you so late?" asked Pickup.

"You must be famished," said Pickup.

"That goes without saying," replied Danwa.

"Hurry in and have some deep-fried cakes," said Pickup.

Entering the cave, he removed the lid from the terra-cotta pot on the *kang*. Inside was a half pot of deep-fried cakes. A half pot of sweet-smelling, bright yellow, golden-brown deep-fried cakes.

"Where did these come from?" asked Danwa.

"Where else? Old Zhuzhu had someone bring them over," said Pickup.

"I, I, I fuck my mother," said Danwa.

Danwa quickly looked away from the pot of deep-fried cakes on the *kang*, where he saw the horde of fly heads, and those pairs of big eyes all staring at him.

Heinu and Her Andi

White-haired and bareheaded, Heinu clutched a red willow stick taller than herself for support as she walked. As she made her way, she called out, "Andi, Andi . . ."

When she ran into someone, she would ask, "Have you seen my Andi? Where did you happen to see my Andi?"

Everyone shook their heads and said that they had not seen her "auntie."

Heinu went elsewhere to look.

She checked the cattle pen, the sheepfold, the threshing ground, the stone roller, and finally every woodshed of every house, but still her Andi was nowhere to be found.

Then she looked beyond the village.

"Andi, Andi," Heinu called as she walked, but her Andi never answered her from its hiding place. Nor did her Andi flap its wings and come running on its long legs, as it had always done in the past, and, with a gust of cool air, leap onto her shoulders. Outside the village, she searched all the places she had taken her Andi to eat bugs. She called everywhere, but her Andi was nowhere to be found.

The sun was setting.

After searching here and there and everywhere, Heinu could walk no farther. Grasping her red willow stick, she sat down on the field embankment on the west side of the village. She scoured the area with her eyes, hoping that she might suddenly spot her Andi. But though she looked this way and that, the sight she longed for never materialized.

The flock of sheep returned.

Shepherd Boy resembled a victorious general leading his troops home. He shouted at the lambs, "Fuck your mothers fuck your ancestors," as he cracked his whip. Several hundred legs flashed chaotically.

Many of the sheep had red or blue patches—large and small, light and dark—smeared on their backs. They were like brands for the privately raised sheep. Most of the privately raised sheep were fat and stout, while those of the Brigade were thin and bony.

Upon entering the village, not one of the privately raised sheep obeyed Shepherd Boy. They bleated, jumped, crowded together, and bumped into one another as they all ran home. The remaining Brigade sheep docilely followed Shepherd Boy back to the sheepfold.

Poor things, the poor sheep, thought Heinu.

Oh, where is my Andi right now?

The Accountant's two piglets came grunting into the village. Shifty-eyed, the two piglets always followed the wall as they walked. They looked as if they were up to no good or had just done something bad.

Where is my Andi? Where could my Andi be? wondered Heinu as she watched a group of chickens approach from the wilds beyond the village.

The red clouds in the sky faded into darkness.

One cloud resembled her Andi. Red cockscomb and red feet, the greenish-black feathers gleaming with a golden light. It really looked like her Andi, thought Heinu.

Suddenly, Heinu heard a sound, a familiar, very familiar sound.

"It's my Andi; it's my Andi," said Heinu as she listened.

"It's my Andi calling me: my Andi is in the wild, overgrown graveyard calling me," Heinu said as she listened.

Heinu stood up and, grasping her red willow stick, set off toward the wild, overgrown graveyard.

It grew darker and darker.

It grew darker and darker.

Andi had been given to Heinu the year before by an outsider who spoke with an accent.

That morning, the laborers had gone with the Brigade Leader to hoe oats on the western slope. Nursing infants were taken to the field and the older children followed their parents to the western slope to take care of their little brothers and sisters. A few useless old men and women remained in the village. They all gathered outside Heinu's cave, where they enjoyed the cool while plucking lice.

An old man who spoke with an accent came down from the southern ridge carrying a large basket. Upon entering the village, he shouted, "Baby chicks for sale, baby chicks for sale!"

No one understood what he was shouting. Only after he arrived shakily with his burden did they hear the peeping of the chicks and the clacking of the steel-colored claws in the bottom of the basket, and understand that he was selling baby chicks.

"Let's see, let's see," said everyone together.

The old man removed the lid from the basket. The basket was filled with downy black chicks with yellow bills. The old men and women praised the chicks and picked them up to examine them and argue about whether they were male or female. But in the end, no one bought any.

The chickens in the village could produce chicks, so why would they want to buy any?

"What breed of chicken do you have? Stupid chickens," said the old man.

"These are Australian Blacks," said the old man.

No one understood what sort of black he said. Anyway, they didn't buy any.

Heinu saw the sweat on his brow, so she brought him a ladle of cool well water from her cave. The water was fresh—Leng Er had brought it from the well that morning when she made breakfast. The old man gulped down half a ladle of water; the remainder he poured into a gourd.

The old man rolled the red and white towel on his shoulder into what looked like a pot stand. He put the towel around his head and picked up his basket to leave. Then he put it down again, removed the lid, grabbed a chick, and gave it to Heinu.

Heinu did not refuse but reached out to accept it. In this way lonely old Heinu received a chicken as a companion for her days.

She held the chick on her open hand; its claws tickled her palm. She put the chick on her index finger to perch, but the chick was afraid of falling so dug its claws into her finger. It then opened its yellow bill and cheeped at her. She said the chick was thirsty. She pursed her lips and gave the chick her own saliva to drink.

"Heinu, Heinu, you've never raised a kid, but you've always raised chickens. You can't give such a small chick water," said one of them to Heinu.

"It's spit, not water," replied Heinu angrily. Heinu always got mad when someone mentioned that she had never had a child.

After Heinu married, she wanted to have a child, but it never happened. It was said that there was an efficacious Guanyin temple in Caofuluo Village outside Datong. She went there to burn incense and bow to the goddess. When she prayed to the goddess, she said, "Maybe there is something wrong with me and I can't have kids, but that wasn't the case before I married. Maybe there's something wrong with my man so I can't have kids, but I've slept with other men. Who is to blame?" The goddess never enlightened her as to who was to blame—herself or all her men. Anyway, she never had a child.

Heinu called her little chick Fluff Ball.

Heinu loved her Fluff Ball.

She paid no attention to the others and continued to give her chick saliva to drink from her own mouth, oatmeal from her own mouth, as well as thin millet gruel from her own mouth. She liked to feel Fluff Ball's hard bill on her tongue. It felt good, even better than doing that.

At night when she went to bed, she covered Fluff Ball with an old unlined jacket and placed it by her pillow. In that way, whenever she woke up she could touch it.

Normally she left an opening in her house so that the neighbor's cats could come and go freely to catch rats, but she blocked the opening after she got Fluff Ball. She was afraid they would kill Fluff Ball or carry it away and eat it. Heinu knew that some cats, unable to catch a rat, might turn their attention to a small chick. Wen Shan's cat, which was called Ratter, liked to kill chicks.

Fluff Ball grew quickly. It developed wings in a couple of weeks and sprouted tail feathers in less than a month. It soon clucked rather than cheeped.

Heinu never prepared a feeder for Fluff Ball, but let it eat from her own bowl. When Heinu took up her bowl, the chicken would leap up onto her elbow. She would take a bite, then the chicken would take a bite. They took turns, and neither one complained, made a mess, or was afraid of making the other sick.

Heinu never built a chicken coop for it; it slept on the *kang* with her. Fluff Ball no longer wanted to be covered with her tattered old unlined jacket. The moment she covered it, it would peck her. It didn't want to peck her, it just didn't want to be covered with the jacket. She stopped covering it. Fluff Ball wanted to sleep on a perch. She placed the stool on which she sat to fan the fire upside down at the head of the *kang*. Fluff Ball would sleep on the horizontal struts. Getting up in the morning, she would see chicken droppings on the bottom of the seat, which she would brush into the kitchen fire. Dry chicken droppings would burn like coal.

When Fluff Ball grew large enough that the cats couldn't eat it, she let it out in the courtyard. Fluff Ball would stretch its legs and run all over the courtyard without tiring; it would scratch and scratch, scratching up things to eat. She took it to the uncultivated places to eat bugs. Fluff Ball would eye and eye a large locust before it would grab it in its beak; then it would stretch its neck and pull back, stretch its neck and pull back several times before the locust went down its gullet. Heinu was always afraid it would choke, so she would squat and catch small locusts to feed it. But she wasn't always able to catch them—sometimes she grabbed for one, but as she opened her hand, there was nothing there. Sometimes she thought she had caught nothing, but as soon as she removed her hand, the locust would hop away. She always chuckled regardless of whether she caught one or not. Fluff Ball's clucking resembled her chuckling.

Wherever Heinu went, Fluff Ball was sure to follow. Wherever Fluff Ball went, Heinu was sure to follow. Regardless of how far Fluff Ball wandered, as soon as it heard Heinu shout its name, it would come running. When Heinu saw Fluff Ball loping around like a camel, she called it "camel." When Heinu shouted "Camel," it knew she was calling it. Fluff Ball could recognize Heinu's call. It would come running to Heinu, flapping its wings, and with a rush of cool air leap onto her elbow or her shoulder.

She would carry it back home like a hunter carrying a hawk.

By the time the threshing was done in the fall, Fluff Ball was fully grown. It stood a neck taller than any of the other big chickens. It was covered with shiny black feathers and its tail and neck feathers gleamed with a golden sheen. Its crest, legs, and eyes were red. No one in the village had ever seen such an attractive chicken.

"Next year when that fucking old outsider comes, we'll have to buy some no matter what," said all the villagers.

On the morning of the sixteenth day of the first lunar month when people worship their ancestors, Fluff Ball squatted on the *kang* and laid an egg for Heinu.

Heinu thought it was a rooster and had never felt its rump to see if it could lay eggs. But after making a hell of a fuss for hours, it actually laid an egg.

Happy as could be, Heinu picked up the warm egg and walked around.

Heinu suddenly recalled that she should let the dead see it.

The dead included, first of all, her husband. Then there was Jinlai, Zhaozhao, Fufu, Guigui, and the old drunk Pothook, as well as several others she could no longer remember. When they were alive, they had been intimate with her and even done that.

Poverty was the one thing that had been handed down over generations in the village. Some men were so poor they could never take a wife. Heinu thought that chickens and dogs all mated. As a woman, she couldn't bear to see the men as less than chickens or dogs. She'd had this thought after a certain incident had occurred.

The incident happened like this:

One day she was taking a noon nap when suddenly she remembered that she hadn't stirred the contents of the bean paste pot in the sun on the roof in several days. If she wasn't careful it would be full of maggots. She climbed up on the roof to stir the contents of the pot. As she was stirring, she saw Zhaozhao. There was an empty piece of land behind her place, in front of which was a sorghum field. She saw

Zhaozho in the empty piece of land behind the sorghum field. He was bare-assed and trying to mount a ewe. The ewe couldn't figure out what he was trying to do and was struggling to run away. He was afraid that the sheep would run away and afraid that it would bleat. He also was trying to lift its tail while holding it by the neck. Trying to do everything at once, he tripped and fell, face up. Heinu couldn't help laughing and almost laughed aloud.

Later, when Heinu ran into Zhaozhao and no one else was around, she said, "Zhaozhao, Zhaozhao, I know all about it." Zhaozhao, who had no idea what she was talking about, just stared at her. She continued, "Zhaozhao, Zhaozhao, I saw you." When she saw that he still didn't understand, she said, "Around the time of the noon nap that day, I was up on the roof." Hearing this, Zhaozhao blushed furiously. He dropped to his knees with a thud and said, "Heinu, Heinu, Heinu. I'll call you Grandaunt, I'll call you Grandmother. Heinu, if you tell anyone, I won't be able to go on living."

It was that time that Heinu took off her trousers and let Zhaozhao do it with her.

From then on, whenever one of the unmarried men wanted to do it, all they had to do was ask, and Heinu would never refuse.

~

Heinu placed the egg in a terra-cotta pot, put the lid on, and let it sit for a while so that the dead could eat their fill. Only after that would she eat it. Actually on the lid of the terra-cotta pot, she placed a pair of chopsticks made of sorghum stalks, which in Heinu's mind served as a spirit tablet for the dead. There was no way to set up a real spirit tablet because it was considered superstitious, and there would be real trouble if the Brigade Leader found out about it; he would revoke her status of enjoying the five guarantees. If her status were revoked she would no longer be able to count on her grain ration, or having Leng Er or the other unmarried men take turns to carry water for her. Nor could she count on receiving three catties of meat at the New Year. With the exception of households enjoying the five guarantees, few households in the village could get three catties of pork to eat for New Year's.

After the deceased had seen it long enough, she made a fire and boiled the egg in a pot. She then peeled the egg. The peeled egg was white and fragrant and shook just a bit because it was soft boiled. She placed it in a bowl and sprinkled it with salt. She then put it back in the pot and offered it to the dead again. If she didn't offer it to them, they wouldn't get anything else to eat that year. She'd see them off in the afternoon with the spirits of her ancestors and could only invite them back in thirteen months to eat and drink. When they were alive they always shared anything good to eat with her. Zhaozhao was even more generous—he would set aside things for her to eat and go hungry himself. One time when he was driving a cart, he picked up an apricot on the road but didn't eat it; he carried it for two days for her to eat. The dead were all in the underworld and would never again partake of things in the world of the living. Furthermore, they had no family. That's why on New Year's Eve, Heinu would always secretly burn some paper money for them, invite them all back to share everything, have something to eat and drink, and pass a comfortable spell at home before seeing them off again on the sixteenth of the first lunar month.

She waited until the egg was nearly cold before she ate it, one small bite after another. Fluff Ball sat on the ground watching her eat. Contrary to its customary practice, it did not join her. Fluff Ball knew that it was wrong to eat an egg it had laid.

Fluff Ball struggled nearly every day to lay an egg for Heinu on the *kang*. The newly laid egg was hot, and at first the shell was soft and could be impressed with a finger; later it would harden.

But after seeing off the dead, Heinu ate no more eggs—she'd save up a dozen or so and, taking up her red willow stick, take them to the commune, where she'd trade them for things such as coal oil, salt, matches, toilet paper, noodles, and alum. There were a lot of things on the commune store shelves, but Heinu traded only for what she needed. She even traded with the commune hospital for several packets of pills in the event of an emergency.

One time she didn't know what to get, so she traded for a pane of glass and pasted it to the hemp paper in the window. That way she could stay indoors and look out through the glass and keep an eye on

Fluff Ball in the courtyard. She couldn't help humming the beggar's song she'd been fond of singing when she was young:

> I think about you, about you, I think so hard about you
> I embrace my pillow and give a kiss.
>
> I think about you, about you, I think so hard about you
> I kiss a mouth full of buckwheat husks.

She hummed and hummed, then she stopped. She found herself funny. Old as she was, she shouldn't be singing such songs. Old people were just not much good for anything. There was that time when Grunt carried water for her and then hesitated to leave. Heinu thought he was hungry, so she told him to stay and eat. But it wasn't eating that was on his mind. Fuck if he didn't say he wanted to do it. Heinu replied, "Oh no. I can't. When a person gets old, they can't do it. Old ghosts." Then she said, "But if you want to look, you can look." Grunt replied, "I don't want to look, it's better not to look at all." So saying, he turned and left. Since then, he had not come back to her house. When it was his turn to help her out as one of those enjoying the five guarantees, he'd ask someone else to take his place. It seemed as if his pride were hurt.

Heinu's Fluff Ball attracted a lot of attention and people found it delightful. And it kept on laying eggs. Her Fluff Ball was the envy of the entire village.

Talking it over with Heinu, a number of villagers tried to convince her to let Fluff Ball mate with the large roosters of the village, because only fertile eggs would produce chicks, produce little Fluff Balls. Seeing nothing wrong with the idea, Heinu consented and told them to bring them over.

Although Heinu promised, Fluff Ball didn't cooperate. Fluff Ball was not as good-hearted as Heinu to let anyone do it who wanted to. Fluff Ball would not allow itself to be mounted by any rooster.

With a shake of its wings, Fluff Ball would frighten the roosters and send them running for their lives. In fleeing, some of the roosters would try to leap over the wall, leaving white claw marks, but they were unable to clear it though they still kept trying. They clawed the wall but always fell back to the ground. They squawked and rushed madly about, leaving feathers everywhere.

Seeing that Fluff Ball wouldn't be producing any little Fluff Balls, all the villagers could do was hope that the outsider would return, the one who wore a towel on his head like a pot stand. They hoped he would come to sell more little black chicks. But the day he should have returned came and went and there was still no sign of him.

One morning, Heinu opened her eyes and saw that it was already light, but Fluff Ball was still asleep, perched on the upturned stool. When she got dressed, Fluff Ball didn't turn to look at her. Normally, it would have leaped and fluttered over the *kang* as Heinu folded up her quilt. Only after Heinu came back from emptying the chamber pot and cleaned up the droppings from off the stool did she notice that the droppings were not the same as usual. They were black and runny. She hurriedly picked up Fluff Ball and noticed that its eyelids were not bright red but rather purple. Its crown and claws were the same. It was cold as winter ice.

Heinu began to sob. Her large tears flowed, dripping on Fluff Ball, falling to the ground.

When Chou Bang came to carry water for her, he suggested that she go see the barefoot doctor. She stopped crying and, without even taking her red willow walking stick, picked up Fluff Ball and left. Unable to find the barefoot doctor, she took it to the veterinary clinic. There they told her they only looked after large livestock and not chickens. She could do nothing but return home with Fluff Ball.

After crying for a time, she suddenly recalled the medicine she had got by trading. Unconcerned with what sort of medicine it was, she opened Fluff Ball's beak and fed it two pills, then washed them down with some water.

That afternoon, Fluff Ball opened its eyes and looked at Heinu. Its cockscomb was no longer such a dark shade of purple and it was no longer so cold. Clearly it wasn't going to die. Heinu hugged it and wept some more. But this time she was so happy. She kissed its crown and went to make something to eat for it. She added more medicine to the food so that it would get better quickly.

In a few days, Fluff Ball made a complete recovery. But after recovering, Fluff Ball ceased to lay eggs.

It just up and ceased to lay eggs, and that was it. Originally she had raised it for company, not for eggs. Having it recover was better than anything else.

Fluff Ball had never been one to wander around on the road, but after recovering it liked to go out, and Heinu's calls were ineffective in making it stay. Once out on the road, it would go in search of other chickens, in search of hens.

Whenever the village hens saw Fluff Ball coming, they would stop what they were doing and hunker down, lift their tails exposing their red rumps, and allow Fluff Ball to mount them. Fluff Ball would strut, its chest thrust forward, over to the most attractive hen. It would spread its right wing like a fan and circle the hen. Round and round it would go before leaping on the hen's back to do it. To maintain its balance, it would grasp the feathers on the hen's neck in its beak.

After mounting one, it would circle and mount another.

This provoked the ire of the other roosters, but none dared to take on Fluff Ball alone, so they ganged up. But they were soon routed by Fluff Ball—one lost an eye, another had its crown torn off. They all squawked and fled, leaving all the hens as spoils for Fluff Ball.

"Heinu stirred up all the men in the village, and now Fluff Ball is getting revenge for them," said someone.

"That's great! Next year the village will be filled with Fluff Balls beyond reckoning," said someone else.

After that, Heinu started calling the androgynous Fluff Ball Andi.

One night around midnight when everyone was sound asleep and dreaming sweetly, they were suddenly awakened by a rooster crowing.

"Cock-a-doodle-doo . . ."

No one had ever heard such resounding and frightening cockcrows.

"Cock-a-doodle-doo . . ."

Everyone in Wen Clan Caves Village was startled.

It was the good deed of Heinu's Fluff Ball Andi.

"Cock-a-doodle-doo . . ."

It not only crowed at midnight, it also crowed at the break of day and at noon. It crowed in the morning and in the afternoon, and at night as soon as everyone had gone to sleep. It crowed whenever the fancy took it. It crowed more times in a day than could be counted.

But worse still, it didn't crow alone, but got the other roosters to crow as well.

Even worse yet, in addition to the other roosters, it got the hens to call.

Andi got all the other chickens in the village crowing so no one could sleep, no one could be confused. Andi wanted everyone in the village wide awake.

No one in the village of the Wen Clan Caves could take it.

"It's disturbing everyone," the villagers told Heinu.

"Kill it," the villagers told Heinu.

Everyone in the village scolded Heinu, but she didn't listen. She couldn't kill her Andi that mated with the hens and laid eggs and crowed.

On this day, she had taken the five remaining eggs to the commune store and traded them for a pack of matches and a bottle of coal oil. She placed the articles on the lid of the clay pot just inside the door and went out looking for her Andi.

Unable to find her Andi, she thought the worst. She couldn't find it anywhere.

After dark, Heinu thought she heard her Andi in the wild, overgrown graveyard. When she went to the graveyard to check, she thought she heard Andi calling to her from West River. When she went to West River to check, she thought she heard her Andi calling to her from home.

Midnight. Heinu hurried home from West River with her red willow stick. She hoped with all her heart that Andi was just playing with her and was not lost. All she had to do was open the door, light a lamp, and it would be there sleeping, perched on the upturned stool.

Heinu hurried into the courtyard. Heinu hurriedly opened the door. Heinu anxiously called "Andi," but the house was dead quiet.

She reached out and felt for the matches on the lid of the pot, but couldn't find them. She managed to knock the bottle of coal oil to the ground. Impatient, she wanted to light the house to see if Andi was asleep, perched on the upturned stool.

She found the box of matches, removed one, and struck it.

Hua! The cave was illuminated.

The stool was empty. Andi was nowhere in sight.

Overcome, she dropped to the floor with a thud. The still-burning match in her fingers fell into the firewood soaked in coal oil.

A fire started with a whoosh.

The fire raged.

Amid the flames, Heinu suddenly caught sight of her Andi. Andi floated down out of the sky on its huge spread wings and landed in front of Heinu. After Heinu had climbed on its back, it soared into the sky with a flap of its wings. It flew higher and higher and farther and farther, leaving Wen Clan Caves Village far below.

Sun-Drenched Nest

It was a cloudless day and not a breeze was stirring. The sun shone brightly in the dry, cold air.

A group of men were congregated after working on several meters of terraced field. They were curled up on the slope, basking in the sun, laughing and talking.

"Wen Bao, tell us again what it was like inside," said Chou Chou.

"That's all I've done the last few days. I keep repeating myself," replied Wen Bao.

"But I haven't heard it all. I heard it's better inside than out," said Chou Chou.

"I never said inside was better than outside," said Wen Bao.

"Everyone says so," said Chou Chou.

"Whatever. People say what they want. I didn't say it, though," said Wen Bao.

"What I said was that inside you can eat white flour and rice, deep-fried cakes, and vegetable buns. Every ten days or two weeks, you get some meat," said Wen Bao.

"There's fish too. You get fish on New Year's and festivals," said Leng Er.

"Fish?" asked Chou Chou.

"Fish," replied Leng Er.

"Leng Er, do you know what fish looks like?" asked Zits Wu.

It's, it's . . . it's like the fish in the picture on the wall above the Brigade Leader's stove. The fish in the baby's hands. It's even bigger than the baby," said Leng Er.

Everyone laughed: "Ha-ha-ha-ha-ha." They laughed, "Ha-ha-ha," and laughed, "Ha-ha," and laughed, "Ha." They laughed until they were breathless.

"Inside you can watch movies and listen to the radio," said Zits Wu.

"Radio? A transistor, a transistor," said Leng Er, looking askance at Zits Wu.

"Doesn't that make it better inside than out?" asked Chou Chou.

"People say what they want. I didn't say it, though," said Wen Bao.

Wen Bao had been released from prison. He told everyone that inside you ate well, dressed well, and never suffered from the cold. At first no one believed him. But when everyone saw his white flesh, his new gray cotton uniform, they believed him. When they saw him bending forward in his doorway in the morning holding a cup and brushing his white teeth like Old Zhao, the cadre who had been sent down to the countryside, they were even more certain.

"Were there women inside?" asked Leng Er.

"All you think of is women. You always go on about women," said Zits Wu to Leng Er.

"Can there be any men without women? Would you be here if there were no women? Is your mom a woman? Is she androgynous? Like Heinu's Fluff Ball?" Leng Er asked Zits Wu.

Zits Wu was left speechless.

"Fuck, that's the way the world is: men and women, women and men," said blind Guan Guan. Guan Guan had not been involved in making the terraced fields. He was one of those who enjoyed the five guarantees. He was bored at home alone, so he always went to where people were gathered.

"Look. Even the sparrows are in pairs," said Dog. Dog was feeling around in his crotch as he watched two sparrows alight on a dried-up tree.

Everyone looked at the sparrows.

The two sparrows were chirping to each other as if considering where to go to eat.

"Fuck your mother," said Leng Er. Leng Er picked up a rock and threw it at the dried-up tree.

The sparrows took flight, worried for their lives.

"Look at you. The sparrows weren't bothering you," said Dog as he felt around in his crotch.

"Who told them to go around in pairs?" said Leng Er.

"You're jealous," said Zits Wu.

"Aren't you jealous? If you're not jealous, why do you go and listen outside Wen Hai's bridal chamber all the time and not even take a noon nap? You want to listen," said Leng Er.

"Aren't you jealous? You're the one who goes around wailing, 'Baibai, Baibai,' every time you get drunk," said Leng Er.

Hearing this, everyone laughed again, "Ha-ha-ha."

Zits Wu was left speechless again and just blinked several times.

Leng Er was a bit slow, but he always wanted to vie for the floor.

Dog finally managed to extract some small object from his crotch. Placing it in the palm of his hand, he said, "Fuck! I thought it was a louse, and after all that it's not." He threw the minute object to the ground and rubbed his hands, as if he were making dough fish at a party.

Grunt squatted and looked until he found the thing. Pinching it up and placing it in his palm, he said, "Fuck! I didn't think it was a louse, and after all that it is." Imitating Dog, he threw the minute object to the ground, then rubbed his hands as if he were making dough fish at a party.

Everyone laughed. Everyone burst out laughing, "Ha-ha-ha, ha-ha-ha." Guan Guan, who was blind, was also laughing in their midst, laughing the loudest of all. When everyone else had stopped, he was still laughing, "Ha-ha-ha."

"Blind as a bat, you can't see a thing. What are you laughing about?" said Grunt to Guan Guan.

"Who are you talking about? Me?" said Guan Guan, raising his chin. It was as if he had an eye under his chin with which he was trying to get a look at who was talking about him.

"Who? You," said Grunt.

"I heard you all laughing and figured it must be funny, so I laughed too," said Guan Guan.

"Laughing blindly. Even if we were laughing at you, you'd still laugh blindly," said Grunt.

"That's life. Sometimes you laugh blindly, sometimes not," replied Guan Guan.

Although Guan Guan was blind, he sometimes said something to make them think. This time, several of them muttered and nodded in agreement.

A night-soil cart went by from the south. The carter sat above the axle singing:

Thirty-three buckwheat seeds, ninety-nine timbers
Kissing someone through a pane of glass, how frustrating!

They watched the night-soil cart depart. Then one of them said to Wen Bao, "Sing something for us. Let's see if you still remember how."

Wen Bao was good-looking. Wen Bao had a good voice. Before going to prison, Wen Bao had been a carpenter and had traveled all over. He had learned a lot of songs; Wen Bao was the opera singer of Wen Clan Caves Village.

"What do you want to hear?" asked Wen Bao.

"Sing the one that goes, 'A soldier's no good, I'm pulled and dragged into the sorghum field,'" said Leng Er.

"That's . . ." said Wen Bao.

"You know, the one that goes, 'My auntie, my auntie,' that one," sang Leng Er, hinting to lead him.

"Not that one, no. It's one of the 'Four Olds.' It's poison. I'll sing you some new opera," said Wen Bao.

As everyone cheered, Wen Bao stood up and moved to the open ground.

"*Pituy, pituy.*" Wen Bao spat forcefully two times. After spitting, he said, "Some sand got in my mouth."

Everyone was a bit confused. He had been fine a moment ago, and then suddenly sand got in his mouth.

"This is called 'Moral of the Day,'" said Wen Bao. He raised his arms and sang:

How many suffering compatriots can be heard to complain
Struggling and suffering under the invader, hatred unassuaged
Waiting for an opportune moment as spring thunder explodes

How meekly the brave Chinese nation submits
To the butcher's knife
Hoping, hoping for the early arrival of Comrade Boshan.

A red lantern hangs high, shining ahead
I give the shout
Sharpened shears clang with cleavers.

Wen Bao sang and gestured. His gestures were neat and direct—a stab was a stab, a cut was a cut, like the real thing. When he finished singing, he returned to where he had been sitting.

No one said a word; all that could be heard was Wen Bao panting.

After a long while, they began to talk. They said they only understood the line, "Sharpened shears clang with cleavers."

"Why are there sharpened shears, clanging with cleavers in opera?" asked Dog.

"It's new opera," replied Wen Bao.

"What damned tune were you singing to?" asked Zits Wu.

"Model opera. Beijing opera," said Wen Bao.

"What gold tools, silver tools, horse tools and ox tools? Did you learn that inside?" asked Dog. ("Beijing opera" is homophonous with "gold tools.")

"Yeah. I sang some big operas," said Wen Bao.

"What? You sang major operas inside?" said Grunt.

"Fuck your mother. He sang major operas inside," said Leng Er.

"I sang whole scenes. We even gave performances to convey greetings and appreciation. Whenever we performed we would be treated to a banquet with six cold and six hot dishes," said Wen Bao.

"Fuck your mother. If you'd had a woman too, you'd have been leading the fucking life of an immortal," said Leng Er.

"Fuck. A woman is just a woman. Plenty of times when we were setting up stage, the woman who sold porridge would take me out back and let me fuck her standing up," replied Wen Bao.

"Fuck your mother. Fucked her standing up," said Leng Er.

"You're just making it up. Who said you could? Did you get a tax stamp for that?" said Zits Wu to Wen Bao.

"If I'm making it up, I'm that thing of yours," said Wen Bao.

"Weren't you afraid of getting stuck fucking her standing up?" asked Zits Wu.

"People are people, not dogs. Bang, bang, and it's done. How could you get stuck? I'd never get stuck," said Leng Er. Leng Er liked to put Zits Wu in his place.

"As if you ever did it with a woman," said Zits Wu.

Leng Er had no comeback, and glared at Zits Wu. Zits Wu paid no attention to Leng Er. He smiled and looked away.

"What else did you do? Let's talk about something else," said Chou Bang, to change the topic. Chou Bang wasn't afraid that Leng Er and Zits Wu would get into a fight—fighting wasn't something that had been handed down over the generations of Wen Clan Caves. Chou Bang just didn't want to hear them talk about women anymore. Whenever people talked about women, Chou Bang couldn't get to sleep at night, and he'd do nothing but think night after night about that damned Nunu, who married and went off to the mines.

"What else did you do inside, Wen Bao?" asked Chou Chou.

"Everything. We played basketball, ping-pong, did calisthenics, tug-of-war, high jump, long jump, and other things. We did everything," said Wen Bao.

Again everyone was silent. They were all trying to figure out what it was to play basketball, ping-pong, tug-of-war, and calisthenics.

"Hey, Wen Bao. You say you're not making this up. Inside you had food, clothes, and even women. Why the fuck would you ever leave?" asked Grunt.

"Um, um . . ." said Wen Bao.

"None of that 'um, um,' just tell us," said Grunt.

"Um, did I have a choice? They wouldn't let me stay there even if I wanted to," replied Wen Bao.

"What do you mean, you didn't have a choice? All you've got to do is get drunk, curse the secretary, and you'll go back in," said Grunt.

"I, I'm not making it up, but I don't want to go back in," said Wen Bao.

"Why not?" they all asked.

"It's freer outside than inside," said Wen Bao.

"There's no freedom inside," said Wen Bao.

"Having food and clothes is enough. What do you want with freedom?" one of them asked.

"Then you guys go in and see," said Wen Bao.

"Oh, that's just being human. Sometimes that's just being human," said Guan Guan.

Hearing Guan Guan, they muttered and nodded their heads. But thinking about it, they couldn't figure out what Guan Guan meant. Nor could they figure out what human nature was.

"Fuck your mother," spat Leng Er. Leng Er always spat the same words and no one knew whom he was swearing at.

Another night-soil cart went by. The carter sat above the axle, singing:

You're in your brother's heart, little sister
When I don't see you for a while, I search the whole village for you.

It was a cloudless day and not a breeze was stirring. The sun shone brightly in the dry, cold air.

The Woman of the Zhu Household

After lunch, Old Zhuzhu, his brother Young Zhu, and his two sons, who were all taller than the door, went to the western room. The four men went to the western room to sleep. They'd get up only when they heard the Brigade Leader shouting from the well platform, "Get up, it's time to go work in the fields." It had always been so—after lunch the four men would go to the western room, where a fire was never lit. It was a great place to take a nap because it was cool, and there weren't many flies.

"There are no wild garlic flowers in the house. I asked Caicai's wife for some yesterday when Old Zhao, who was sent to the countryside, was coming to have his arranged meal here," said the Zhu woman at lunchtime.

"I won't take a nap the next two days. I have to go to the wild, over-grown graveyard and pick some wild garlic flowers," said the Zhu woman while eating lunch.

"It's scorching hot this afternoon. You'll be cooked," said Young Zhu.

"I'm not afraid of the heat. I have to go at noon so I don't lose work time in the fields," said the Zhu woman.

"It doesn't really matter if you go to the fields or not. To heck with it. It won't change our being poor," said Young Zhu.

"The afternoon sun makes the wild garlic flowers all the more fragrant. The heat brings out their aroma," said the Zhu woman.

Zhuzhu listened to them without saying a word. Ever since he and his younger brother had started sharing the same woman, he'd had nothing to say. Even when it was his turn to go sleep with his woman in the eastern room, he said nothing. He didn't say anything when they did it. She didn't concern herself with his not speaking. She figured he still felt injured and resentful. Hold back your anger and you'll slowly be able to hold yourself in check. That's the way people are. You cry until you don't cry; you're angry until you're no longer angry.

The Zhu woman was neat and orderly. It took her no time at all to clean the dishes and the eastern room.

Old Zhao had said so yesterday. "Eating at your place, the food is clean, the house is clean. You are the only clean woman in the village and the cleanest in the commune." While he spoke, Old Zhao's eyes grew more besotted, even more so than the Accountant's.

Hearing nothing but the sound of snoring coming from the western room, the Zhu woman tied a white kerchief around her head, picked up her straw hat, and left.

The venomous sun rendered everything a glaring white brightness.

The street was silent and not a soul was to be seen. Regardless of whether they were full or hadn't eaten well, everyone in the Wen Clan Caves took a nap after eating.

The Accountant's big, filthy white pig, food smeared around its mouth, was resting comfortably in the shade, unperturbed, and went on snoring even when a small chick pecked at the food around its mouth.

Look how comfortable it is, thought the Zhu woman.

Such luxury, thought the Zhu woman.

Leaving the village, the Zhu woman shaded herself from the venomous sun with her straw hat.

But she didn't head for the wild, overgrown graveyard as she had just said. She turned down the road along West River.

Suddenly two piglets ran out of the potato field beside the road; they ran nervously back to the village. No doubt they had been stealing something to eat.

The two piglets belonged to the Accountant.

Most people can hardly take care of themselves, thought the Zhu woman.

When will we ever be able to raise a pig? wondered the Zhu woman.

"Pei!" spat the Zhu woman. *Such comparisons only make a person angry. We can't aim too high. It'll be enough to do it right and get a job for the oldest boy as a laborer on public projects. That way we won't have to worry about getting a wife for him. It's foolish to aim too high; it'll just shorten a person's life*, thought the Zhu woman.

"*Pei, pei,*" the Zhu woman spat twice. Whenever the Zhu woman felt the need to keep evil at bay, she would spit a couple of times.

She took the white kerchief from her head and wiped the sweat from her face. Replacing the straw hat on her head, she quickened her pace along West River.

West River was the only nice place in the vicinity of the Wen Clan Caves.

West River was four kilometers long, was wide, and had a flat bottom, and water ran in it all year. The water flowed, meandering down the riverbed, resembling a snake. Sometimes Old Guiju grazed his animals there. The grass grew as high as chives and always grew back, grew back after being grazed.

A number of poplar groves grew at points in the bed of the river. The trees grew thin and tall. Some of the trees grew taller than nine meters out of the riverbed. Lots of sparrows were heard twittering in their limbs.

It was a wonderful place, but few people came except for Old Guiju, because they said it was haunted. It was said that the crooked tree at the outlet of the river resembled a banner for calling the spirits of the dead, one that always seemed to call people from the Wen Clan Caves.

The Zhu woman was not afraid. She didn't believe in ghosts. Before she had married into the Wen Clan Caves, she had heard the adults talk about this haunted place, but she was not afraid. She often crossed the ridge to get there. She would pick bitter herbs, cut cattails at the edge of the river, and carry water from the river to flush out ground squirrels, which she would roast and eat. She would often strip naked and jump into the water of the dammed river. After she married Old Zhuzhu when she was thirteen, she came even more frequently.

This time, she again stood by the edge of the river.

No one knew when or what ancestor of the Wen Clan Caves had laid the large stones to create the reservoir. During the dry season, it was two *mu* in size, and the still water reflected the green trees along the shore, the blue sky, the white clouds, and even the darting dragonflies.

No one dares come to such a wonderful place. It's their loss, thought the Zhu woman.

Will you be fortunate? Will your oldest son become a public projects laborer? the Zhu woman asked herself.

She looked back along the road on which she'd come. Not a soul was in sight. She looked at the river. Not an animal was in sight. She looked up at the sun. It would be a while before anyone got up from the noon nap.

Certain that no one was around, she unbuttoned her jacket and undid her underwear. She took off her shoes and slipped out of her clothes, exposing her white body for the sun and the sky, the sparrows and the butterflies to see.

Feeling the hot stones on the soles of her feet, she quickly shifted her footing to the cattails. Treading on the cattails, she entered the water. But suddenly she stopped. Looking up and across the river, she climbed out of the water to the edge of the reservoir. She decided she ought to wash her clothes. Squatting, she put her clothes in the water, bubbles rising, *gudu, gudu.* Several large tadpoles fled, while several others approached, their tails wriggling. They were curious about the *gudu, gudu* of rising bubbles.

Nearby, the Zhu woman saw a couple of white-bellied toads in the middle of doing it by her feet. The male was on the back of the female; the female was under the belly of the male. The two long legs of the male clung tightly to the female's waist. The female's waist was narrowly compressed. They were making little toads. She wondered if they were conscious of producing thousands of little toads or not.

Can you afford to feed them? You are concerned only with your own pleasure, thought the Zhu woman.

Her face felt warm. She kicked the two toads into the water, but the two of them clung just as tightly to each other without letting go.

People know shame, but are never satisfied; animals are satisfied but know no shame, thought the Zhu woman.

What is satisfaction? What does it mean to have no shame? the Zhu woman asked herself. She asked without answering. She simply shook her head.

Only after she had spread her washed clothes on the large stones of the dam did she wade out into the middle of the water, swinging her white arms, and then sit down. It was really dry and the water was very low. Even when she sat down, the water didn't come up to her neck.

There was warmth in the coolness of the water and coolness in its warmth.

The water was clean and bright and the bottom could be seen.

The Zhu woman felt very comfortable; she felt good all over.

When she washed her breasts with the white kerchief, she thought of her brother-in-law, Young Zhu.

Young Zhu was different from his older brother. When his older brother finished doing it, he would roll to one side and snore, fast asleep, and pay no more attention to her. Young Zhu was different. Young Zhu would use his big hands in turn to squeeze those mounds of flesh on her chest. Only after he fell asleep did he release his grip. If he woke up at midnight, he'd have to hold them again.

"Sister-in-law, when I was little I liked to hold my mother's. I could only get to sleep if I held them."

"What did you do before our arrangement?"

"I always had a hard time getting to sleep."

"You're hopeless."

"Sister-in-law, you are my mother."

"You're funny."

"I'm okay."

"Young Zhu, you are a child. You're almost forty and you're still a kid," said the Zhu woman.

"Some people never grow up," said the Zhu woman.

Do I really not look like I am approaching forty? Old Zhao insists that I don't look thirty. He says, looking at my body, that I don't even look as if I've had kids. What a funny Chinese, thought the Zhu woman.

Thinking these thoughts, the Zhu woman left off washing and scrubbing. She pressed her breasts and the flesh of her thighs with her fingers; she turned this way and that to look at her naked body in the water.

"Fucking Old Zhao really knows how to talk," said the Zhu woman.

"Those sent down to the countryside just know how to talk," said the Zhu woman.

I'm sure Old Zhao knows about our arrangement. He said, "I hear your family dug out a third room. Is that so your eldest can get married?" That's what he said. Why didn't he ask if it was so that my brother-in-law could get married? Our family ought normally to be more concerned about my brother-in-law. But he didn't ask about him.

"He knows. The fucker found out," said the Zhu woman.

"Who cares if he knows? We're so poor," said the Zhu woman.

There's no shame in being poor. Being poor doesn't mean a person knows no shame.

Even Blackie shares his wife with his in-law from far away in the mountains, doesn't he? People say he planted both gourds and melons. Who can say anything about the two brothers in our family sharing? thought the Zhu woman.

Besides, Zhuzhu isn't much fucking good; he has to have some help to get by. If they didn't share, we wouldn't have the three rooms. Relying on Old Zhuzhu is just no good.

To me, a woman can be compared to a cart. Men are hitched to the cart between the shafts. It's always better to have help than not alongside the shafts to pull the cart. If there is help, the cart goes more smoothly while the one who is hitched to the cart has an easier time. That's the way it is, thought the Zhu woman.

That's the way I see it, thought the Zhu woman.

Who rides in the cart? Any need to ask? The kids, mainly the kids. They ride in the cart. They ride first and pull later. That's the way it is, thought the Zhu woman.

If you can't pull a cart, you get a helper. If you can't feed the kids, you get another man. There is nothing wrong with that. In our house, for example, sharing is pretty good. It's good for my brother-in-law because he doesn't have to live like a bachelor. It's good for his older brother because he needs help to feed his family. It's good for the kids too, because how would we ever have three rooms? And last, it's not bad for me. At most it keeps me busy, but that's nothing, that's just the way women are. It's like Dog is always saying in his beastly way: men are not afraid of suffering; women are not afraid of . . . doing it.

Thinking such thoughts, the Zhu woman touched her breasts once again.

After washing and scrubbing all over, the Zhu woman looked up at the sun. They ought to be waking from their naps about then. The fucker ought to be coming soon.

She stood up and looked down the road. Not a soul was in sight.

The fucker better not be playing games with me and make me wait here for nothing. No way, not the fucking way he behaved yesterday. He was ready to do it then and there, and wanted me to take off my pants. He'll be here, he'll fucking be here for sure, thought the Zhu woman.

A gadfly flew and bumped against the Zhu woman where her thigh joined her hip, then flew off again. But it circled back and flew straight at her crotch. The Zhu woman hurriedly covered her crotch with one hand and with the other picked up her kerchief to meet it and strike at the gadfly.

Weng! Off flew the gadfly.

Figuring her clothes must be dry, the Zhu woman walked toward the dam. Afraid that she would slip in the mud, she spread her arms. Before she had taken two steps, she felt something hit her where her thigh joined her hip.

The gadfly had returned, determined to bite that tender flesh.

"What? What? The fucker wants inside me," said the Zhu woman.

"Why would I let it? Give my second son a job as a laborer on public projects and I'll let you in," cursed the Zhu woman as she struck at the gadfly.

"Ha-ha . . ."

The Zhu woman suddenly heard the sound of laughter. Without a second thought, she sat down in the water. But she was in a shallow place and, though she splashed the water, her breasts were still visible. She quickly covered them with her kerchief.

"Ha-ha . . ."

The laughter grew more delighted and more explosive.

The Zhu woman collected herself and looked in the direction of the laughter.

It was Old Zhao, who had been sent down to the countryside, standing by the grove of trees.

Old Zhao, who had been sent down to the countryside, had been there for some time.

Old Zhao was a man of his word. He had arrived some time ago, but remained concealed in the poplar grove, watching as the Zhu woman performed for him. He watched as she undressed, stripping off her clothes to expose herself to him. He watched as she kicked the two shameless toads into the water, as she squatted opposite him to wash her clothes. Later he watched as she waded to the middle of the water. As she walked, her naked body was doubled: one above the water and one reflected in the water. He watched as she washed herself. How she swore and swore at that shameless gadfly. . . .

Old Zhao, the cadre who had been sent down to the countryside, sure knew how to enjoy himself.

"So it's you, Old Zhao," said the Zhu woman.

"You kill me, you're so funny," said Old Zhao.

"Keep your voice down, Old Zhao. Someone might hear," said the Zhu woman.

"Didn't you say there'd be no one here?"

"Sometimes someone comes unexpectedly."

"I won't shout. But you can't sit in the water forever and not come out."

"How can a person get dressed with you standing there?"

"Oh . . . okay. Okay."

"You just say 'okay, okay,' but don't move."

"Okay, okay."

Only then did Old Zhao unwillingly step back, step back into the poplar grove.

~

That afternoon, Old Zhao lay on the grass in the poplar grove. He was as dizzy as if he had been drinking. Soon he dozed off. A breeze blew cool and soft over him.

The Zhu woman came out of the poplar grove and, as if her legs had been oiled, made her way quickly from West River to the wild, overgrown graveyard.

After she had filled her hat with wild garlic flowers, she left the wild, overgrown graveyard. Her heart seemed well oiled and comfortable.

Far up on the ridge, someone sang a beggar's song for her.

Black cattle and white horses rest in the grass
Seeing her far away, my legs give way.

The Zhu woman fixed her eyes on the person in the distance but couldn't tell if it was someone from the village.

Her straw hat by two blowing ribbons knotted
The more you look at her, the more you love her.

"Like kissing through glass, trying in vain to relieve your desire," said the Zhu woman.

Fanning the fire, the bench upside down
How pitiful are the unmarried men.

"Pitiful, be pitiful," said the Zhu woman.
"But my Sorghum won't be pitied long," said the Zhu woman.
The Zhu woman could no longer make out what the man on the ridge was singing. She had long since walked away.

Lucky Ox, Lucky Ox

Immediately upon entering his house, Lucky Ox stripped off his clothes and burrowed under his quilt.

Throughout the year, his quilt was spread on the *kang*. He never rolled it up or folded it. He never even piled it up. All the unmarried men found this approach the least troublesome. Whenever they wished to burrow under the covers, all they had to do was burrow. All the unmarried men in the village did the same. But there was a bad side to the practice. One year Chou Bang set off to work on an irrigation project. When he returned a month later, he heard a squeaking sound at his feet. He struck a match and saw a nest of hairless baby rats. When the rats felt the quilt move, they thought it was their mother returning, so they began squeaking and moving about, seeking her teats. After that Chou Bang would shake out his quilt every three to five days in the afternoon, for fear the rats would move in again. Nothing of the sort ever happened to Lucky Ox.

Lucky Ox got up early to relieve himself. As soon as he stepped out the door, he took a piss. With a stream of urine, he made a hole in the dry earth that was neither large nor small, nor round nor square. He thought the hole resembled something. He thought it looked like the thing called "heavenly sun" as described by Grunt.

"Brother Lucky Ox, Brother Lucky Ox."

Lucky Ox was looking at the puddle of urine, which was neither large nor small, nor round nor square, when he heard a woman's voice calling his name.

Looking up, he saw Wen Hai's woman from next door up on the wall, smiling at him.

Immediately his face felt warm. He quickly lowered his eyes and saw that hole. His face felt even warmer.

"Brother Lucky Ox, that lousy Wen Hai still hasn't come back. He said he was going out to make some money to pay off some debts. He's been gone two months and still hasn't returned."

"Brother Lucky Ox, the Production Brigade said my household can open half a *mu* of uncultivated land. Soon all the good land will be taken, and that lousy Wen Hai still isn't back," said Wen Hai's woman.

"Brother, go with me this morning to have a look to find some land to cultivate," said Wen Hai's woman.

Lucky Ox stared at the puddle of piss without speaking.

"Brother, I'm talking to you, but you always ignore me," said Wen Hai's woman.

"Elder Sister, I'm listening," replied Lucky Ox.

"Elder Sister, I'm listening," replied Lucky Ox.

"Come over and have breakfast," said Wen Hai's woman.

"No, I still have leftovers that will spoil if I don't eat them," said Lucky Ox.

So saying, he quickly went back inside and wouldn't come out again regardless of what Wen Hai's woman said from the wall.

There was no good land nearby. Lucky Ox and Wen Hai's woman found a piece near the hollow below the southern ridge. It was a little far, but not bad.

"You go on back and let me do the digging," said Lucky Ox.

"How could I leave you here to dig by yourself? You'd be lonely," said Wen Hai's woman.

They started by digging the rocks out of the field.

When Wen Hai's woman dug rocks on the eastern side, Lucky Ox would move to the western side.

When Wen Hai's woman dug rocks on the western side, Lucky Ox would move to the eastern side.

Once all the rocks had been dug out, they had to be piled around the field. In that way, the Production Brigade could measure the field to see if it exceeded half a *mu*; then the rocks could serve as a retaining wall to prevent the soil from being washed away if it rained.

"Elder Sister, you go back now. Little Dog must be crying," said Lucky Ox.

"He's all right. Big Dog is looking after him," said Wen Hai's woman.

Wen Hai's woman competed with Lucky Ox in carrying the rocks. When she bent over, a strip of white flesh was visible at her waist. *Shua!* It was as if Lucky Ox's eyes had been blinded by the sun. He quickly looked away. But for some reason, the same patch of flesh flashed at him again. A short while later, it flashed at him again.

"Brother, why is your face so red? You must be tired. Let's rest a bit," said Wen Hai's woman.

"You take a rest; I'm not tired," replied Lucky Ox.

So saying, he felt his face get even warmer. He knew why his face was so flushed.

When the field wall was half piled, Old Man Heaven sent down rain. Suddenly raindrops the size of elm seed fell, *pili-pala*, from the bright red sky.

Wen Hai's woman stood up and saw that there was shelter from the rain to be had at the foot of the cliff behind her. "Hurry up! Hurry up!" She motioned to Lucky Ox to run for it. She ran to the foot of the cliff. When she got there, she saw Lucky Ox still piling stones on the field wall. She covered her head with her hands and ran out again. She seized Lucky Ox by the sleeve of his jacket and dragged him to the foot of the cliff.

"Look, you're all wet, Brother," said Wen Hai's woman.

Wen Hai's woman took a white hankie from her belt and reached to wipe his face. Lucky Ox snatched it from her and wiped his face himself. It seemed okay to him to wipe, but he began to itch uncomfortably all over. He smelled an enchanting fragrance on the hankie. It had to be the enchanting aroma of a woman's body that Grunt had talked about. He quickly handed the hankie back to Wen Hai's woman. It seemed okay to give it back to her, but he saw her breasts. She was soaking wet and her blouse clung to her breasts. Two bulging round mounds protruded before Lucky Ox's eyes.

Lucky Ox felt faint and quickly leaned against the cliff face.

"Brother, I recall you are twenty-eight this year," said Wen Hai's woman.

Lucky Ox nodded.

"You're two years older than me," said Wen Hai's woman.

Lucky Ox nodded again.

"See, I remember," said Wen Hai's woman.

Lucky Ox nodded yet again.

"Actually, what's all this 'Elder Sister' this and 'Elder Sister' that?" said Wen Hai's woman.

But this time, Lucky Ox didn't nod. He suddenly rushed out into the rainy field.

Wen Hai's woman looked at the raindrops illuminated by the brightly shining sun; she looked at Lucky Ox madly piling stones in the brightly shining rain. Wen Hai's woman heaved a long sigh.

After having lunch at Wen Hai's woman's place, Lucky Ox didn't stop to rest. He shouldered a shovel and stepped out the door. Wen Hai's woman went to the western room, where she spread the white sheepskin, which was part of her dowry, for him to rest on. But he didn't say anything and insisted on going to the hollow beneath the southern ridge.

When it was nearly dark, Wen Hai's woman arrived.

"Oh, look how you have leveled the soil, Brother!" exclaimed Wen Hai's woman.

"It's a good piece of land," said Lucky Ox.

"Brother, it is as smooth and level as a *kang*. Just looking at it would make anyone want to lie down on it," said Wen Hai's woman.

"It's a good piece of land," said Lucky Ox.

"Brother, it's so quiet all around the field, not even a sparrow is stirring," said Wen Hai's woman.

"It's a really good piece of land," said Lucky Ox.

"I'm talking with you, and all you know how to say is that it's a good piece of land," said Wen Hai's woman.

"It's dark. Let's head back," said Lucky Ox.

All the way back, Wen Hai's woman stumbled along, bumping into Lucky Ox. When she didn't bump into him, he wished she would; when she bumped into him he could hardly stand it. Lucky Ox wanted to throw the shovel on the ground, but he didn't.

Throw it down, throw it down—still he didn't.

Throw it down, throw it down—still he didn't.

They stumbled along home without him throwing down the shovel.

For dinner, Wen Hai's woman prepared potato strips, fried eggs, and poured wine for him.

"Look, Elder Sister, I can't eat a thing," said Lucky Ox.

"I poured you a cup of wine," said Wen Hai's woman.

"I can't drink," replied Lucky Ox.

"I understand you. Have you forgotten that time?" asked Wen Hai's woman.

Hearing Wen Hai's woman speak so, he felt his face gradually begin to warm.

Wen Hai's woman took a needle from a sorghum-stalk basket; with it she poked the wick, and immediately the kerosene lamp flared up. The entire room was brightly illumined.

Wen Hai's woman placed some potato strips and some egg in the Big Dog's bowl and said, "Eat, then go sleep in the other room."

Wen Hai's woman held Little Dog and unbuttoned her blouse to nurse him. Her bulging white breasts suddenly appeared. Those bulging white breasts were like the sun, blinding Lucky Ox. It didn't matter where Lucky Ox turned his eyes, he was still dazzled.

Lucky Ox quickly picked up his chopsticks and held up his cup of wine. Then he began shoveling food and wine into his mouth. He shoveled food into his mouth as if he had been famished his entire life; he ate like a beggar, and didn't have the slightest idea what he was eating.

Wen Hai's woman watched Lucky Ox eat, then lowered her head to kiss Little Dog.

Za'r! one kiss.

Za'r! another kiss.

Za'r! Za'r! kiss after kiss as Lucky Ox ate.

Za'r! Za'r! kiss after kiss—it was simply killing Lucky Ox.

Eating and eating, Lucky Ox suddenly noticed that the wine bottle was half full.

Fuck, if I have any more to drink, I'll make an ass of myself, thought Lucky Ox.

Lucky Ox knew himself. He knew that if he drank more than half a bottle, he wouldn't be able to control himself. He wouldn't be responsible for his actions. He would say things he normally wouldn't dare say; he would also do things he normally wouldn't dare do. Once when he was working for the County Opera Troupe he got drunk and chased Xi'er and Tie Mei. On that account Da Chun and Huang Shiren, as well as Li Yu and Jiu Shan, pinned him down and made him pay for it. When he returned to the village he went crazy. Later he crowned himself with a rock, and only then did he recover. Last year, Wen Hai and his woman had a fight. He came over and broke it up. After they patched things up, they invited him over to eat. He had too much to drink that time as well. He was determined to touch Wen Hai's woman's back to see if she was sweating or not.

"Brother, why aren't you drinking?" asked Wen Hai's woman.

"I've had enough," replied Lucky Ox.

"Have a couple more cups," said Wen Hai's woman.

"Elder Sister, I can't because I'll make an ass of myself again," said Lucky Ox.

"What's there to be afraid of? I'm no stranger. It's all right to make an ass of yourself, so long as no one else knows about it," said Wen Hai's woman.

"Really, Elder Sister, I can't drink any more," said Lucky Ox.

Lucky Ox jumped to the floor; Wen Hai's woman followed suit.

"So don't drink if you don't want to. Let's sit a while longer. We seldom sit together," said Wen Hai's woman.

"I can't. Elder Sister, you really don't understand. I've already had too much," said Lucky Ox.

Lucky Ox pushed aside Wen Hai's woman, and without using the gate, leaped over the wall into his own courtyard.

Immediately upon entering his house, he stripped off his clothes and burrowed under his quilt.

His whole body felt hot and his head was spinning. Tossing and turning, he couldn't sleep.

Lucky Ox threw aside his blanket and stared at the ceiling of his dark cave. His eyes fixed, he felt a hand touch him, touch his chest, his stomach, touch him there.

He felt good. He shouted out "Elder Sister" and suddenly realized what had happened.

The hand he thought was touching him wasn't that of Wen Hai's woman, but his own.

"You're not a man. Fucking Lucky Ox," cursed Lucky Ox.

"You can't count yourself a man. Fucking Lucky Ox," cursed Lucky Ox.

"Die, die. Fucking Lucky Ox," cursed Lucky Ox.

He cursed himself viciously, repeatedly, without taking a breath. After cursing himself, he covered his face with his large hand. *Shua-shua-shua*, the tears rolled down his face.

Lucky Ox wept.

Cursing himself, Lucky Ox wept.

Shepherd Boy died.

Shepherd Boy hanged himself.

As soon as the lamps were lit, *pa'a'er*, a whip was usually heard on the outskirts of the village. It was Shepherd Boy leading a flock of sheep back to the village.

But that day, as people were getting ready to blow out their lamps, still they hadn't heard his whip; Shepherd Boy hadn't yet been heard driving the sheep, "Lamby, lamb, lambkins"; Shepherd Boy hadn't been heard swearing at the sheep, "Fuck your mothers, fuck your damned ancestors"; nor had the bleating or the hooves of the sheep been heard.

The Brigade Leader gave orders to several of the unmarried men, "Go up to West River and look. Maybe he's in a dark mood."

The Brigade Leader was right.

They found Shepherd Boy at West River. Shepherd Boy was hanging from that crooked tree at the outlet of the river, swaying in the wind like a banner. The round toads in the bottom of the river had become silent; not a single one croaked. Only the sheep seemed aware that something was wrong. They looked up and faced Shepherd Boy, bleating, "*mom—mom.*"

"Ai, such a wrongful death."

"All because he wanted to see some heavenly sun."

"But he died without seeing it."

"Why? Why?"

And so people talked about Shepherd Boy as they cut him down from the tree.

Shepherd Boy was also an unmarried man. His situation matched Grunt's: his dad was dead, his mom was remarried, and his grandparents were all gone. There was no one left in his family but him.

Shepherd Boy had been obsessed for the last two days. He had spent an entire day thinking only about a story Grunt had told. What Grunt said didn't amount to anything, but Shepherd Boy couldn't stop thinking about it.

This is the story:

There was a girl who went to pick bitter herbs with a bunch of boys on uncultivated land. As they were picking herbs, the girl suddenly stood up and said to the boys, "If you can guess which way my 'heavenly sun' faces—backward or forward—I'll give you all the herbs I have picked. If you guess wrong, you have to give me everything you have picked." One of the boys asked, "What's a heavenly sun?" The girl replied, "It's that little thing between my legs." The boys thought together and replied, "It faces forward." The girl pulled down her pants and turned her backside toward the boys and asked, "Backward or forward?" After that, she took all the bitter herbs the boys had gathered and put them in her own basket.

That's all Grunt had said, but Shepherd Boy had thought about nothing else for the last two days. He was obsessed.

That day, Shepherd Boy took the sheep to the outlet of West River.

In the river there were some poplar trees and tender grass that never stopped growing. But Shepherd Boy didn't dare go down into the riverbed because people said there were ghosts there. Shepherd Boy didn't go because he was afraid the ghosts might eat him or his sheep. He took the sheep to the outlet of the river and stopped. At the edge of the river there was a crooked tree; down in the channel there were grassy slopes and a basin of fresh water.

Looking at the sun, he decided it was time for a noon nap. He herded the sheep together. The sheep all tried to hide their heads under the rump of another sheep, to find someplace cool where the sun couldn't cook their brains. After that they were able to stand still without moving all afternoon.

The fuckers, all they care about is their heads and not heavenly sun.

Heavenly sun, heavenly sun . . . only a fucking girl could think up such a name.

A sheep's faces backward; so do those of donkeys and horses. How could a girl's also face backward?

Thinking such thoughts, Shepherd Boy went down into the riverbed, where he lay prone, putting his mouth to the water basin, drinking like an animal for a while from the basin. After drinking, he removed a greasy black bag from his belt. Inside was some toasted oat flour, a piece of dry, pickled yellow turnip, and a chipped bowl. He scooped out half a bowl of toasted flour, sprinkled some water in the bowl, and began mixing the flour and water. After mixing the flour and water, he ate pinches of the mixture using his fingers. He kept the bowl under his chin lest the flour fall to the ground. The village provided the shepherd with what was considered a good amount of grain, a catty and a half as opposed to the half catty for other commune members. But Shepherd Boy was always hungry. After finishing off the flour, he put the piece of turnip in his mouth and chewed. The dried turnip was tough and rubbery. He chewed it on the left side of his mouth, then on the right side, and then back again. He chewed it into a salty liquid before swallowing it. It was like eating vegetables and drinking soup. The liquid had the flavor of pickled turnips. It was very good.

After eating, Shepherd Boy made his way back up the slope of the riverbank. He hummed a beggar's song to ask for oat flour to eat. They don't want fresh cooked meal because it doesn't keep; they want flour they can take home to feed their families. There have always been too many beggars over the generations in the Wen Clan Caves, just as too many beggar's songs have been created over the generations in the Wen Clan Caves. In the Wen Clan Caves, men and women, the old and the young can all sing such songs.

Returning up the slope of the bank, Shepherd Boy sang:

Before the lamb takes milk, it must kneel on its forelegs
The shepherd without a wife has a hellish life.

After the lamb takes milk, it kicks its rear legs
The shepherd without a wife is miserable indeed.

He was going to continue singing, but he heard someone laugh and keep on laughing.

It was a woman! Shepherd Boy looked all around but saw no one.

Could it be a ghost in the river?

Ge-ge-ge, he heard the laughter again.

Shepherd Boy bent and moved in the direction from where the laughter was coming.

Squatting next to the crooked tree was a girl. She watched as a ram tried to mount a ewe. But the ewe was not cooperating. In a flash, the ram fell off, again and again. The girl laughed. It took forever before the ewe was subdued and the ram mounted her to do it.

"Cool! People and animals are the same. Cool! People and animals are the same." The girl clenched her fists and swung them again and again to egg on the ram.

Cool? The same? Fuck your mother. Fuck if it's the same. An animal does it with whoever's around and does it as many times as it wants. Can a person do that?

The more Shepherd Boy thought about it, the angrier he became. In a loud voice he shouted, "Can a person do that?"

Hearing this, the girl turned and looked at Shepherd Boy.

"Are people just like animals?" asked Shepherd Boy.

"Why not?" said the girl.

"Can a person do it as often as they want?"

"Why not?"

"Can a person do it with whomever they want?"

"Why not?"

"Doesn't that make them an animal?"

"You're the animal."

The girl stood up and stormed off in a huff.

Is she pregnant? The fucking girl is pregnant. Shepherd Boy thought it was hilarious. Watching the girl, her big belly sticking out, walk away, Shepherd Boy squatted against the crooked tree.

Could they be the same? I've never even seen a heavenly sun. I'm thirty-five and I've never seen a heavenly sun. Could they be the same? Fuck, an animal is better off than me.

The more Shepherd Boy thought about it, the more he realized how different people were from animals. The more Shepherd Boy thought about it, the more he realized an animal was better off than he was. As he was thinking, his thoughts returned to Grunt's story.

If it'd been me, I would have said it faces backward and not forward.

A donkey's is black, a sheep's is white. What color is a human being's?

As he was thinking these thoughts, he heard someone shout, "Bring my bitter herbs."

Bitter herbs? What bitter herbs?

"Bring my bitter herbs."

The girl with the big belly who had just walked away was shouting at Shepherd Boy from the other side of the flock of sheep.

Shepherd Boy looked to his left and right until he spied a willow basket nearby. It was half full of bitter herbs and a small trowel.

Shepherd Boy pulled the basket toward him, held it close to him, and said, "I'll help you pick bitter herbs."

"You'll pick bitter herbs with me?"

"Let me see your heavenly sun, and I'll pick bitter herbs with you."

The girl shook her head.

"I just want to look. I won't do anything else but look."

"Look at what?"

"Heavenly sun, your heavenly sun."

"What is 'heavenly sun'? I don't have one."

"Yes, you do. People have them just like animals. I have one too."

"Then let me see yours first."

"Okay, I'll show you."

Shepherd Boy lifted his skirtlike old trousers and said, "Look." Something popped out of the crotch of his pants.

When the girl approached and saw what it was, she turned and ran. She ran and she shouted, "My dad will beat me again, my dad will beat me again."

Shepherd Boy was stunned and stood there without moving, holding the basket. He watched until the girl disappeared.

That afternoon, Shepherd Boy didn't go anywhere. He squatted against the crooked tree, waiting for the girl to return. He hoped the girl would come and ask him to help her pick bitter herbs.

The girl didn't come.

That day, Shepherd Boy came back later than usual.

At midnight, the Brigade Leader opened Shepherd Boy's door and came in. The Brigade Leader struck a match and lit the lamp, and saw a willow basket in the middle of the floor. In it were bitter herbs, on top of which was a small trowel. The Brigade Leader woke Shepherd Boy.

"You're supposed to report to the commune tomorrow."

"What for?"

"There's a foolish girl there. They are trying to figure out who made her pregnant."

"Whether she's pregnant or not has nothing to do with me. I didn't do it. I just wanted to see her heavenly sun. But she refused and ran away."

The Brigade Leader asked a number of questions to understand what was going on. He said, "Take the sheep out as usual tomorrow. I'll talk with the commune." Then he picked up the basket and left.

Early the next morning, Shepherd Boy took the sheep to the outlet of West River.

~

The unmarried men took turns carrying dead Shepherd Boy on their backs. They said nothing the entire way. The sheep too were silent the entire way. The only thing that was heard was the hooves of the sheep on the road and the tails of the sheep slapping their rumps.

The moon shone white on the group of people and on the sheep.

Before entering the village, one of the people shouted and cursed:

"Fucking heavenly sun!"

"If you have to take a piss, just take a piss," said Dog.

"I don't have to take a piss," said Guan Guan.

"If you don't have to take a piss, why do you keep scratching your ass?"

"Just rubbing."

"When I have to take a piss, I always scratch my ass."

"You're you and I'm me."

"Then why do you keep scratching your ass?"

"I feel like scratching it."

"Rub, go ahead and scratch."

Dog had just told Guan Guan about the dream he'd had the night before, when he dreamed about Widow San. He said that Widow San had slept with him. He said that his dream was vivid, so vivid that he had seen Widow San's plump white thighs, her full white waist, and her large white breasts. As Dog told Guan Guan about his dream, Guan Guan began to squirm on the ground.

"Right you are. Widow San's body was that kind of white," said Guan Guan.

"You know? Blind as you are, you know?"

"I know."

"You know what the color white is?"

Guan Guan suddenly blinked and said nothing.

"See, you can't fool me," said Dog.

"Who doesn't know?" said Guan Guan.

"What was it like? You tell me."

"You know, white. Not dark."

"Fuck you. What a bunch of nonsense. Tell me what her heavenly sun looked like."

"Aren't you afraid that Uncle Pothook might strangle you?" asked Guan Guan.

"Uncle Pothook would strangle you if he were drunk," said Guan Guan.

Hearing Guan Guan's words, Dog glanced behind him at the large blue boulder. Widow San and Uncle Pothook had been buried together beside the big blue boulder.

It was pitch dark behind the boulder because the firelight didn't reach there.

Dog pricked up his ears but heard nothing. Only then did he turn back.

"I'm not afraid. If you were in my shoes, you wouldn't be afraid," said Dog.

"If you don't believe me, then try tonight. There's nothing to be afraid of," said Dog.

"Widow San spreads her legs like a pair of shears for you, showing you her heavenly sun. Are you afraid? You wouldn't have time to be," said Dog.

Guan Guan didn't rub his ass. He knelt, tucking his feet under his rear. He seemed as if he were afraid his rear end would run off and so used his feet as an anchor.

"Widow San was really a good person," said Dog.

"She was said to be pretty old, but her breasts were big and plump," said Dog.

"Are you finished? You talk too much," said Guan Guan.

"What are you afraid off? You're not Chou Bang. You shouldn't be afraid of a little talk."

"Check and see if the porridge is ready."

Only then did Dog stop talking and go check on the porridge.

~

Being masters of their own fate, the people of the commune had repaired the irrigation ditch all the way to the wild, overgrown graveyard west of the Wen Clan Caves. As soon as it grew dark, the laborers from the various villages returned home, except for Dog, who had the graveyard shift. If no one took the graveyard shift, then someone would walk off with the rubber tires from the small flatbed, take them home and make wheelbarrows with them. Others would steal the ten red flags planted on the side of the ditch and take them home and put them away until they were needed for a rare wedding or to be used to pay a bride price. The red flags were silk and could be made into wedding quilts or mantas. But they couldn't be used to make red belts, because the fabric was slick and couldn't hold up a pair of pants. If you weren't careful, your pants would fall at the most inopportune time, and you'd make an ass of yourself.

In addition to keeping an eye on these things, a graveyard shift worker had to get up early and make a huge pot of millet porridge for the morning workers as well as slice up a pot of salted yellow turnips, to which he had to add some sesame oil. Everything was provided by the commune. You could eat for free. Everyone wanted to eat but was afraid of being late.

Working the graveyard shift was great. The work points were high and you could fill up on porridge. You could also carry some millet and salted turnip home on your back, and you could also sneak some sesame oil for the family. The graveyard shift had its good points, but no one in the Wen Clan Caves wanted to work it. They were all afraid of the ghosts in the wild, overgrown graveyard. They were afraid the ghosts would spring on them in the night and eat them. No one wanted the job.

The Brigade Leader knew that Dog was like a beast of burden that would do as it was bidden. He always gave him the jobs no one else would touch.

The Brigade Leader said, "Dog, you go work the graveyard shift." Dog said, "I'll go, I'll go." The Brigade Leader said, "Working the graveyard shift has its good points—you can take some food home." Dog said, "I won't take anything home—eating and drinking for free is good enough. Why take some? I won't."

On the first night, Dog slept alone in the wild, overgrown graveyard.

The next night, he secretly went and got the blind Guan Guan. Dog knew that Guan Guan wasn't afraid of ghosts either.

He fetched Guan Guan when it was nearly dark. Guan Guan was in his pitch-dark cave boiling some corn mush. The cave was filled with the odor of burned leaves and the smell of rotten cloth. Dog said, "Don't bother boiling the mush." Guan Guan asked why.

Dog said, "Come to the wild, overgrown graveyard around midnight."

Guan Guan said, "It will be dark."

Dog replied, "Fuck, it's dark for you even during the day."

Guan Guan asked, "Go there for what?"

Dog said, "I'll give you millet porridge and potatoes to eat and also let you do something good."

Guan Guan asked, "What good thing?"

Dog said, "You'll find out when you get there."

Dog went on ahead to the wild, overgrown graveyard.

The workers repairing the irrigation ditch had long since departed. Big Chin, the commune engineer, was waiting anxiously for him. The guy with the big chin was really big, and his chin looked like it was made of stone.

Big Chin said, "Fuck your mother. What took you so long? If you throw the flags in the ditch or they don't look straight, you'll be in for it." Dog thought, *I fuck your mother, Big Chin.* The guy with the big chin pushed his bike across the ditch. *Te'er*, he rang the bell on his bike as he rode off. Dog thought, *Go make noise for the soul of your dead mom.*

He listened as Big Chin rang his bell as he rode away, *te'er, te'er, te'er.* Dog thought, *Fuck your mother, I'm gonna throw the red flags in the ditch.*

The first night around midnight, Dog had been sleeping soundly on the flatbed when he got up, pulled up the red flags, and tossed them into the ditch. When Big Chin arrived early the next morning and saw that there were no red flags flapping, *hua-la, hua-la,* on the edge of the ditch, he thought someone had carried them off. Later he saw them scattered in the bottom of the ditch. He asked Dog why he'd thrown the red flags into the ditch. Dog smiled without saying a word. Big Chin said, "I think you want to rebel. You must want the Committee of the Dictatorship of the Masses to get you." Dog continued to smile without saying a word. Then the Brigade Leader, speaking for Dog, commented that he had done what he did because he was afraid the flags would be stolen. Only then did Big Chin drop the matter and have someone throw the flags up out of the ditch so that they could be positioned once again.

In front of Dog and Guan Guan were three large blue stones, on top of which was placed an unmovable cauldron. The cauldron was huge and couldn't be budged by one person alone. A charcoal fire burned under it. Potatoes ringed the burning charcoal.

Dog flipped the potatoes so that the side away from the fire now faced the charcoal.

Dog lit a corncob to illumine the inside of the cauldron to see how the millet porridge was coming.

Originally, Big Chin had issued Dog a flashlight like the one that hung on the Accountant's belt all year round. But Dog couldn't use it, he couldn't make it work. The Accountant said it was broken and that he would take it and have it fixed. He never returned it to Dog. Dog didn't dare ask for it back, nor did he dare tell Big Chin. Dog was afraid of the Accountant. Dog wasn't afraid of anyone except for the Accountant. Dog felt like peeing his pants every time he saw the Accountant.

"The porridge still isn't ready," said Dog.

"The potatoes aren't ready yet either," said Dog.

Guan Guan was silent.

"Is your ass bothering you again, Guan Guan?" asked Dog.

"Why are you rubbing your ass?" asked Dog.

Guan Guan paid no attention to Dog. He rubbed his ass against his feet, *ba, ba.*

Ba, ba, ba, he rubbed.

Ba, ba, ba, he rubbed.

Dog watched Guan Guan rubbing.

Dog found Guan Guan's rubbing quite energetic.

Dog thought that the way Guan Guan rubbed his ass was the same as a child who wants its mother to pick it up.

Guan Guan rubbed and rubbed until he rubbed no more.

Guan Guan heaved a huge sigh.

"Worn out," said Dog.

"Guan Guan, you're all worn out," said Dog.

Guan Guan ignored Dog. His eyes stared into the dark without blinking, as if he were counting the stars in the night sky.

"Guan Guan, why do you think people hang couplets, red couplets at New Year's?" asked Dog.

"Is it to scare the ghosts away?" asked Dog.

"Why are ghosts afraid of red? Do bad and good ghosts all fear red?" asked Dog.

Guan Guan ignored Dog. His head remained lifted toward the starry sky.

Dog looked at Guan Guan. Then he looked up at the dark sky.

"A shooting star," said Dog.

"Someone died," said Guan Guan.

"Who?"

"What I mean is, as soon as you see a shooting star fall to the ground it means someone will die."

"Guan Guan, can all blind people tell fortunes? Who do you think died?"

"Fucking waste of time. Let's eat."

Dog and Guan Guan ate the pickled yellow turnips and the roasted potatoes. They gulped down a lot of millet porridge as well. They stuffed themselves to bursting.

"Guan Guan, I want to ask you something."

Guan Guan lifted his chin and inclined an ear toward Dog.

"Grunt says that ghosts come out at night and sleep with men. Is that true?"

"No such thing. That's a story concocted by the unmarried men for a bit of relief."

"But last night Widow San really did come. Plump white legs, plump white . . ."

"You're at it again, you."

"I want to talk about it."

"Go ahead and talk about it, I'm going to bed."

"Widow San said she was going to come back again tonight."

"Let her come, I'm going to bed."

"Sleep if you want, but if someone comes at midnight, don't scream and shout. Just pretend it's a dream."

"Who's coming? You're dreaming. Who's coming?"

"If you don't believe it, you don't believe it, but I do."

Dog pushed a flatbed over for Guan Guan. Then he spread a layer of cornstalks inside. Dog helped Guan Guan to lie down. Lest his feet get cold, Dog refused to let Guan Guan take off his shoes. Dog took off his own shoes and placed them under Guan Guan's head as a pillow.

Originally Dog had wanted to prepare the next morning's pickled turnips and a cauldron of millet porridge so he wouldn't have to listen to Big Chin grumbling if it wasn't ready. But Dog knew that no ghosts would appear after first cockcrow. By third cockcrow they had to leave. He was afraid to be late. He left off work. He covered the coals beneath the cauldron with ash and then pulled the flags from along the edge of the ditch. This time he didn't throw them into the ditch but rather piled them neatly and then covered them with some cornstalks. He pulled another flatbed over and positioned it next to Guan Guan's. He spread a layer of cornstalks and lay down inside.

Dog sincerely believed that Widow San would come after he fell asleep. Widow San said she was afraid of the color red. Not only had he concealed the flags, he had also covered the burning coals with ash. Fire was red too.

While Dog was still sunk in thought, Widow San came again, and he let her sleep with Guan Guan too. Dog thought that Guan Guan had had a pretty rough life. Guan Guan was blind.

A star fell, cutting a long, bright line across the belly of heaven, and vanished.

"Another shooting star," said Dog.

"It's a bad star," said Guan Guan.

"Did you see it?"

"I saw it."

"Can you?"

"I can't, but I did see it."

Dog, Dog

Dog saw the Accountant out when he left.

"Look how dark it is. Even with the stars it's so dark," said Dog.

The Accountant ignored Dog. The Accountant ignored Dog. The Accountant had no fucking need to pay attention to fucking Dog. With a *click*, the Accountant turned on his flashlight.

When Dog heard the *click*, he opened his hands with his palms out and covered his face to shield his eyes from the Accountant's flashlight.

The Accountant liked to shine his flashlight at people. The entire village was afraid of him shining his flashlight. Standing or sitting, the Accountant was never without his flashlight, even during the day. There was a ring on the rear of the flashlight. The Accountant would flip it up and hook it on his belt.

The flashlight was the Accountant's talisman.

If anyone was caught snoring at a meeting of the commune, the Accountant would click on his flashlight and ask, "Who's that? Who's that?" as he shone a blinding ray of light at them. It would make your scalp tingle and frighten you; you'd even dream about that evil light. If anyone laughed aloud at another's fright, the Accountant would say, "Who's that? Who's that?" and then turn the light on him, leaving him no room to escape. If someone's nose itched, he wouldn't dare sneeze lest the Accountant accuse him of doing it on purpose. They feared the *click* of the Accountant's flashlight and having no place to run and becoming the target. If the Accountant was present at a meeting, no one dared to make a sound. They all listened. They listened even when they couldn't hear; they listened even when they didn't understand, lest the Accountant shine his light on them.

But this time, the Accountant did not shine his light at Dog the way he had done in the cave. He walked away without shining his flashlight.

Dog waited, but when no light shone on his face, he opened his eyes and lowered his hands.

The ray of white light that shot from the Accountant's flashlight was like a stick sweeping back and forth across the road. Dog felt as if the light could chop down a tree, knock down a wall, or split open the earth.

Dog watched the Accountant's shadow, a black shadow that blocked out half the sky.

How could that ray of light give rise to such a large and tall shadow? The sun couldn't do it. The flashlight was more venomous than the sun. No wonder the entire village was afraid of his flashlight. The fucking flashlight was possessed of magic arts, thought Dog.

After the Accountant had walked some distance, he heard him whistling, *xu-xu-xu-xi-xi-xi*. Dog couldn't make out the exact tone of the whistle, but he knew that the Accountant was very happy, spirited, and very alive. Dog knew that when the Accountant was feeling spirited and alive, he would whistle.

Xu-xu-xu-xi-xi-xi, he whistled.

The Accountant was a lot like Heinu's big rooster—the village hens were all his, for him to mount when he wished. It would mount the hens, willing or not.

The Accountant led a glorious life, thought Dog.

The Accountant really led a damned glorious life, thought Dog.

The fucking Accountant lived more damned gloriously than the emperor, thought Dog.

The Accountant lived like a human being, thought Dog.

The fucking Accountant really lived like a damned human being, thought Dog.

The fucking Accountant lived like a damned human being, better than the damned emperor, thought Dog.

He thought and thought as he watched from a distance. Suddenly, Dog lost sight of that white light shining like a stick. It was pitch black in front of him. The Accountant had turned into his own house. Although his flashlight could no longer be seen, his whistling could still be heard, *xu-xu-xu-xi-xi-xi*.

From a distance, the whistling sounded different. It wasn't a sharp or clear difference, but it made Dog think of his distant childhood.

In those days his mother also whistled, with an equal lack of clarity and sharpness. That was when she had to take Dog Girl out to pee. His mother held Dog Girl in her arms, Dog Girl's back against her chest, and two legs spread apart. As soon as his mother whistled, *xu-xu-xu-xi-xi-xi*, Dog Girl's pee would start to flow from that messy place in the crotch of her trousers. At first it was just a dribble, like water leaking from a cracked pot. Later the drops would spurt forth in an arc, gushing into the distance. Then the gushing arc would dwindle down. In the end it would again be like water leaking from a cracked pot, dribbling. Dog would watch his sister pee from nearby. His mother scolded him and told him not to watch his sister, but rather stand at a distance behind her. Still, he wanted to watch her pee. He wanted to watch regardless of his mother's scolding. When he heard his mother's unclear whistling, *xu-xu-xu-xi-xi-xi*, he'd come running. One time when his mother took his sister out to pee, she turned suddenly and that stream of pee, *shua*, sprayed all over his face. Dog Girl laughed. His mother said, "You got what you deserved, you got what you deserved." But Dog didn't care. As the pee ran down his face, he stopped it with his tongue, tasting its saltiness and the sweetness.

Dog thought about Dog Girl.

Dog was afraid to think about Dog Girl. But the Accountant's whistling, unclear and lacking in sharpness, made him think of his little sister, Dog Girl.

What are you thinking? What are you thinking? It's always the same old story; it's always the same old shit. What are you thinking? Dog cursed himself. Cursing himself, Dog turned and went inside his cave house.

Entering the central room, Dog suddenly stopped. He saw his beloved big silver-dollar box. He stood there, dumbly staring at his beloved big silver-dollar box.

Compared to the Accountant's flashlight, the coal-oil lamp in the eastern room more resembled a will-o'-the-wisp over the wild graveyard. The coal-oil lamp gave off such a weak light. The weak yellow light shining through the doorway was enough to illuminate the red paper couplets pasted on the big box.

Dog couldn't read, but he knew what the couplets said. The couplets said: "Prosperity ever flows like the eastern sea; Longevity greater than the old pine on the southern mountain."

Fucking prosperity, thought Dog.

Fucking longevity, thought Dog.

The previous autumn, Dog had been sent to work the graveyard shift for the Wild Graveyard irrigation project. A month later, the location of the work changed. After doing the repair work, Dog was replaced by someone else and sent home. Returning to the village, he fell ill almost immediately. At first he coughed, but later he couldn't get off the *kang*. Guan Guan said he had run into a ghost from the wild, overgrown graveyard. If he wanted to recover, he would have to have a coffin made to counteract his bad luck. Dog was very popular, so the villagers pleaded with the Brigade Leader. The Brigade Leader gave his consent, but said that there was no wood in the village and that they'd have to try their luck at the commune. He went to the commune. When the commune heard it was for Dog, who had saved their bricks from the big hail, they immediately consented. They provided a pine log and wouldn't take a cent for it. They gave it for free.

Just like Guan Guan said, before the coffin was finished, Dog began to recover and was able to work in the fields. He was able to carry the wood shavings and pieces of bark from the pine log to his western room.

By the time the coffin was finished, Dog had completely recovered. For this, Dog invited Guan Guan for a meal of dough fish. When Guan Guan was about to leave, Dog also gave him a box of pine kindling. Dog told him to use a little each time he cooked and his house would be filled with pine fragrance.

After the coffin was finished, it was placed in the main room. The Brigade Leader had the Accountant write a pair of red couplets and pasted them on the face of the coffin.

The entire village turned out. Everyone wanted to smell the pine fragrance in Dog's house. They all wanted to pat the coffin and hear the *peng-peng* sound. Everyone in the village praised the coffin.

Old Guiju said, "Good. Dog, Old Cai didn't have it any better."

"Good. Good. Good," said Dog.

Dog called his coffin his "big silver-dollar box." But it was more than just a name. He actually put the oats, corn, and sorghum in his terra-cotta urns in his "big silver-dollar box."

Dog loved to look at his big silver-dollar box. He so loved to look at it that at times he began to doubt it had ever happened. If he found himself unable to sleep at night, he'd get up, pick up his coal-oil lamp, and go to the main room to see if the coffin was really there. Seeing it, he would feel assured, but just as soon begin to doubt his own eyes. He'd pat it with his hands. Hearing the *peng-peng* it gave when tapped, he'd be certain of its existence.

Dog really liked to look at his big silver-dollar box.

After seeing off the Accountant, Dog stood in the main room. First he stared dumbly at the coffin, then he felt his heart thump and begin to beat wildly.

He'd felt the same way that day many years ago.

His mother died of consumption, leaving him alone with his sister Dog Girl. As usual, he wanted to watch her pee. He couldn't watch, so he listened on the sly. He often waited till well into the night to listen to her pee. Only when he heard that trickling sound would he peacefully go off to sleep. When she grew older, he wondered if that place of hers was the same as when she was little. One summer, it was very hot in the cave. Dog Girl threw off her blanket, and he struck a match to get a better look. He often did the same after that. When it came time to go to bed, he would tightly shut the windows, claiming he was afraid of mosquitoes. He did it so that Dog Girl would get hot and throw off her blanket.

Then he was conscripted by the Japanese to build a gun turret and was away for three whole months. During those three months he thought constantly of Dog Girl. Every night he wanted to dream he could hear the trickle of Dog Girl's urine into the terra-cotta pot.

He wanted to dream about that place of hers. But it never happened; the more he wanted to dream, the less likely it was to happen.

Three months later, after the work was completed, he hastily returned to the village.

"Brother, brother, brother."

"Don't worry, don't worry, don't worry."

"You can't, you can't."

Dog Girl, his sister, bitterly implored him that night. But he heard nothing. He heard absolutely nothing.

The next day, someone came to tell him that Dog Girl had hanged herself from the crooked tree by West River. At first he just stood there stunned; then he felt his heart thump, and then it began to beat wildly. Then he fell to the floor on his ass.

He felt the same way again now.

He regretted what he had done very much. At the time he felt he had truly wronged his sister, Dog Girl. He now felt he had wronged himself. He had done two things in his entire life that he was sorry for—first he had lost his sister, Dog Girl, and now he was about to lose his beloved big silver-dollar box.

Dog had lain down without eating dinner. He often went without dinner. As soon as night fell he would get under the quilt. That way he saved food, the time spent cooking, and coal oil.

In this confused state, Dog suddenly felt a white light in his eyes.

It was a flashlight!

Dog thought he was at a meeting and had committed the offense of dozing off. He hurriedly said, "I didn't sleep. I wasn't sleeping." When he opened his eyes, he realized he was in his own house. The Accountant was standing before him.

"Oh, it's you, it's you. I didn't realize it was you," said Dog respectfully, sitting up.

Dog was afraid of the Accountant. Dog had feared no one his entire life, not even the Japanese who burned and murdered, but he did fear the Accountant. All the Accountant had to do was cough, and Dog's legs would nearly collapse under him. All the Accountant had to do was look at him, and his heart would beat wildly. All the Accountant had to do was shine his flashlight at Dog, and he would go numb.

When the Accountant told him to do something, he would do it. The Accountant never had to tell him twice. All he had to say was, "Dog, the latrine is full," and Dog would show up at the Accountant's latrine to shovel the shit out of the pit, then pile it outside the gate before carrying yellow soil with which to cover it. All he had to say was, "Dog, the well rope is almost worn out," and Dog would tuck a sickle into his belt and set off for West River to cut reeds with which to braid a new rope for the well.

Dog was the Accountant's hired hand who was never paid.

"Dog, here, have this bowl of millet porridge." Dog dared not refuse, but he knew that if he ate the Accountant's leftovers, his stomach would give him trouble. But he didn't dare refuse. He would take the bowl in both hands and squat beneath the window in the courtyard and slurp up the porridge like a beggar.

Dog feared nothing more than the Accountant. They were like cat and mouse, natural-born enemies.

Seeing the Accountant standing before him with his flashlight, Dog wondered what the Accountant had for him to do. He wondered in silence, not daring to open his mouth and ask.

Dog dressed, piled his quilt to one side, and got off his *kang*. He lit his coal-oil lamp. He stood silently, waiting for the Accountant to give his orders. But the Accountant did not utter a word. He simply looked at Dog. Dog, of course, dared not look back; he just looked down at his neck. He glanced at his lips to see if he was speaking. But the Accountant had not uttered a word.

Dog finally spoke when he couldn't take it any longer and was on the point of fainting.

"You, you," said Dog respectfully.

"What about me?" said the Accountant.

"I didn't say anything about you. I just wondered what you have for me to do. Just tell me."

"It's this."

"Uh huh."

"My father-in-law is ill."

"Goodness."

"He won't last much longer."

"My goodness."

"That's it."

"Oh."

"I want to borrow your coffin to counteract the bad luck."

"Um. Um?"

The Accountant clicked on his flashlight and thrust it in Dog's face. Dog felt as if the venomous sun had entered his house. He immediately spread his hands with his palms out to shield his eyes from the light.

"Did you say 'um'? Did you just say 'um'?" asked the Accountant.

"No, not at all. I didn't say 'um.' I said 'um,'" replied Dog.

Dog still shielded his face with his two outspread hands. The venomous sun that had entered his house was hot enough to make him sweat.

"What I mean is that the coffin is full of grain and I have to put it in terra-cotta urns. You can send someone for it tomorrow morning," said Dog.

"That's a promise, then," said the Accountant.

Off went the flashlight with a *click*.

"That's a promise, then," said the Accountant. So saying, he turned on his heels and left.

"Stay a little longer, stay a little longer," said Dog, following him into the courtyard.

⁓

After seeing off the Accountant, he returned to his main room and stood there transfixed. First he stood dumbly looking at his silver-dollar box, then he fell to the ground on his ass. His mind was empty, and it was a long time before he returned to himself.

"Was the Accountant just here?" The words fell from Dog's lips.

He was here, his mind replied.

"Did the Accountant just ask to borrow my silver-dollar box?"

Yes.

"Borrow?"

Rob.

"Fucker! Asshole! He whose asshole is fucked by ten thousand!"

But why did I agree?

"I should have said that the whole village gave it to me. Go ask all the villagers."

I fuck your ancestors eight generations back. Accountant, you are a fucker. You are the balls between my legs! Dream on!

"Dream on!"

~

The next morning after breakfast, the Accountant dispatched a few unmarried men to Dog's place to get the coffin, but the door to Dog's house was locked.

The people like Dog had never locked their house before. The people like Dog had never possessed a lock.

The Accountant examined the lock; he recognized it as belonging to the Brigade Leader. He went to inquire of the Brigade Leader. The Brigade Leader replied that Dog had asked for leave to go to his uncle's house and that he would be back in three to five days.

The Accountant looked through a crack in the door. The coffin was still there. He said, "The monk might run away, but the temple cannot. I'll be waiting."

The Accountant waited for three days, waited for five days, waited for fifteen days, waited for thirty-five days, but still Dog did not return.

The Accountant sent someone to the house of Dog's uncle. His uncle said that Dog had not been there.

The Accountant was furious. Without consulting the Brigade Leader, he broke down Dog's door and ordered some of the unmarried men to carry the coffin to his house.

But the Accountant had no idea that the coffin already contained a dead man.

The dead man lay face up on top of the oats, corn, and sorghum. His mouth was wide open as if to speak, laugh, cry, or shout.

"What a good Dog," said the villagers.

"What a good Dog," said the villagers.

Chou Bang Herds Sheep

In the years Shepherd Boy worked as shepherd, some sheep would inevitably die during the hottest days of summer. For this reason, the Accountant deducted work points. If a sheep died, three months' work was for nothing. When bonuses were shared out at year's end, Shepherd Boy rarely received a single cent; everything was taken without a word. To make matters worse, he owed the work unit money.

After Shepherd Boy hanged himself, no young person in the village was willing to shoulder his work.

The sheep were not taken out to graze for several days. People were sent out to cut grass for them, but it was never enough. The sheep were so famished that they couldn't even bleat. Occasionally one would open its mouth, but the sound that came out was less a bleat than a cry for its mother. Soft-hearted, Chou Bang took pity on them and told the Brigade Leader that he would graze them. The Brigade Leader replied, "Good young man, good young man; such a good man should receive an award." The Brigade Leader ordered the Accountant to give Chou Bang two and a half work points per day, which was a whole point more than Shepherd Boy had received.

Chou Bang was very happy.

The other young people all regretted not having taken the job. If they had but known that one day grazing sheep was equal to two and a half days' work for them in the village. One year was equal to two and a half years; two years was equal to five years.

Chou Bang was very happy.

Fearing lest a sheep die in the heat, Chou Bang took the advice of the old people, and taking a bag of toasted oats and several pickled turnips, herded the sheep into the western mountains as soon as the hottest days of summer arrived.

131

That day, his older brother Chou Chou saw him to the mountains.

"Bang, if we save for a few years, we won't have to worry about finding the money for a woman," Chou Chou said.

"That depends on if we get several good years," replied Chou Bang.

"This year can't get any worse."

"Nope."

"When bonuses are handed out at the end of the year, you can get engaged."

"To whom?"

"Nunu. Who else?"

"That sounds good, but you know her mom is letting her see Heizi."

". . ."

"My God. Where are you running? Lamb, lamb!"

"We'll wait for a good year. With money, we won't have to give him a second thought."

"When we have money, we'll have to make arrangements for you first."

"Me? I'm already thirty-five. No matter what, you shouldn't delay."

"Here's the ravine. You go on back," said Chou Bang.

"Oh, okay," replied Chou Chou.

"Why are you crying?"

"My nose itches."

"You go on back."

"Hang on to the galvanized bucket."

"Oh."

"Keep your matches dry."

"You go on back."

"Eat all the toasted oats; don't bring any back. I overcooked them."

"You go on back."

". . ."

"I told you not to cry. Why are you crying again?"

"My fucking nose itches."

Chou Bang urged the sheep ahead, and didn't look back at his older brother.

He talked with the sheep as they made their way into the mountains following the ravine. He was searching for a place with water. As night fell, they arrived at the foot of a sheer rock face. The cliff rose straight up like a wall. Below the cliff was an open area a *mu* and half in size. Smooth and flat, it looked like someone's courtyard; there wasn't much chance of finding a better place to tie the sheep.

But what made him even happier was the sight of a spring trickling from a crevice to the left of the cliff face. The trickle of water ran into a small stone basin below the crevice. The water overflowed the basin and flowed into a pool. The water flowed no farther, but vanished into the sand.

Chou Bang, who acknowledged his misfortune and resigned himself to his fate, was very happy to find this place. He couldn't help but shout like Leng Er did all the time. He shouted as loud as he could.

"Ah . . ."

"Ah . . . ah . . . ah . . ." echoed the distant mountains.

"*Ma* . . ." echoed the sheep.

"*Ba* . . ." echoed the goats.

Whether it was echoed by the mountains or the goats, or the sheep, they were all happy to find this place. Chou Bang had led the sheep on a long day, and he was tired. After he used a rope to pen the sheep below the cliff, he lay down on a flat rock and went to sleep.

He dreamed of Nunu.

Nunu said, "Look, it's cold and you haven't covered yourself with your coat." When she said this, he woke up. He opened his eyes and when he looked, there really was a girl standing in front of him.

He sat up with a start. The girl retreated a couple of steps.

"Nunu?" he asked.

The girl was silent.

The day was just dawning. He saw that she was stark naked, without a stitch of clothing on. He'd always thought that a naked woman would look this way.

"Who are you?" he asked.

The girl remained silent. She turned and walked away. Without thinking, Chou Bang stood up and followed her.

Chou Bang dodged and walked lightly and slowly behind. But the girl seemed to fly along the mountain road, and she was soon out of sight.

Was she a ghost?

Chou Bang believed in fate, not ghosts. Grunt didn't believe in them either; nor did Old Zhao, the cadre who had been sent to the countryside. Like them, he didn't believe in ghosts. Chou Bang spat and pinched his thigh to make sure that he wasn't dreaming.

Then he was confused.

Chou Bang undid his pants and took a piss. He recalled how Grunt had said that if a person were confused, they could clear their mind by taking a piss. After a piss, Chou Bang concluded that he was not confused.

But who was the girl who walked on mountain roads as if they were flat?

Human? Ghost? Immortal?

Thinking, Chou Bang returned to below the cliff. He didn't sleep again. He developed a chill and covered himself with his coat and sat on the flat rock until morning.

The sheep also awoke. Wanting out, they bleated from within the cordoned-off area.

Sheep are among the dumbest animals. All you have to do is pen them in with a rope a meter off the ground and they will stay inside and not try to get out. They don't realize that all they have to do is step forward, nor will they try to jump over the rope. That's the way sheep are. If you put a knife to their throat, they have no idea that you intend to kill them. If not, why are stubbornly stupid people cursed as sheep?

Two goats were butting heads to see whose head was hardest and who would give in first and walk away.

Chou Bang gathered some dry wood and made a fire. He made a pot of oatmeal. When he finished eating, he drove the sheep down into the ravine.

A hawk soared in the clear blue sky. It saw the sheep scattered over the ravine as it circled overhead. It circled for a long time before flying off. It decided that it didn't have the strength to carry one of them off and make a meal of it. It went elsewhere in search of a rabbit, pheasant, or snake, something it could handle.

A hawk has sharp eyes. *If only I were a hawk, I would fly high in the sky to spot that girl*, thought Chou Bang.

At dawn on the following day, Chou Bang had the feeling that someone was sitting next to him and pressing down on a corner of the leather coat that covered him.

It's her! he thought. He dared not move and just opened his eyes a crack.

It was her! The same girl as on the first day. She was facing Chou Bang and sat beside the flat stone.

He saw that she was still naked.

He considered sitting up suddenly and grabbing her, but changed his mind. He was afraid of frightening her.

"So, you're here," said Chou Bang.

The girl said nothing, and she didn't move.

"If you are cold, take my leather coat and cover yourself," said Chou Bang.

The girl remained silent and didn't stir.

"Tell me who you are," said Chou Bang.

The girl stood up slowly, after which she slowly set off as quickly as she had done the first time.

"Hold on, hold on," said Chou Bang.

Chou Bang got to his feet and set off after her. Despite his efforts, she disappeared.

Chou Bang was filled with regret.

He wondered if she would come back the next day when he woke up. If she did, he would grab her first and then worry.

But Chou Bang waited in vain many mornings. His hopes came to naught, waiting for the naked girl.

He searched for her many times along the path she had taken, but never encountered her. Every place seemed uninhabitable. Farther on, the path ran out.

Chou Bang decided that she must have flown.

Normally, Chou Bang drove the sheep into the ravine and let them graze the grass on both sides. Half of the herd was composed of sheep.

They were not as proficient as the goats in navigating the mountainous terrain. One slip and they would roll into the ravine and die. He always led them into a depression to graze.

On this particular day, he drove them into the ravine. He went in search of mushrooms in a wooded area. There were mushrooms in these mountains. He tried some and found that they were not poisonous. Afterward he often picked them. He boiled them and ate them, but regretted that he had not brought any salt. With a little salt, they'd be tastier.

He picked and picked the mushrooms. Suddenly, the sun seemed to cloud over. He felt something was going to happen. He shouted and herded the flock together and drove them to the mountain, cracking his whip. As they reached the foot of the cliff after a great deal of effort, the thunder exploded and the lightning flashed. The strong wind was followed by a downpour of rain, accompanied by walnut-sized hailstones. Luck was on their side as they found shelter under the cliff. Neither Chou Bang nor the sheep had been soaked by the rain or struck by the hail.

Chou Bang stood close to the cliff face. He covered himself with his tattered sheepskin coat, the fleece facing outward. That's what Widow San would have done. She said that when it was hot, sleep on top; when it was cold, put it on top; and when it rained, turn the fleece out.

Chou Bang looked at the open area a few meters in front of them and saw the white hail piled there. Farther off he heard a sound, growing louder and louder. He knew it was a mountain torrent of rainwater rushing down the ravine.

Ga . . . ga . . .

As the rain was letting up, a peal of thunder clapped above.

It was extremely loud. Chou Bang thought a piece of the cliff had broken off and would smash him and his sheep to a pulp. He shouted "quick" and ran toward the open area. There was no way of knowing if the sheep had listened to their master's command or if they had decided it on their own, but they ran amok en masse.

The lightning had not toppled the cliff; it stood there just as steep and precipitous as ever.

With a great deal of effort, Chou Bang managed to calm the sheep and herd them back to below the cliff, where the rain and hail had failed to reach.

The lightning had probably parted the clouds; the sky grew bright and the rain stopped.

Chou Bang wanted to catch his breath, but he heard the bleating of what sounded like more than five or six of them. He set off toward them at a trot while calling for them. As if ill, the sheep didn't seem to recognize their master. Seeing him approach, they distanced themselves farther along the ravine. When he ran faster, they ran faster to make sure their master didn't catch them.

Chou Bang pursued them for more than two *li*, but was not able to bring even one of them back. He watched as each one fell into the ravine, only to be swallowed up by the rushing yellow torrent, like some cotton balls that had been swallowed. At first he wanted to dive in and rescue them, not considering whether they were dead or alive. After several false starts, he decided it was no good if even if he had been extremely able. He knew he would die the moment he hit the water. He knew he would be swept away like a cotton ball. He would never see his older brother Chou Chou or Nunu again. He would never hear his older brother say that his nose itched. At this, he wept. Nor would he hear Nunu sing to him, "I am so infatuated thinking of you; carrying firewood, I fall into a potato cellar."

There was no hope; all he could do was go back. He was afraid that the flock of sheep below the cliff might have scattered, and hurled themselves into the ravine to be swept away. But that was not the case. When he got back, they were still penned there under the cliff.

Most of the sheep were trembling, frightened by the recent thunderclaps. Several shook severely, their hind legs anchored to the ground as if to take a piss. Several of the braver ones sat there chewing grass. They were the ones that didn't run off.

He counted the sheep and recounted them

"Fuck, I'm short ten."

"Ten of them."

He dropped to sit on the flat rock.

He realized that the rock was already dry and the sun was burning overhead. The sky was blue, without a cloud to be seen.

The hail on the flat area had melted and run down to join the torrent in the ravine. The drops of water hanging on the grass reminded Chou Bang of tears hanging on Nunu's eyelashes. The taller grass had been knocked to the ground by the hail and had not stood up again. The insects and the birds had not broken the silence; the moths and butterflies had not dared to take wing. The sheep and the goats were also silent, wondering if it all had not been a nightmare.

Only the mountain torrent continued to roar without pause, sweeping away rocks, harming the people who only tried to live a happy life downstream, ruining fields and crops.

A hawk approached and circled overhead. Its shadow faded and grew dark as it rose and fell over slope, ridge, ravine, and ditch. Then suddenly it plummeted out of the sky and just as it was about to hit the ridge, it turned and shot straight into the sky. Holding something in its claws, it flew high up in the sky before descending to the top of a mountain, where Chou Bang lost sight of it.

At that moment, he turned to his left and stared dumbly toward the east, where, fifty *li* away over three rows of mountains, lay his Wen Clan Caves.

He thought again of his older brother. He recalled how he had wept and how he had brushed his tears away with dirty black hands. He thought of how his older brother always said his nose itched. With such thoughts filling his mind, his own nose began to itch, and he too felt like crying.

Ai—I should have stayed in the village. Although sheep died in the heat under Shepherd Boy's care, the bodies remained. The Accountant would eat mutton and deduct three months' work points from his pay. But not even a hair of the ten sheep I lost is left for the Accountant. I have no idea how the fucker will fine me. Big brother will cry his eyes out when he hears about it. Just a few days ago, he was hoping we could work hard for a few years and save money to get a wife. Now it's just a dream.

Chou Bang thought of Nunu. She often came to their house to help them with their chores. She patched their clothes and washed their quilts. On the fifth day of the fifth lunar month, she made cold glutinous rice cakes, and on the fifteenth day of the eighth lunar month, she made moon cakes. When she entered their house during the day, it was as if the sun itself had entered their abode. When she entered their house in the evening, it was as if the moon itself had entered their abode.

Ai—she was such a good person, but we're not so lucky. Nunu, go find Heizi, your man, in the coal pit. That's fate. I don't believe in ghosts, but I do believe in fate. I have suffered all my life. My unlucky fate! Fuck my fate!

"It's almost dark. Why aren't you cooking dinner?"

Chou Bang was cursing his fucking fate when he heard a woman's voice.

He turned his head and saw a girl standing behind him.

"Why have you just been sitting around all afternoon?"

"I lost some sheep," said Chou Bang.

"I saw them. They were swept away by the torrent."

"Yeah."

"When you went after them, I penned in the ones below the cliff with a rope."

Chou Bang then realized that when he had gone in pursuit of the fleeing sheep, he had failed to pen the others. Then he knew that the sheep below the cliff had been penned by someone else.

"Who are you?" asked Chou Bang.

"Look, you've been so upset that you haven't eaten. No matter how upset you are, you still have to eat."

"Who are you?"

"I live on the peak. Come on. I cooked for you."

"So it was you the other two days?"

"Let's go."

Chou Bang stared at her.

She looked about twenty. She was wearing homemade clothes of coarse blue homespun. Although the people of the Wen Clan Caves were poor, they'd given up weaving their own cloth a long time ago; they now bought cloth at the commune store. But she was still wearing the old stuff. She was barefoot too; poor as they were at the Wen Clan Caves, any girl her age would be wearing shoes, but not her.

"Let's go," she said.

"Okay," said Chou Bang.

From the large rock, they descended to the open area below the cliff and then began ascending, switching back now and then until she had led Chou Bang to the top. The sharp-toothed rocks there looked impassable. Chou Bang had never ascended to this point.

The girl paused in front of a withered sea buckthorn bush. She pushed the withered sea buckthorn bush aside, revealing a cave.

"Go on in," said the girl.

Chou Bang was afraid and dared not enter.

"Go on in," insisted the girl.

Chou Bang still dared not enter. He turned to look back the way he had come.

"I'll go in," said the girl.

The girl bent over on all fours and entered the cave.

"Still not coming in?" asked the girl from inside the cave.

"If you're not coming in and you want to leave, go ahead," said the girl.

What the heck. She isn't a ghost if she dares show herself in the middle of the day. She knew enough to pen my sheep, so she can't be a ghost. Besides, I don't believe in ghosts. If I'm going in, I may as well go in. So thinking, Chou Bang entered the cave, following the example of the girl.

It was pretty big inside, like a cave dwelling. Near the cave wall was a small *kang* made of piled stones about a meter and a half high, on top of which was spread oat straw. On the straw was spread a dog skin, which served as bedding, and a sheepskin for a quilt. In front of the *kang* stood a squat stone, on top of which was a lighted bean-oil lamp.

"Have a seat," said the girl.

"Is this your home?" asked Chou Bang.

"Yeah."

"Just you?"

"Yeah."

She cooked mushrooms, potatoes, and oat flour-dough fish. She used a small pot, just big enough for one person. There was only one bowl too. The girl let Chou Bang eat first. He didn't decline and wolfed it down in one go.

It was delicious. He had never had such delicious food in the mountains, nor at home for that matter. While she was cooking and he was eating, she asked him all sorts of questions but never said a word about herself. When Chou Bang asked her something she never replied. After many interruptions, he gave up.

When she finished eating, he stood up and said, "I'm leaving."

The girl replied, "If you don't want to stay, then go ahead and leave."

Chou Bang said, "I'm going down to check on the sheep."

The girl said, "I guarantee your sheep won't be eaten by a wolf." Chou Bang took his seat again.

Seeing him yawn, the girl said, "If you're tired, go to bed."

Chou Bang stood up and said, "I'll sleep down below."

The girl said, "If you don't want to stay here where it's nice and warm, then leave."

Chou Bang said, "The *kang* is too small." The girl said she could fix something up on the ground where he could sleep. Chou Bang said okay.

The girl removed some straw from the *kang* and spread it on the ground. Then she placed the sheepskin blanket on top with the fleece up. "Go to bed. I have to go out for a moment," said the girl.

The girl pushed aside the withered sea buckthorn bush blocking the mouth of the cave, then replaced it after she went out. Chou Bang heard her footsteps, *cha, cha, cha, cha,* fade in the distance.

If you can hear footsteps, she can't be a ghost, thought Chou Bang.

How could a ghost make such delicious dough fish? There's no way she is a ghost. If she's anything, she must be a fairy that descended to this mortal world, thought Chou Bang.

Why had she gone out? She had me stay, but she went out. Is she coming back? Why does she dare let me sleep here? Who is she? She probably has something she wants to keep secret. But she didn't tell me what. She was the naked girl I saw those two days, but she never admitted to it. Why did she want to do that? She takes a stroll naked early in the morning and doesn't let me catch her. She walked really fast. Is she married or not? If I were Grunt, I'd know in a minute. Fucking Grunt has it all together, thought Chou Bang.

Married or not, I shouldn't offend her. No one from the Wen Clan Caves would ever harm a girl. It would be a great sin to do so. Even if she's someone's wife, she shouldn't be bothered. But a married woman who lives in a cave and doesn't go home to her husband, must mean there is trouble. Anyway, I shouldn't offend her, thought Chou Bang.

Furthermore, she considers me a good person; that's why she has me stay here to sleep. Then all the more reason not to have bad thoughts about her, thought Chou Bang.

Thinking such thoughts, Chou Bang decided it would be best if he left. He thought and thought, but didn't want to leave. He really didn't want to leave.

Such a nice girl; such a nice fairy girl, thought Chou Bang.

As Chou Bang was thinking, he heard footsteps approaching.

He had been sitting up on the small *kang,* but as soon as heard the footsteps, he hurriedly lay down, and even turned to face the wall.

He heard the girl enter the cave and seal its mouth.

He heard the girl pick up something and brush her hair, *cha-cha-cha-cha.* He felt cool drops of water fall on his face and neck.

"Hey," said the girl.

"Are you asleep?" she asked.

"Asleep so soon?" she said.

"Some people," she said.

Chou Bang heard the girl speak, then lie down on the sheepskin blanket. He heard her roll up the sheepskin to use as a pillow. Then he heard her blow out the lamp.

Suddenly the cave was pitch black. Chou Bang relaxed a bit, but dared not move.

Slowly he fell asleep.

He didn't know when, but he heard a movement. He thought it was a sheep. He listened again. No, it wasn't. Then he remembered he was in a cave and not below the cliff.

He opened his eyes and saw the mouth of the cave was open. It was already light outside. He looked at his side; the girl was gone. But it looked as if something was on top of the sheepskin. He reached out to touch it. It was the girl's clothes.

There was a sound outside the cave. It was the sound of the withered sea buckthorn bush being moved aside. It was the same sound he had heard not long ago. Shortly, the mouth of the cave darkened a bit. It was the girl crawling in and blocking the light. Chou Bang saw her naked body. She came in and lay down on the sheepskin again.

He quickly shut his eyes. He didn't hear her dress nor cover herself with her clothes. Gradually, he heard her snore lightly.

She was stark naked, lying right beside him looking up. He could reach out and touch her, Chou bang thought.

Chou Bang opened his eyes just a crack to look at the girl. But it was so dark he could see nothing.

Yes, yes, she was lying naked right beside him, face up, thought Chou Bang.

Chou Bang's heart pounded. It had never pounded so hard. When he held Nunu's hand and they kissed, his heart never pounded in such a way. But he had never seen Nunu naked. He had never been so close to a naked woman, and one who was lying face up.

Chou Bang felt like stripping off his own clothes to keep the girl company. But he didn't. He didn't do it. He just thought about it.

If Nunu were lying naked by my side face up, I'd get on top of her. No matter what, I'd want to kiss her entire body from head to toe.

Occupied with his thoughts, he heard the girl move. Then he heard her move again. Then she yawned and sat up. Then he heard her groping for something and hurriedly begin dressing.

Chou Bang dared not move. He almost dared not breathe. He was afraid she would know he was awake. He was afraid that she would know he had been looking at her.

"Hey!" said the girl.

"Hey! Are you still asleep?" she asked.

"Hey, it's time to wake up," said the girl.

Speaking, the girl reached out and touched Chou Bang.

To Chou Bang, the girl's hand felt like something crawling on his chest. Crawling, crawling under his shirt.

"I know you're an honest guy," she said.

Chou Bang suddenly grabbed her hand.

At that moment, they heard a sound outside the cave. The girl snatched her hand away.

Chou Bang sat up.

Two people entered the cave.

"It's bad. People are going to search the mountain today. They want to burn you to death."

"Last night, hail destroyed the crops."

"The shaman said that you were still here."

"He said the hail destroyed the crops on your account."

"He said they have to search the mountain to get you today."

"And burn you."

The two people who had entered the cave spoke in turn.

Cha! The cave was suddenly alight. The shorter of the two had struck a match and lit the oil lamp.

"Who's he?"

"Don't worry about who he is. I'm leaving with him," said the girl.

"Are the sheep below the cliff yours?"

"Yeah," said Chou Bang.

"I'm leaving with him," said the girl.

"Are you taking her with you?"

"I want to leave with you," said the girl.

"Okay, I'm taking her with me," said Chou Bang.

"Then you'd better hurry up and get moving."

"Don't plan on coming back here."

"Okay," said Chou Bang.

"Okay," said the girl.

So Chou Bang took the girl and led the sheep away from the cliff early in the morning, and set off for the Wen Clan Caves. Just before leaving, Chou Bang said, "You can each have one sheep." They didn't refuse; each selected one fat sheep, which they drove off deep into the mountains.

On the way back, the girl said that the two men were her brothers.

"Why would anyone want to burn you to death?" asked Chou Bang.

"They all say I'm an evil spirit of the mountain. They've said so for years. This year, a shaman said that if they didn't burn me, there would be disaster," said the girl.

"I'm not an evil spirit of the mountain," said the girl.

"I'm a human being," said the girl.

"A human being," said Chou Bang.

"A good person," said Chou Bang.

They arrived at the Wen Clan Caves as the day was darkening.

People asked Chou Bang who the girl was. Chou Bang said nothing, but the girl said she was Chou Bang's wife.

Entering the cave, the girl put down her bundle and started to work. She went with Chou Bang to the well to draw water. She had never seen a well before and didn't know how to draw water with the bucket, but she insisted upon learning.

When night fell and the neighbors had left, Chou Bang spread the dogskin mat and the sheepskin blanket in the western room for her to sleep. Chou Bang and his brother slept in the eastern room.

"You should stay with her in the western room," said Chou Chou.

"I brought her back for you," said Chou Bang.

"Nonsense. She's yours."

"You go first."

"Enough of such talk."

"We'll talk about it later."

"No matter what, there'll be a woman in the house. Coming and going, talking and laughing," said Chou Chou.

"Yeah," said Chou Bang.

"It seems like a dream, but it isn't."

"Yeah."

Brother, your fate is good. You exchanged twelve sheep for a woman. It was worth it. Your fate is a good."

"I told you, I don't want her."

"Nonsense. If you persist this way, I'm going to West River."

"We'll talk about it later."

"Chou Bang."

"Yeah?"

"..."

"Look, you're crying again."

"I'm happy because there is a woman in the house. I don't know why my fucking nose itches when I'm happy."

"Go to bed."

"Okay. Go to bed."

They blew out the lamp. Although neither one made a sound, they couldn't sleep. Later they got up and talked in the dark.

"Chou Bang."

"Yeah?"

"I keep thinking that this is all a dream."

"It's not a dream. It's real."

"I say it's real too, but it's still like a dream."

"It's not a dream. If you don't believe it, let's go have a look."

"Let's go. We don't have to look, just listen."

"Let's go."

Barefooted, the two of them slowly left the main hall and felt their way to the door of the western room. They pricked up their ears to listen. After listening for a while, Chou Chou tugged at his brother. The two of them quietly made their way back to the eastern room. Entering their room, they covered their mouths and laughed.

"I didn't hear anything," said Chou Bang.

"She must be a light sleeper," said Chou Chou.

Lying on the *kang*, the two men continued talking. They were trying to decide what sort of fabric to get for her, what sort of scarf for her head, what sort of stockings, and what sort of shoes. They also decided to have two new quilts sewn. They talked until cockcrow, and only then fell silent.

Chou Bang heard a vague sound in the courtyard. As he listened, it sounded like someone thumping a water bucket. At first he thought it was his older brother going for some water, but he reached out and touched Chou Chou, who was still asleep on the *kang*.

He looked at the paper window. Dawn was beginning to break.

He stooped down to look through a hole in the window and saw a figure carrying a bucket through the gate.

It was the girl.

He climbed off the *kang* and followed the girl, who was already standing on the well platform. She was stark naked, stooping over to lower the bucket into the well.

"Let me, you don't know how . . ."

Before Chou Bang had finished speaking, the girl had vanished. She was gone that suddenly. After a while he heard a splash in the well.

Later, the village barefoot doctor said to the two of them, "The girl suffered from sleepwalking. Once a sleepwalking girl marries, she will get well." He continued, "That night one of you, no matter which one, only had to sleep with her and do it, and she would have been okay and nothing would have happened."

Chou Bang looked at his brother without saying a word.

Chou Chou was already melting into tears.

The Taste of Oat Flour

Blue sky. White clouds. Green mountains.

Under heaven, people were cutting a field of oats.

Back straight, Chou Bang wielded his scythe. He gazed at the green mountain slope ahead and saw a person descending.

He gazed, eyes wide open, for a while; then his heart began to pound. His scythe fell from his hands. Again he gazed, eyes wide open, for a while. Suddenly he took off running through the field.

The oats grew waist high. Chou Bang leaned forward, his arms swinging as if he were rowing.

The person descending the slope saw Chou Bang and leaped into the waves of grain. Chou Bang saw the person cut through the waves like a boat.

Rowing and swimming; rowing and swimming. When they were about three meters apart, they stopped. They looked at each other for a long time before they spoke.

"It's you."

"It's me."

"I knew it was you as soon as I saw you."

"Me too."

So speaking, they fell silent. Panting, trying to catch their breath, they remained looking at each other for a long time.

"You're cutting oats?"

"I'm cutting oats."

"There has been plenty of rain this year."

"Plenty of rain."

Panting, they nearly choked trying to catch their breath. They looked at each other for a long time. They both wanted to say something, but for the moment didn't know what to say.

"Let's talk later."

"Okay, we'll talk later."

"We'll talk tonight."

"Okay."

"The same place."

"Okay."

She turned and rowed off. Taking a few steps, she turned and looked; taking a few more steps, she turned and looked.

He watched her as she left the oat field and watched her descend the terraced slope.

After she disappeared, he raised his fists in the air and brought them down forcefully. Then he turned and ran. He suddenly tripped in the oats and fell and drowned amid the waves of grain.

Then someone began to sing:

The mountains, rivers, and stones are all here
Everyone is here but you.

The east wind blows, the river flows west
I think of you when I see others.

At night, everything shone white under the moon.

Off in the distance, the frogs croaked and the flying insects of autumn were calling.

They made a nest for themselves from the piles of naked oat straw facing the moon, where he and she had made a nest for themselves last year. To avoid bumping into the nest and having it collapse as it had last year, they burrowed inside one after the other.

"Have you thought of me?"

"Is there any need to ask?"

"I still want to ask."

"And you?"

"You don't have to ask."

"What are you thinking?"

"Thinking in spite of myself."

"Me too."

His left arm around her waist, he caressed her breasts with his right hand. When he first placed his large hand on her breasts, she trembled. She hurriedly pushed his hand away. But he touched her again. He said, "I want to touch you; I want to touch you here. It's been a year since I touched you."

"Okay, go ahead," she said.

He stopped caressing her and asked, "Are you going to let me guess what your mouth tastes like? Last year you let me guess, but I always got it wrong."

"Okay. Guess."

"You have to let me kiss you before I can guess."

"I never said you couldn't."

Hearing her, he clasped her tightly to himself and kissed and kissed and kissed until he had to come up for air. Only then did he stop.

"What did you taste?"

"What do you mean, what did I taste?"

"Didn't you say you were going to guess?"

"Oh, I forgot, I was so busy kissing you."

"Try again."

He kissed her again and said, "Rock candy."

"Wrong."

"Malt sugar?"

"Wrong."

"Candy?"

"Wrong."

"I know, I know. Licorice shoot."

"No, that's not right."

"I don't know what else is sweet."

"You're a fool. It's oat flour."

"Oat flour? That's not sweet. I'll just have another taste to see if you're fooling me."

She offered him her lips. He tasted, and took a breath.

"Well, do you know?"

"What?"

"Whenever I do it with him, I close my eyes and imagine it's you."

"Me?"

"Yeah."

"It's no use, there's no point."

"I'll have a son for you."

"I don't want one."

"Why?"

"I'm afraid he won't be able to get a wife, like me—be unmarried."

"Huh . . . you are a fool."

"I don't even have a woman, how can I have a son?"

"I've saved lots and lots of money for you. In three years you can get a woman."

"I don't want one."

"Why?"

"I already have a woman."

"Who?"

"You."

"What?"

"I want you to be my woman."

"What?"

"I want you to be my woman tomorrow and the next day and the next and the next and . . ."

"Yeah? Yeah?"

They knocked over the oat straw. They were buried ever so gently under the shiny yellow oat straw.

Off in the distance, the frogs croaked and the flying insects of autumn called.

Wen Shan's Woman

Wen Shan's woman had been sick for two days. She lay curled up on the *kang*. No one cared for her except Mouser.

Her husband, Wen Shan, was suffering from tympanites, which was brought on by his anger during the land-reform proceedings. Furious, he wanted to know why the land that had been handed down by generations of his family was supposed to be shared out to others. He was so angry that he fell ill. Although he was treated and his condition improved, he never fully regained his health. He lived another seven or eight years, and on the very day he joined the cooperative, he keeled over. The moment he gasped his last, outside was filled with the sound of exploding firecrackers and the beating of drums and cymbals.

Her son, Hehe, and his milk sister, Bannu, stole white flour from the Accountant and made skillet cakes. The following day, the Committee of the Dictatorship of the Masses of the commune checked house to house and found the flour. He was tied up and beaten and then sent to jail. Bannu's half-wit husband broke one of her legs.

After Hehe was thrown in jail, Bannu would visit Wen Shan's woman once a week. Dragging her leg, she also carried water to fill her water jar. Bannu was a good person, but she hadn't been over in the last two days.

Wen Shan's woman was also very close to one other person—that was Old Guiju, who worked as a hired hand for them. It was because she was so close to him that she didn't allow him to visit. After Wen Shan died, Old Guiju pressed her several times to marry him legally, but she would not consent. But as soon as he left, she would cry. In years past, she would keep her door open for him at night, and he often sneaked over to her place after feeding the animals. The last two years, she hadn't let him in. If she saw him on the street, she avoided him or ignored him. She was a landlord's wife and was afraid their meeting would be bad for him.

Only Mouser had looked after her the last two days. He sniffed her face, licked her hands, dilly-dallied in her arms, and lay opposite her, purring as if asking her something.

Old Guiju had caught Mouser that year and given him to her.

It was spring, and Wen Shan's tympanites had deteriorated and he had to be hospitalized in the city. Everyone avoided him because of his class status; even his close relations did not help him. It was as if he were a pile of dog shit and everyone was afraid of soiling themselves, except Old Guiju. Old Guiju said that in those years he had lived off him and that he couldn't be ungrateful. The Accountant said he had exploited and oppressed him, so why should he care? Old Guiju said fuck it. He carried him to the county hospital in a wheelbarrow.

One day midmorning, the sun was shining brightly. The people of the Wen Clan Caves, their chickens and beasts, all came out to soak up the warmth in the courtyards. Wen Shan's woman was sitting on the platform to wash clothes in her courtyard. As she washed, she tried to calculate how many days had passed since they left. As she was thinking, Old Guiju entered the courtyard gate and strode toward her, carrying a cloth sack.

She knew his walk well. He walked as if he were pushing an invisible wheelbarrow.

She stood up, smiling at him. First she shook her wet hands, then she wiped them back and forth on the front of her clothes like a barber sharpening his razor.

"It's been ages since I've seen you," she said.

"Altogether, it has been nineteen and a half days," he said.

"You're very precise," she replied.

"Here's a kitten for you," he said.

He proceeded to dump the kitten out of the bag. The kitten stood there looking all around. He didn't know where he was. Wen Shan's woman bent down and picked him up.

"Meow . . . Mouser. Meow . . . Mouser."

"Why are you calling the kitten Mouser?" he asked.

"It just popped into my head," she replied.

As they spoke, they went into her house.

"Put Mouser on the *kang*," he said.

"Why put him on the *kang*?" she asked.

"I'd like you to put him on the *kang*," he replied.

Her face flushed red because she knew what he wanted to do when she put the kitten down.

"Wen Shan is suffering in the hospital, the poor thing," she said.

"Well then, just forget it," he said.

"Look, I'm just talking. I didn't say forget it," she said.

She put Mouser on the *kang*.

He put her on the *kang* too.

Wen Shan died that very month.

Old Guiju went to get Hehe at his old wet nurse's village. But Hehe refused to return. So saying, Hehe left with his milk sister, Bannu. Watching Hehe depart, he thought that the young man walked as if he were pushing an invisible wheelbarrow. Old Guiju shook his head.

From then on, Wen Shan's woman lived alone. Her only companion was Mouser.

When he was nineteen, Hehe moved back to the Wen Clan Caves from his wet nurse's village, but he didn't live with his mother. He lived in a deserted cave dwelling at the north end of the village. He would go to his mother's place once a week to carry water for her. At the end of the year, he would have the Accountant set aside some of his work points for his mother, and in this way he supported her.

Wen Shan's woman slept at the foot of the wall. She moved. Her arms folded across her chest; her fingers curled, twitching. She was dreaming. She was dreaming about the Dragon Boat Festival.

She dreamed of Old Guiju shouldering a huge bundle of silvery wormwood and carrying it back to the village. As he passed her door, she softly called, "Elder Brother Guiju." Normally she did not call him Elder Brother Guiju, but once in a while, she would secretly and softly address him in such a familiar fashion.

Sitting beneath the window in the courtyard, she braided wormwood rope with Old Guiju. He braided one rope after another, each of which was about one meter in length. She was different. She wanted to braid one very long rope and coil it like a well rope.

"Why are you braiding it that way?" he asked.

"I feel like it," she said.

"Braid it, braid it."

Wen Shan could be heard reading in the western room, which was his study. Wen Shan liked to read. He was happy so long as he had something to read. He would read all day long and do nothing else. All he did was read. When the Japanese were there, they wanted him to serve as an official, but he declined, saying he was not cut out for it. When he read, he had to read aloud, otherwise he wouldn't know what he was reading.

At that time he was reading:

The gentleman is bamboo, the official is a pine tree. The butterfly steals the fragrant pollen, the bee gathers nectar. The breeze wafts the lotus fragrance, the shadows dense with the sun high overhead. Dageng Mountain is crowned with a shimmering plum; at the foot of Gusu Tower, a confusion of grass. A man on horseback rides through a garden to look at the flowers and enjoy the beautiful scene; the old pig herder in the field prays for a bountiful year.

Hearing Wen Shan read, he looked at her and she looked at him. They both had to cover their smiles.

"Let's go and have some glutinous rice dumplings," she said.

They entered the eastern outbuilding, which was used as a dining room. She peeled the bamboo-leaf wrappings from the rice dumplings and placed three in a bowl, on top of which she sprinkled some malt syrup. He took the bowl and wolfed down the glutinous rice dumplings.

"Don't choke, don't choke," she said.

The very moment she hastily uttered these words, she heard a cat miserably crying, "Meow."

Wen Shan's woman woke up. She didn't hear Wen Shan reading, nor Old Guiju's laughter and talk. Nor did she see the malt syrup canister or the basin of glutinous rice dumplings. Only then did she realize she had been dreaming.

She could hear the *sha-sha-sha-sha* of the falling rain outside. It was a spring rain with no thunder or lightning.

She lay there without moving. Her head no longer ached, nor was she feverish. She was a bit hungry and wanted to drink some water.

Which meant she was getting well, she thought.

She calculated she had been lying there for two days. She discovered it was the day of the Dragon Boat Festival.

No wonder I dreamed about eating glutinous rice dumplings, today is the Dragon Boat Festival, she thought.

She thought she could detect the aroma of glutinous rice dumplings. At first she was suspicious and thought she was dreaming, but after inhaling a couple of times, she decided the aroma was, in fact, real.

After she opened her eyes, she sat up and was stunned. There were three glutinous rice dumplings beside her pillow.

Her mind was a blank and, without taking so much as a breath, she devoured the three glutinous rice dumplings. Several grains of rice were stuck to the edge of the bamboo-leaf wrapper; she licked them off and ate them. She plopped a date pit in her mouth and sucked on it as if she were sucking on candy.

No wonder she had dreamed about eating glutinous rice dumplings—she had, of course, smelled them.

But where had they come from? Who had brought them? Bannu? Old Guiju? Why hadn't they wakened her?

As she was thinking, she heard a strange sound coming from the floor. She leaned forward to look down. She saw that something had fallen in over the threshold. Startled at first, she took a closer look and realized that it was her Mouser.

Mouser was wet and covered with mud. He dragged himself across the floor toward her. In his mouth was something covered with mud, which he was struggling to drag to her. She reached out and took it. It was a glutinous rice dumpling covered with mud. She then realized who had brought the glutinous rice dumplings she had just eaten, but she wondered where her Mouser had gotten them.

"My Mouser. My poor Mouser." She spoke as she bent down to pick the cat up by its front legs and put him on the *kang*.

"Meow!"

It was a sharp and miserable sound.

She immediately let go of him. She thought she had heard the same sound when she was dreaming.

Mouser was in pain, injured. Then she recalled how he had tumbled in over the threshold. She climbed down off the *kang* and pulled back the door curtain. She saw a trail on the bricks between the courtyard door and the door to the main room. A broad, wet, and muddy mark left where Mouser had dragged himself.

Mouser had been hurt and couldn't stand on his feet.

She ran out into the courtyard. A light rain was still falling. She saw the mark Mouser had left when he dragged himself from the foot of the west wall to the courtyard door. It was a dirt courtyard, softened by the rain. The trail left by Mouser as he dragged himself left an impression in the ground. She could also see some red stains in the trail before her. Squatting, she saw that it was blood. As she looked at the trail before her, she saw that the amount of blood increased. It was blood.

Poor Mouser had dragged himself home. But he had refused to drop the glutinous rice dumpling. *He brought it home for me.*

"My Mouser!"

She ran into the eastern room. Mouser was still in the doorway. Squatting, she looked to see where Mouser had been injured, but Mouser refused to be touched. He absolutely refused to be picked up. She used two fingers and slowly felt the cat's whole body before determining that his lower back was broken. His neck was also injured. He refused to let her touch those two places. When she did, he would give a sharp, miserable wail.

Later, she realized that Mouser was missing more than half his tail. Flesh, bone, and hair, all gone. That was the source of the blood.

"Mouser, who could be so cruel? Mouser, I know who could be so cruel," she said, weeping.

Hearing her weep, Mouser struggled to lift his head and look at her. He looked at her for just a moment before lowering his head again in pain. Head on his forelegs, he closed his eyes.

Around midnight, Wen Shan's woman discovered that Mouser was nowhere to be seen. She had no idea when her Mouser had left, dragging himself painfully across the courtyard. She took the lamp and went in search. She found him, mouth wide open, stiff and stretched out outside the main room.

Her Mouser was dead.

Wen Shan's woman went to the commune and bought a can of fish. She opened it and placed it in front of her dressing table, on the old-fashioned square table for eight people.

The dressing table had two drawers side by side, one large and one small. Mouser was laid out in the larger drawer. After he died, Wen Shan's woman washed him and dried him. She spread her white hankie in the bottom of the drawer and placed Mouser on top. She planned to use the larger drawer as a coffin for Mouser.

She filled a bowl half full with millet, in which she inserted three sticks of burning incense. She then knelt on a rush mat and kowtowed three times to Mouser. As she kowtowed, she said to herself, *Mouser, you were beaten to death because you stole glutinous rice dumplings for me. Mouser, please forgive me. Mouser, I will not let you die in vain.*

"Wu-ah, ah . . ." Wen Shan's woman began to cry. She wailed for her Mouser.

Wen Shan's woman wanted to conduct a funeral ceremony like the one for her dead husband Wen Shan. She would wait seven days before removing the coffin and burying her Mouser.

Every day Wen Shan's woman thought about her Mouser, her poor Mouser.

In nine years, her Mouser had encountered all sorts of disasters and difficulties that never seemed to end, she thought.

The Accountant had a fight with his wife and beat her, so his wife went home to her parents. She only returned to the Wen Clan Caves two months later. The Accountant insisted that when his wife went home to her parents she had a man on the side. His wife denied it. The Accountant went outside and caught a cat on the windowsill and stuffed it down his wife's pants. The unfortunate cat had been none other than Mouser. The Accountant took a whisk and, while beating the woman's pants, asked her if she had a man outside. Stuffed in the woman's pants and beaten in the dark, Mouser began to scratch and claw but could find no way out. He just let out a miserable yowl. Unable to bear the cat's clawing, the Accountant's wife hurriedly confessed to having a man outside. But the Accountant wouldn't let it go at that— only after his wife had admitted to having had a whole village of men did he relent. Only then did he let Mouser out. The Accountant said, "From now on, don't mind my business." After that, the Accountant's wife developed an intense hatred for Mouser. She transferred all the hate she dared not express toward her husband to Mouser.

"Oh, poor Mouser," said Wen Shan's woman.

"Today's the seventh day, Mouser. I won't let you die for nothing," she said.

Next door, at the Accountant's house, there were two cats. She called the female Big Eyes and the male Black Bandit. Big Eyes had a soft, sweet cry; "*Nian'r, nian'r*," she called. Black Bandit called "*Mie'r, mie'r*," which Wen Shan's woman found odious.

Big Eyes and her Mouser were often together. On account of this, Black Bandit often fought with Mouser. But Black Bandit was no match. One time, Mouser took a chunk out of his ear. A few days later, Mouser lost a bit of his right ear. One look told Wen Shan's woman that someone had cut his ear with a pair of scissors. She also knew that the Accountant's wife was the culprit. No one else could be so cruel.

"It was she who chopped off Mouser's tail," said Wen Shan's woman.

"She knows that without a tail, a cat can't climb and will fall," said Wen Shan's woman.

"Mouser lost his tail and fell from the wall and died," said Wen Shan's woman.

From the day Mouser died, Big Eyes wanted to come over several times a day. "*Nian'r, nian'r*," she would cry, searching for Mouser. "*Mie'r, mie'r*," cried Black Bandit, following her. But Wen Shan's woman had long since blocked the cat hole with a pillow, and they were unable to come in.

Wen Shan's woman had taken a spade from the southern room and dug a hole two *chi* square and one *chi* deep in the courtyard, where she planned to bury Mouser.

She heard Big Eyes crying on the windowsill, *"Nian'r, nian'r."* After she removed the pillow that blocked the cat hole, Big Eyes immediately entered the house and leaped up on the square table. She heard Black Bandit as well, but he dared not enter. He lifted the flap of the cat hole and peeked in, crying to Big Eyes. He kept his eyes fixed on Wen Shan's woman to see if she was going to throw something at him.

Wen Shan's woman threw a piece of fish on the floor. As if pouncing on a rat, Black Bandit pounced on the fish and gulped it down. Unlike Big Eyes, he did not remain in the same place to eat. He retreated into a corner.

Wen Shan's woman blocked the cat hole with the pillow again.

She had long since closed the door to the house.

The Accountant's two cats never made it home.

Big Eyes and Mouser slept together in the drawer of the dressing table. Black Bandit was wrapped in half a cement bag. Wen Shan's woman buried them all in the grave in the courtyard. When she buried them, she heard Big Eyes, *"Nian'r, nian'r"* and Black Bandit, *"Mie'r, mie'r."* Later they were silent, or they cried a few times, but Wen Shan's woman never heard them. The sound was cut off when she filled in the hole.

Wen Shan's woman immediately planted some henna seeds and some sunflower seeds in the bare soil.

Within a few months, Wen Shan's woman's courtyard was filled with the sweet aroma of pink blossoms and golden sunflowers.

By autumn, the sunflower heads were as large as pot lids. Everyone thought it was strange and curious and asked Wen Shan's woman about it. She also said it was strange and curious. They asked her to give them some seeds when the heads dried so they could plant them. Wen Shan's woman said nothing could be easier.

Old Yinyin

Fucking Guan Guan left at midnight. Old Yinyin put on a new pair of pants and a new sash to go to West River.

Old Yinyin held the four cooked lamb's feet and the less than half bottle of wine against his chest and stepped out his door. Once outside, he returned to blow out the lamp. At first he hadn't planned to blow it out, as if to keep an altar lamp burning. Departed souls could only find their way and ascend to heaven by the light of an altar lamp. But he regretted his decision once out the door. *Fuck your mother. Keeping the thing lit all night long will waste a lot of oil.* So thinking, he returned home. He groped around for the lamp stand and blew on the red speck of flame. The flame flickered but stayed lit. He blew again; the red speck went out. This time he knew he had extinguished the flame.

Stepping out the door, he stopped again and thought for a while. Then he went back to his cave, where he fumbled around on the *kang* for his Locomotive brand cigarettes and some matches, which he also placed against his chest. Only then did he shut the door with no worries. Standing on tiptoe, he chained the door to indicate that there was no one at home; the only living things were a few flies sleeping on the bowls or pans or wherever, and a nest of rats sleeping behind the water urn. There were no lice. Old Yinyin's blood was far too bitter for lice.

There were a lot of holes, ruts, and bumps all along the five *li* of the mountain road, but Old Yinyin didn't need any support and he never stumbled, making his way with ease all the way to West River without resting.

Old Yinyin was blind. To a blind person, night and day were all the same.

Old Yinyin arrived beneath that tree, that crooked tree. He took off his shoes and banged them together like cymbals. Then he sat down on top of them. If he didn't knock the dirt off his shoes, his new pants might get dirty. The Accountant had given the pants to him, saying that the leadership had issued them as a comfort to a householder enjoying the five guarantees. Later, he had heard that others like himself had also been issued a short jacket. The fucking Accountant had most likely taken it. Let him take it. If he wanted to take everything from you, what could you do? A new pair of pants was better than nothing. Besides, the Accountant was a member of the same clan. As an uncle, he would have felt uncomfortable asking about such things. Anyway, if you didn't wear it, he would; it was all the same whoever wore it.

Old Yinyin took the wine bottle, the Locomotive brand cigarettes and matches, and the lamb's feet out of his coat.

One, two, three. One, two, three. One, two, three.

He only had three lamb's feet left. No matter how many times he counted them, there were always three of them. One was missing. He didn't know where he'd lost it. If it was lost, it was lost. If it was lost, he wouldn't find it. Even if he could see, he wouldn't be able to find it in the middle of the night, not to mention with no eyes. Just one less to eat. *Anyway, if you don't eat it, he will; if he doesn't eat it, a dog will. Whoever eats it, it's all the same.*

Glug, glug, glug, Old Yinying drank his wine; *naming, naming,* he gnawed on the lamb's feet; *puff, puff,* he smoked a cigarette. After finishing everything, Old Yinyin planned to hang himself from the crooked tree like Shepherd Boy and Dog Girl.

The crooked tree was a damned good tree—nothing better for hanging. The tree was treasured by the Wen Clan Caves. It had been very helpful to generations. Even now it was still of use. Even people from other villages coveted the tree. Last year, a girl from a mountain village came and hanged herself on it.

A good tree. A good tree.

The crooked tree was a damned good tree. It was no wonder that the people from the girl's village wanted to come and chop it down, but the people of the Wen Clan Caves came to protect it with spades and carrying poles. The people from the girl's village didn't chop down the tree; all they did was carry the dead girl home. The crooked tree continued to grow at the source of West River, where it extended its crooked neck to look at people and extend its crooked arms to wave at people, urging them to come quickly.

A good tree. A good tree.

The crooked tree was a damned good tree.

Old Yinyin had visited it more than a few times in the last few days.

Oh, living in this world is such a burden. It wouldn't be so bad to end it quickly like Shepherd Boy. Why go on living?

Blind people can't terrace fields, can't repair irrigation works, and can't guide a seed plow. All we can do is eat, and sleep, and eat. Why go on living?

Such thoughts had filled Old Yinyin's mind the last few days. His head always filled with such thoughts, Old Yinyin decided to end his life.

At first he thought of throwing himself into a well. Throwing himself down a well was good. He'd just jump head first and wouldn't have to walk very far. But later he thought he'd dirty the water if he threw himself down a well. Who could drink dirty water? The whole village would end up cursing him. A person couldn't think of themselves alone; they had to think of others. Old Yinyin heard that electrocution was the way to go. It was pretty simple—one *hua* and it would all be over. But there was no electricity in the Wen Clan Caves. The commune had electricity, but he didn't know what it looked like or where to find it. And even if he found it, he didn't know how to electrocute himself. No, he decided to do it like Shepherd Boy and hang himself from the crooked tree.

Once he had made up his mind, Old Yinyin was very happy. As happy as when the Accountant had arranged a wedding engagement for his son. Those days, the Accountant whistled even more resonantly than ever. He didn't even swear at anyone, nor did he shine his flashlight on anyone. He didn't look that gloomy and he smiled when he saw people. He even went from house to house inviting people to come to his place for deep-fried cakes.

Old Yinyin also decided he wanted to celebrate. Such a big event had to be celebrated. He couldn't afford deep-fried cakes, but eating a meal of oat cakes with no millet flour mixed in, he could handle.

There had to be wine. No matter what, there had to be wine. He had to spend money one last time. He had to do things in a grand way—he didn't want people to laugh.

Old Yinyin bought a sheep's head and four lamb's feet at the commune for two *yuan*. He bought a bottle of strong wine for eight *mao*. He also spent one *mao* five for a pack of Locomotive brand cigarettes. The people in Wen Clan Caves who could afford to smoke claimed that Locomotive cigarettes were both good and inexpensive. The poor people would always buy that brand for any kind of celebration or when relatives visited. So Old Yinyin bought a pack.

What was a train? According to Grunt, a train could travel a thousand *li* in one morning. Damn, it must be magic. Old Yinyin knew that there was a picture of a train on the pack of cigarettes. But he couldn't see, and rub it though he might, he couldn't feel anything.

Forget it. He was going to die soon, so why care about a train? Besides, there were plenty of things a person never saw in their lifetime. There was that time the cadre came and didn't know what flax was. He said, "What are you villagers doing planting the fields with blue flowers?" A real fuck. Didn't understand.

If there was to be a celebration, people had to be invited. He couldn't invite that many. He decided to invite only Guan Guan to come for a meal. For one thing, Guan Guan was also blind, and secondly, Guan Guan was also a fortune-teller. He wanted him to pick a good day. He wanted to choose a propitious day.

Guan Guan didn't put on airs. He came when he was invited.

"I think we should light the lamp today," said Old Yinyin.

"I only light one at the New Year; normally I never light one," said Guan Guan.

"We'll just say that we are celebrating the New Year."

"You can see the lamp holder, I can't."

"Everything is red in front of my eyes as if a lamp were lit."

"I heard the barefoot doctor say you have a white skin over your eyes and all you need to do is have it removed."

"Where would I get the money for that?"

"That's right. You can't afford to have it removed."

Old Yinyin carried the sheep's head and the wine to the *kang* as he spoke.

The two of them ate and drank. They drank until midnight.

"I guess people who can see are the same as us—it's still just a sheep's head and some wine," said Old Yinyin.

"People live and do this and fight over that. They do things over and over again, and it all comes down to this, right?" said Guan Guan.

"The emperor rules all under heaven just for this."

"Yeah, the emperor can have all sorts of delicacies, but he just fills his belly."

"But he dies too."

"Yeah, but deaths are different."

"They're all the same. What makes his different?"

"Shit, an emperor dies in pleasure, common people in suffering. How can they be the same?"

"See, you talk animal talk."

"That's how Grunt puts it."

"Anyway, a good death is still a death. A bad death is also a death. I'm saying it's better to die sooner than later."

"Then why don't you die?"

"Do you think I'm afraid of dying? I want to pick a good day for it."

"Okay, then I'll pick one for you."

"Tell me which day is auspicious."

"Drink your damned wine."

"What day would be the best?"

"The best day is to have been drowned by your mother the day you were born."

"I'm serious."

"Drink, drink."

"Oh, drink."

They talked and drank this way till late at night.

Under the crooked tree, Old Yinyin gnawed on the three lamb's feet and drank what was left of the wine. He also smoked several cigarettes, one after another. Afterward, he put on his shoes and stood up. As he stood up, he suddenly recalled how in the midst of eating and drinking, he had forgotten to have Guan Guan select a day for him.

Ai, wine is a bad thing—drink a little and you forget what you have to do. It had always been so. It would be bad not to consider the day.

Damned Guan Guan, fuck your mother. You ask him something serious and all he does is drink. See, as the end nears, he forgets, doesn't he?

Old Yinyin regretted not having handled the situation better. But there was nothing to do about it now. Since he was already there, let it be done.

He moved a stone, which he had readied earlier, from behind a tree and placed it beneath the crooked tree. He took off his sash.

He had bought the red cloth for his sash at the commune and then had Leng Er's mother sew it for him. There was nothing better for a noose than his red sash. It was an auspicious color and it wouldn't hurt his neck.

He stood on the rock and was about to hang his sash from the crooked tree when his pants fell down around his ankles. Flustered, he fell from the rock.

Fuck your mother. Why hadn't he thought of it before? He had forgotten to put on his old sash. But fortunately his pants had fallen now. If they had fallen after he had hanged himself, it would have been too late and a hell of a mess. Hanging himself bare-assed would have made him the laughingstock of the village. Even when he arrived in the land of shadows, he'd be a laughingstock.

After much consideration, Old Yinyin cut several thin twigs from the tree and managed to fasten his pants around his waist with them.

Once again, he tried hanging his sash from the crooked tree.

He wasn't sure if the crooked tree was too high or he was too low. On the stone, even standing on his tiptoes, he was unable to reach the crooked tree.

Then he came up with a solution, which was to tie a small stone to one end of his sash and then toss it over the crooked tree.

He smiled. Even those who could see couldn't do it any better.

Once his sash was in place, he tied a noose and put his head through it to try it out and check the length. It was a little long, so he unhurriedly untied the noose and retied it. There was no need to hurry; hurrying might lead to mistakes. Sunrise was still a ways off. Nor was there a wolf in pursuit. Even if a wolf were in pursuit, it wouldn't matter—Old Yinyin knew that no wolf would eat him. Once when he was little, he and the other children were playing the blind man catches the cripple outside the village. The other kids placed a hat with ears on his head and fastened it tightly at the back of his neck. In the middle of their play someone shouted "Wolf, wolf." All the other kids ran away. But he didn't run because he didn't know where the wolf was, nor did he know where to run. While he stood there trying to untie the hat, he heard a *sou-sou-sou*. It was the wolf going by. The wolf was pursuing the other children and didn't stop to eat him. One of Zits Wu's older brothers was eaten that time.

Some people said that Yinyin had a powerful fate and would not die that easily. Others said that his blood was bitter and the wolf avoided him when it smelled him. Anyway, he hadn't met his end that time.

He redid the noose. He tugged on it with both hands. It was good and strong.

He wondered if there was anything else. It would be all over when he hanged himself.

He thought for some time, but there was nothing he could think of that could keep him. He had eaten and drank. There were still a few cigarettes, but he decided to leave those for the people who took him down. He couldn't let them go to all that trouble for nothing. Besides, they still had to carry his dead weight back to the village.

That was all.

Standing calmly on the rock, Old Yinyin loosened the noose to pull it over his head. He moved his head back and forth and wiggled the noose down, right around his neck.

That was done.

"Fuck your mother!"

Old Yinyin swore ferociously and forcefully kicked with both feet. The rock rolled to one side.

For a moment he felt himself swinging in midair.

Tong!

Old Yinyin heard the sound.

What was it? Had his pants fallen down again?

Old Yinyin felt with his hands and knew it wasn't his pants, but that he had fallen to the ground.

Fuck your mother! You'll always run into a snag when you worry about everything.

I knew there would be problems if I didn't pick an auspicious day. Fuck your mother, Guan Guan.

I have to blame myself. I shouldn't have gone back to blow out the altar lamp in order to save the coal oil.

Ai, living is a lot of trouble, and so is trying to die. Fuck your mother.

After Old Yinyin felt around for the rock, replaced it under the crooked tree, and went to hang his sash again, he realized that it had snapped in half.

Damn, and a new sash at that.

He threw the sash over the tree and tied the two halves together, but it was still no good. He couldn't get it over his head. He untied the lumpy knot and pulled his sash down off the crooked tree.

People said that there were ghosts at West River. That seemed to be the case.

He was still upset that he hadn't checked the day.

He was also upset that he had blown out the altar lamp.

When he got back, he'd have to have Leng Er's mother fix his sash.

Next time he'd have that fucking Guan Guan check the day.

The other thing was that under no circumstances could he forget to light the altar lamp burning day and night.

Old Yinyin set off for the village, talking to himself.

Someone followed him from a distance.

Watching the Fields

Thanks to the Old Man in Heaven, the crops grew better than in any year in memory. Harvest time was coming in fifteen to twenty days. The Revolutionary Committee of the commune ordered that everyone in the Production Brigade be mobilized to guard the crops to be harvested. It was also to deal with the starving people who had survived all summer by eating relief grain. The relief grain had been allocated from above in the amount of eight *liang* of unhusked grain per person per day. One might not be full, but one wouldn't starve to death either. By adding some bitter herbs or tree leaves, one could make it through the long days of summer.

"In the past, didn't the Production Brigade close one eye so that the children might eat what was in season?" said the Brigade Leader.

"But that was in the past. Raising a ruckus was nothing more than that. That's not the case now—no one can raise a ruckus, not even my wife," said the Brigade Leader.

"Let's say the ugly words up front. Whoever we catch will be turned over to the commune and will be punished by the Committee of the Dictatorship of the Masses," said the Accountant.

All of this was said at the general meeting of commune members.

None of the commune members said a word, but neither did they lower their heads. If you lowered your head, the Accountant would accuse you of dozing off and shine his flashlight at you, embarrassing you by not letting you dodge left or right.

During the meeting, a dozen or so unmarried men were chosen to take care of this and that, and were sent out to watch the fields. Each one was also given a rope with which to bind any thief.

The people of the Wen Clan Caves let the field watchmen eat their fill. The Brigade Leader and the Accountant both knew that if you didn't let them eat, they'd find a way, so it was better to take care of them publicly. But they were not permitted to take anything home with them.

Whatever the case might be, the job of field watchman was a good one.

Zits Wu was sent to watch the corn on the west slope.

Midnight. Nothing was stirring; even the legless red spotted toads in the riverbed had ceased their incessant croaking and were sleeping. If there was a sudden croak, it was nothing more than a dream.

"Shepherd Boy, you fucked it up. You killed yourself and you won't be back."

"You can't even have an ear of roasted corn. You fucked it up. Messed it up."

Zits Wu sat at the foot of the field wall, a fire burning in front of him as he gnawed on an ear of corn and swore at Shepherd Boy. Occasionally he would look up at the constellation Orion to see if it was midnight yet.

Far off on the slope on the other side of the river, a fire also twinkled like a star.

Fucking Grunt was no doubt at that very moment feasting on potatoes. *I don't feel like corn—maybe I should go trade the fucker for some potatoes*, thought Zits Wu.

Still, it's better to be alive, thought Zits Wu.

Zits Wu stirred the fire until it blazed. Then he placed the cobs of the corn he had eaten in a circle around the fire to dry them out so that they could be easily burned. Although the field watchmen were permitted to eat their fill, still the corncobs and corn husks couldn't be left for all to see. First, it would look bad—it all had to be burned. Second, in this way the watchmen need not collect that much firewood.

He looked up again at the constellation Orion. It was almost midnight.

Zits Wu took off his pants and with some branches, tied off the legs to form two sacks, and then entered the cornfield.

At first, he loudly yanked the ears of corn from the stalks. After pulling off several, he felt he was making too much noise. He began twisting the ears of corn from the stalks. That was better. There was no sound. No one would ever know there was anyone in the field. After a while, Zits Wu had filled the legs of his pants to bursting with ears of corn.

He dumped the ears of corn beside the fire and kicked them into a pile. Then he took his pants to a different part of the field. He came out a short while later, the bulging pants legs riding across his shoulders.

When he was little, he liked nothing more than to let Baibai ride on his shoulders. His mother got Baibai in a marriage exchange for his sister. She was only six when she arrived, and she would become his wife at thirteen. Everyone said that when a girl reached thirteen, she was pretty much like her mother. Zits Wu could hardly wait till she reached thirteen. Little Baibai had a way of saying good things to people, so much so, in fact, that Zits Wu and his mother came to treat her as their own sister and daughter. She also had a way with Zits Wu so that he would carry her around all day long and play horse with her. When he played horse, she would spread her plump little legs and sit astride his shoulders. The year Baibai turned nine, Zits Wu's own sister turned fourteen. The espoused came to complete the marriage. His sister refused and ran off with a camel driver beyond the pass. The family of the espoused took Baibai back by force. On account of this, he went beyond the pass many times. He carried a cleaver with the intention of hacking up the young camel driver and bringing back his sister to trade for his Baibai. He went beyond the pass many times but never found them.

Zits Wu took up his bag again and busied himself for a while, sitting to shuck the corn. He shucked until there was only one thin layer of husk on each ear. He also removed all the corn silk. When he was small, he would shove the corn silk in his nose and pretend he was an old man, but now . . . he rubbed his chin and cheeks.

"There's no point, no point. I'm almost fifty," said Zits Wu.

He thought the ears of corn, without their husks and silk, looked like a . . . He smiled at the thought. He shook his head. He stacked the ears of corn on the ground, then built a circle around the fire with them. He looked up again. It was midnight.

As a rule, this was the time she would leave. His Little Aunt would leave now, thought Zits Wu.

He looked in the direction of the village, but it was too dark to see anything. But the fire on the slope on the other side of the river looked larger than before.

The fucker was probably waiting for someone too, thought Zits Wu.

Zits Wu squatted and stirred the fire and added the dry corncobs.

Crack! A spark shot out from the fire and burned him there.

"Fuck, it knows to pick the right place to shoot," he said, pressing his legs together. Then he pulled his pants toward himself.

He really didn't want to put on his pants. Shucking corn a moment ago, the husks rubbing against his skin had produced a damned pleasurable sensation. When he was small, his mother would let him go without pants when the weather warmed up. He walked around bare-assed even after ten. But his mom had Baibai wear pants. She would say, "She's a girl, and it looks bad for a girl not to wear pants." Actually, most girls went around without pants too. But not Baibai. Baibai was going to be her daughter-in-law, and one's daughter-in-law had to wear pants.

But in fact everything was handed down. It would have been great if the ancestors had said everyone should go naked. *If that had been the case, then that poor devil Shepherd Boy wouldn't have hanged himself over not having seen some heavenly sun,* thought Zits Wu.

People had to make it so complicated and mysterious. *Everyone knows who's who with or without clothes on, so why bother wearing clothes?* thought Zits Wu.

What would Little Aunt look like without clothes? Big ass, slender waist, big boobs. No woman in the village was better looking, with the exception perhaps of the woman of the Zhu household. *Little Aunt is really like my Baibai. Identical, exactly the same,* thought Zits Wu.

My Baibai would be about the same age as Little Aunt, and I can be pretty certain that they would look about the same. Big ass, slender waist, big boobs, thought Zits Wu.

It had been many years and Little Aunt never got pregnant. Who was to blame? wondered Zits Wu.

"Fuck your mother. What nonsense. What the hell does someone being pregnant or not have to do with you? What difference does it make who is to blame? They're not blaming you," said Zits Wu.

He heard footsteps in the distance. Zits Wu grabbed his pants but couldn't get them on. Then he realized that he had tied the legs shut. He hurriedly untied them.

The moment he got his pants on, the person was already standing in front of the fire. It was total blackness behind her.

"Nephew, you'll catch cold in just your shirt sleeves."

"I won't—here's a fire."

"Nephew, what are you looking at?"

"Nothing."

"Nephew, that looks like a sash over there."

Zits Wu flushed. His face wasn't flushed by the fire, but one word from Little Aunt set him afire.

"Over there. Right, right. Over there. Look, it looks like a sash."

Zits Wu took his sash from among the corn husks. It looked like a burning mugwort cord—half of it had already been burned up. He hurriedly stamped out the burning end. But too much of the sash had been consumed by the flame and there was no way he could fasten it.

"I'll make you a new one out of red cloth tomorrow."

"Auntie, let's pack up everything first. I've husked it all. Take as much as you can."

"I noticed. You are a very considerate nephew."

Zits Wu took the sack that Little Aunt had taken from her waist in his right hand. He squatted and opened the sack with his left hand. The sack was warm and smelled good.

Every time Little Aunt placed an ear of corn in the sack, Zits Wu felt her hair caress his face. It was more pleasurable than the corn husks rubbing against his naked flesh a little while ago. Every time Little Aunt placed an ear of corn in the sack, Zits Wu was aware of the pleasant fragrance wafting from her.

"Little Aunt, what did you keep in this bag? It smells so good."

"It held muskmelon."

"That's it; it smells like muskmelon."

Zits Wu inhaled deeply as he spoke. He liked to inhale the aroma deep into his lungs.

"Nephew, you picked too many; they won't all fit in the sack."

"Try again."

Zits Wu dumped the ears of corn on the ground. He had Little Aunt hold the sack while he filled it. He managed to squeeze in a few more ears, but five remained.

"Little Aunt, since you're here, don't leave anything."

"What can I do?"

"I heard that Bannu can really fill a sack. She can get ten *jin* of potatoes into her trouser legs."

"That would make it hard to walk."

"I also heard that she can put eight ears of corn around her waist, eight big ones."

"Let's try. Oh no, it's so itchy, oh, oh, it's so itchy."

As Little Aunt placed the five ears of corn around her waist, Zits Wu took the rope the Brigade Leader had given him to tie up thieves and tied it around her waist.

"Let's go, Little Aunt. I'll see you part way back."

"Aren't you going to keep watch over the field?"

"I have to look after Little Aunt first."

"You really are a nice person."

Zits Wu picked up the sack and started north. Little Aunt threw some more wood on the fire and then followed.

Little Aunt's household plot was three *li* to the north. The land was planted with corn and potatoes. He had to hide the corn there overnight; then she could carry it home in broad daylight the following day. No one would pay attention to someone carrying anything from their own household plot. This is what they had decided earlier.

"Nephew, we're almost there. Let's rest for a spell here, then you go back."

"Might as well not stop."

"Nephew, you really are a nice person."

Arriving at the household plot, Zits Wu put down the sack.

"Little Aunt. There's no need for you to come out tomorrow night. I'll manage to find time to carry a sack over. Uncle can bring a sack and pick it up during the day."

"Nephew, you really are a nice person."

"The next two days, I'll go up to where Grunt is and get a couple sacks of potatoes and bring those over."

"Nephew, how can I ever thank you?"

"There's no need to thank me."

"Just tell me."

"...Aunt, I've got to go."

"What's the hurry? Take a rest."

"I'm not tired; I'm not tired."

"I added fuel to your fire."

"I don't care about the fire. I'm going to take off."

"But I haven't thanked you."

"There's no need."

"Tell me. We're all flesh and blood."

Zits Wu stood without moving. Zits Wu kept saying he was going to leave, but he just stood there.

Baibai, thought Zits Wu.

"Come here. I can't reach the ears of corn in the back."

Baibai, thought Zits Wu.

"Come here and help Auntie get the ears of corn."

Baibai, thought Zits Wu.

"Do I have to beg you?"

Zits Wu couldn't just stand there any longer. He walked toward his aunt. He went to help his aunt remove that large ear of corn from the back of her waist.

The stars in the sky were white, blue, red, and yellow; there were even some whose color was hard to determine. The stars hung high up in the sky, entirely unconcerned with the trivial affairs of the people on earth. The stars had their own affairs; they had to endlessly blink their unseen eyes.

"Aunt, can you come again tomorrow night?"

"Didn't you tell me I didn't have to?"

"I'd like you to come."

"Okay. Auntie will give you your share the next two weeks."

The next day, men from the dozen or so households of the Wen Clan Caves, carrying willow baskets on their backs or carrying bags, set off for their household plots, smiling broadly, to harvest the ripe crops. Those that were not ripe could wait and be harvested later.

It was a fine autumn.

Old Guiju and His White Neck

Old Guiju drove the animals up the southern ridge. He shouted *"Hei!"* thinking to drive them to graze farther on. Ignoring him, they kept their heads glued to the ground where they grazed. *"Hei!"* he shouted again. The animals pretended not to hear him. "Rebellion, rebellion," he said as he picked up some stones. He was finally able to get them moving by throwing stones at them.

He didn't even want to look at them. It was the first time in so many years that he did not wish to look at them. Looking at them, he was vexed.

The animals scattered in all directions. He pursued them with his eyes, wanting to see only one thing. But however he looked, his White Neck was not among them.

They are castrating him, he thought.

The fuckers are castrating him, he thought.

Old Guiju turned to look in the direction of the village.

From the southern ridge, the village looked very small, like several boxes of matches that had been flattened underfoot. But he could immediately pick out the cave where he lived with the animals.

He recalled that White Neck had been born there three years before. He recalled White Neck's birth.

White Neck emerged with a black foot first from his mother. The person who served at the veterinary clinic forced the black leg back in. Then he reached up into the cow's belly and pulled White Neck out by the head. His body then followed.

"It has a white ring around its neck. It's a white neck," the people said.

White Neck lay on the straw. His body was sticky, and he shivered.

"He's very cold. The calf is cold," said Old Guiju.

As he spoke, Old Guiju took off his padded coat to cover the calf with it. The vet told him not to cover it, so he relented. Soon, the cow turned and began to lick White Neck. Licking here and there, it licked White Neck all over. White Neck opened his big eyes and looked at his mother and looked at the people. In a short while, White Neck got up on the knees of his front legs and then, ever so slowly, stood up.

"What a good animal. Without so much as a blink, he was on his feet. Damn, people can't compare with animals," said Old Guiju.

White Neck wanted to step forward, but as he did, he fell to his knees. He knelt and stood up to take a step forward again. Once more he fell to his knees.

"It's doing obeisance to the four directions, it's doing obeisance to Heaven, Earth, and Dad and Ma," said someone.

White Neck did indeed fall to his knees four times. On the fifth try, he managed to step forward without falling. He walked toward Old Guiju. He approached as if he had long recognized him.

"Damn people can't compare with animals. Damn, people only bow to Heaven and Earth when they get married," said Old Guiju.

Twelve days after White Neck was born, Old Guiju carried him to see the Brigade Leader and asked to celebrate the calf's twelfth day. The leader said that only a child's twelfth day was celebrated. Old Guiju said that the landlords used to celebrate a calf's twelfth day. The leader replied that that was the landlords and the brigade did not celebrate such things.

At one month, Old Guiju led White Neck to see the Brigade Leader and asked that the brigade celebrate the calf's first month. Lest the Brigade Leader protest, he reminded him that the calf belonged to the brigade and that it would suffer working for the brigade. The leader said that Old Guiju got no smarter with age, that in recent years even one-month anniversaries of children had not been celebrated, much less those of animals.

Old Guiju replied, "If you don't celebrate, I will." Old Guiju got a bottle of wine at the commune and cooked up some potato strips. He then invited a couple of old bachelors for a meal. He even bought a small brass bell, which he hung around White Neck's neck with a strip of red cloth.

When White Neck took a step, the bell rang. When White Neck ran, the bell rang and rang. White Neck seemed to like the sound—he would run, jump, and cavort all day long. Old Guiju listened to the ringing bell all day long and found it more pleasing to the ear than an opera.

They're castrating him right now, thought Old Guiju.

The fuckers are castrating my White Neck at this very moment, thought Old Guiju.

After breakfast and after slowly washing his dishes, he had to drive the animals out to graze. With the exception of White Neck, he released the animals from where they were tied to the mangers. The animals all scrambled to get out, knocking the broken gate frame and making it squeak. Old Guiju carried a half basket of feed—a mixture of black soybeans and hay—from the inner room, dumped it into the manger in front of White Neck, patted his flat brow, and departed. He left White Neck penned there alone.

Ascending the southern ridge, Old Guiju and the group of animals looked much like a bunch of dung beetles slowly climbing the ridge. The four unmarried men started to work.

Zits Wu tied White Neck to the mortar in the courtyard. White Neck drank some water and then in a circular motion, licked his lips, then raised his head and lowed a couple of times to the sky. White Neck wanted to turn around and see what work was in store for that day—pulling cartloads of coal up at the mine or following the tiller to pull a plow in the fields. Those were the most strenuous tasks. There was no other reason to be fed so well on black soybeans and hay. He tried to turn but found that he couldn't move his body or his legs.

Leng Er had grabbed hold of his tail with his two large hands so that he could not swing it. Ropes had been looped around his forelegs and hind legs so that he couldn't move. Grunt held the rope binding his hind legs and Wen Bao the rope that bound his forelegs. Zits Wu had a firm grasp on his two horns.

White Neck still did not understand what was going on when, *putong*, he staggered to one side and fell to the ground.

Frightened, White Neck kicked with his legs and desperately lifted his back from the ground, trying to right himself, all to no avail. The more he struggled, the tighter the ropes were pulled; the tighter the ropes were pulled, the harder he struggled to right himself.

Seeing White Neck struggling on the ground and hearing his brass bell ring, the four unmarried men laughed. They thought they had done a pretty good job.

The kids watching the excitement from a distance also laughed; Big Dog and Little Dog laughed the most stridently.

A young man came east along the ridge, singing as he walked:

Onion-white face, flower-bud mouth
For love of you, I am dying.

He walked over and stood in front of Old Guiju.

"Look, Old Man, your animals are gnawing on the bark of the trees," said the young man.

"Let them gnaw," said Old Guiju.

"But that will kill the trees."

"Let them die, let them die."

A lot of trees had been planted on the southern ridge, every eight or ten paces. The trees had died a long time ago; otherwise Old Guiju would not have brought his animals to graze there. One year, several truckloads of people had come from the county and planted the trees, but the trees never grew. They were always stunted and twisted and never amounted to anything. Later, they all simply died.

The young man knew the trees were dead, but had been trying to strike up a conversation before sitting down to rest his feet. When he saw that Old Guiju didn't look very happy, he started off to the west again, singing as he went:

The calf goes down to the river to drink
I kiss my girl on the lips.

White Neck wouldn't eat the bark off these dead trees. White Neck knows which stones to turn over to find tender grass, thought Old Guiju.

White Neck is the most intelligent, thought Old Guiju.

On the days the animals worked in the fields, Old Guiju would feed them twice every night. The second feeding was after midnight. All the animals were asleep, standing or lying down. Only White Neck was aware of his presence, and he would look up at Old Guiju with his big, beautiful eyes as if to say, you are busy, so busy on our behalf.

White Neck would stretch his head to the mangers of the other animals and take up the hay in his lips or eat the black soybeans. "*Hei,*" Old Guiju would shout at him. White Neck would flick his ears but pretend that his master was not talking to him, and go on eating. "Rebellion, rebellion!" Old Guiju would shout at him again. Only then would he pull his head back and slowly turn to look at Old Guiju. Seeing his master staring at him, he would quickly turn away. Old Guiju would laugh and give him several more handfuls of feed. White Neck was happy but wouldn't eat the feed right away. He knew that when the feed was done, there would be no more. He would stretch his neck, making the brass bell ring. He also pulled his head from the manger and placed his lips on the back of his master's hand.

Old Guiju recalled that time, a time he would never forget.

It was winter then. In the vicinity of the village, there was no grass to be found to assuage the hunger of the animals, so Old Guiju took the animals to West River. There was grass at West River. Normally he didn't like going there and wouldn't if there was any other option. He suspected that there were ghosts there.

He fell seriously ill before returning. He shivered all over and his teeth chattered. He figured he had come in contact with a ghost.

He clenched his teeth and climbed up on White Neck's back, but he didn't have enough strength to steady himself there. Before White Neck took two steps, Old Guiju fell to the ground. He knew he wouldn't make it home. He struggled to climb to the base of a cliff. He felt cold and wanted to hide there to avoid the wind. But unexpectedly, as he took shelter there, he passed out.

Around midnight he vaguely heard a cow bellowing. As he opened his eyes, he saw White Neck bounding toward him. Following White Neck was a group of men with torches.

Later, Old Guiju heard that if White Neck had not led the other animals back to the village and begun bellowing, no one would have known that Old Guiju had not returned. People also said that if White Neck hadn't led them to West River, Old Guiju would have frozen to death beneath the cliff.

One time, Grunt took White Neck out to spread manure. When he returned that evening, one of White Neck's hind legs was lame from a beating by Grunt. At midnight, Old Guiju had massaged the lame leg with alcohol. As he rubbed the lame leg, he said, "We're beasts. When someone tells us to come, we come; if they tell us to do something, we do it. Otherwise we suffer."

White Neck stopped chewing its cud and sighed. Old Guiju said, "That's fate. Everything is predetermined. That's the reason why no one would want to come back as a beast in their next life." White Neck sighed again. Of Old Guiju's nine animals, only White Neck could sigh. He often sighed.

Old Guiju also heaved a long sigh.

I wonder how those fuckers are castrating him, thought Old Guiju.

Seeing that White Neck was tired of kicking, had stopped struggling, and was panting, Wen Bao said, "That should do it." Grunt said, "Not quite." He took up a corn stalk and began beating White Neck's belly. White Neck wanted to catch his breath but didn't get a chance, and began kicking wildly again. When White Neck grew tired of kicking, Grunt passed the corn stalk to Wen Bao, who beat him again. After Wen Bao beat him, it was Zits Wu's turn, then it was Leng Er's turn. And so the four unmarried men tormented White Neck until he could scarcely move. He no longer moved when struck with the corn stalk; he merely snorted.

Grunt had Zits Wu tie his four hooves together and then bind them again to a wooden pole. He ordered Leng Er and Wen Bao to hold either end of the pole. He then called to the kids watching the excitement. A few of the braver ones approached. He had them get on top of White Neck to hold him down.

Seeing that there was no more fight left in White Neck, the unmarried men felt they were quite capable and skillful. They were also very happy and felt that they had got even.

Little Dog sat on White Neck's neck; Big Dog sat on his shoulders. They laughed and found it amusing. Later, the two of them pulled with all their might on the strip of red cloth around his neck, trying to get the brass bell.

White Neck closed his eyes. He felt like crying but didn't. He had no idea what he had done wrong. When he plowed, he pulled the plow with all he had; when he plowed, he never slacked; when he had something to do, he spared no energy. But why were these people punishing him so cruelly? Why? He had no idea where his master had gone and why he didn't come and take charge and chase them away. Why? Why?

⁓

Old Guiju took a wormwood cord from his back. He took off his felt hat and removed a half box of matches. Turning his back to the wind, he lit the wormwood cord. Whenever Old Guiju was upset about something, he would light a wormwood cord, regardless of whether it was night or day, or if there were any mosquitoes around or not. Smelling the aroma of the wormwood, he felt more at ease, dispelling his troubles and thinking about something else.

"The calf goes down to the river to drink, I kiss my girl on the lips." Old Guiju recalled the beggar's song the young man had sung a while ago.

Too aggressive, my ass. It's you, you fucker, who ought to be castrated to make you less aggressive, thought Old Guiju.

With this thought, Old Guiju's heart gave a thump. Old Guiju thought of his White Neck again. At night, when Old Guiju drove the animals home, the Accountant had stopped them at the entrance to the village. The Accountant said, "Everyone is saying that White Neck is not behaving these days, and doesn't work as it should. The animal has become too aggressive." Seeing that Old Guiju remained silent, the Accountant continued, "People say that if it is castrated, it won't be so aggressive. It'll behave."

Old Guiju said, "Is it really necessary?"

The Accountant replied, "Yes. Why doesn't it behave and do its work? Any animal that doesn't behave will be castrated."

Old Guiju said, "He's old enough to breed; why not get him a cow from another village?"

The Accountant explained, "The brigade keeps it for work, not for its own pleasure. It'll be castrated tomorrow."

Old Guiju replied, "Then I'll take him to the veterinary clinic at the commune tomorrow."

The Accountant said, "That foreign way isn't good for anything. We'll do it ourselves, the old way."

Old Guiju said, "But, but, that will hurt."

The Accountant said, "Shit, it's not you who is being castrated. What are you afraid of?"

Thinking of this, Old Guiju became furious.

"Fuck. Are those the words of a man? It's more like a beast," said Old Guiju.

"'You're not being castrated. It won't hurt you.' It hurts me. You beast," said Old Guiju.

~

Grunt's felt hat had a hole in it. He stuck his fingers in the hole rather than take it off. From under the wraps he pulled out a straight razor. He opened the razor and wiped it several times on his sleeve. Then he scraped his chin a few times.

"You do everything like an expert," said Wen Bao.

"I was testing its sharpness. It's pretty sharp," said Grunt.

Grunt squatted, placed the razor between his teeth, and with a hand moved White Neck's tail to one side and pinned it under his knee. He pulled the mass of White Neck's large scrotum out where it could be seen.

"Hold on tight, real tight!" shouted Grunt.

Leng Er put pressure on his end of the pole, as did Wen Bao on his. Zits Wu held the horns with both hands and held White Neck's head down. Seeing the razor, the kids looked away.

"Hold on tight. Ready to cut!" shouted Grunt again. As he shouted, he sliced with the razor, opening White Neck's scrotum. Immediately the blood began to pour out. White Neck jerked in pain. He tried to lift his body but couldn't.

There was a puddle of blood between White Neck's legs.

Grunt's hands were covered with blood, but he couldn't locate the testicles. They were on the point of popping out when they slipped back in again. He could almost squeeze them out, but they would shrink back. Grunt grew angry. He squatted to get some leverage with his feet. He tried to squeeze the testicles out by stepping on them.

White Neck was in so much pain that sweat seeped out of his pores, and soon his entire body was wet as if he had been standing in the rain.

"Fuck your mother. Its eyes are bulging out," said Little Dog.

"Hurry and look. Its eyes are popping out of its head," said Little Dog.

"Slap it. Slap its eyes," said Big Dog.

Obeying Big Dog, Little Dog slapped White Neck's eyes.

"Don't slap it. It's in pain, and that's making its eyes pop out," Leng Er scolded Little Dog.

Little Dog didn't dare slap him.

"Fuck your mother. I can't hold him down," said Leng Er.

"Fuck your mother. I feel sorry for White Neck," said Leng Er.

"You feel sorry for it. Who feels sorry for you?" Zits Wu scolded Leng Er.

"If you don't hold it, you don't get to eat any mountain oysters," Zits Wu scolded Leng Er.

Only then did Leng Er hold his tongue.

⁓

"Fuck. Are those the words of a man? More like a beast," said Old Guiju as he blew on the burning wormwood cord, cursing the Accountant.

"It doesn't hurt because I'm not being castrated. It hurts me. You beast!" said Old Guiju as he blew on the burning wormwood cord, cursing the Accountant.

Old Guju hurled the burning wormwood cord ferociously to the ground. He slowly made his way down the ridge. He walked a ways before returning to tie the hungry animals to the stunted trees. Only then did he hurry back to the village.

By the time he reached the village, the unmarried men had already left with White Neck's testicles. They went to Zits Wu's place. It had been ages since they had eaten any meat. They wanted to have a party with the more than one pound of testicles.

There was a trail of blood on the road. The drops of blood had dripped from the bull's testicles. By the light of the sun, the fresh blood shone bright. A wild dog appeared out of nowhere to lick up the blood.

The unmarried men were afraid of being gored by White Neck, so they dared not untie him. They merely shoved some ashes between his legs to stanch the flow of blood.

Steam rose off White Neck's body where he lay outside the livestock pen. The side of his body touching the ground was all muddy.

Hearing the quick pace of his master's feet and his shouts, White Neck opened his eyes. When he saw his master before him, he made an effort to raise his head and bellowed. At the same time, hot tears mixed with blood rolled from his eyes.

White Neck wept.

Seeing White Neck weep, Old Guiju also wept.

White Neck and Old Guiju were both given over to tears.

Flushing out Ground Squirrels

After getting up in the morning, the adults all went to the threshing ground to work.

Like two thieves afraid to make a sound, Big Dog and Little Dog carried a metal bucket on their shoulders. Little Dog walked in front, Big Dog behind. To avoid making any sound, Big Dog kept a firm grip on the bucket, not allowing it to sway and creak on the carrying pole. Just as they were about to turn the corner of an alley, someone hurrying from the opposite direction suddenly turned the corner, nearly running smack into Little Dog. It was their mother.

"What are you doing carrying the bucket?" their mother asked.

"We're getting water for home," said Big Dog.

"Yeah, and the sun rises in the west," said their mother.

"That's right. We're going to go fetch water," said Little Dog.

"Don't tell me—I was young once too and tricked your grandma my whole life," said their mother.

"Use your pants," said their mother.

"Use your pants to flush out ground squirrels. Now put the bucket down," their mother said.

There was nothing to do about it but put down the bucket.

"Are we still going?" asked Big Dog.

"I don't know yet," said Little Dog.

"Go on, go. Learn how to do it using your pants. Go on, go," said their mother.

The boys watched as their mother entered the courtyard, carrying the bucket. They turned and set off for West River. Big Dog walked in front, dragging the carrying pole, scraping out a track in the dirt road. Little Dog followed. Intent on breaking the track, he left one footprint after another on top of it. It looked as if someone had strung the footprints together on a string.

Big Dog suddenly came to a halt.

"It's no good," said Big Dog.

Little Dog looked at Big Dog.

"Our pants are full of holes," said Big Dog.

"Wait here," said Big Dog.

Big Dog left Little Dog and ran back to the village.

Little Dog squatted in the middle of the road, drawing people in the dirt with a twig. First he drew two naked people who slept side by side, face up, on the ground. He straightened his back and looked at the figures for a while before drawing two circles on the chest of one of them, and then in the center of each circle he added a dot. Then he straightened his back and looked at the figures again. He shook his head, smiling.

"That one's Mom," he said.

The he added something between the legs of the other figure. At first he drew it a bit long, like a pole. Later he shortened it.

"That one's Dad," he said.

He stood up and looked at them; they looked back at him. He thought his drawings were pretty good, but not as good as his brother's. His brother could draw a man on top of a woman. Uncle Grunt had taught him. He couldn't draw that, though. He could only draw a man and a woman sleeping side by side. They looked like two corpses pulled from the river lying there.

Big Dog returned as Little Dog was examining the father and mother on the ground. He had an empty metal bucket over his shoulder.

"That bucket's not from our house," said Little Dog.

"Whose house is it from?" asked Little Dog.

"Who cares whose house it comes from?" replied Big Dog.

"It'll do. Let's go," said Big Dog.

So saying, Big Dog set off ahead. Little Dog could hear the *cling-clang* of the brass bell hanging around his brother's neck with each step he took. It was the bell they had taken from White Neck's neck as it lay bound on the ground when Grunt castrated it. Fearing that

Grandpa Guiju would take the bell away from them, they had hidden it. They had only removed it from its hiding place the last two days. They took turns wearing it for a day.

The crops in the fields had all been reaped and transported to the threshing ground. The open land was barren. On the distant ridge, a man was turning up the soil. He was followed by a passel of children. They carried baskets in which they were collecting the potatoes. It was hard to tell if the man was trying to slow the ox down or make it speed up. He swore at it continuously.

"Fuck your mother," he swore.

"Fuck your mother," he swore.

Sometimes his swearing was drowned out by the shouting of the children collecting potatoes.

"Who are those kids?" asked Little Dog.

"They're not from our village; that land doesn't belong to our village," said Big Dog.

"How come we can hear what they're saying? I know if we wanted to get to where they are, it would be a long walk," said Little Dog.

"That's the way the hilly fields are," replied Big Dog.

"Let's cuss at them," said Big Dog.

"Okay! Let's do it. Hey wait, there's more of them than us," said Little Dog.

"What are you afraid of? There might be more of them, but they can't get over here without circling around several *li*," said Big Dog.

"They could throw dirt clods at you," said Little Dog.

"Oh, well, forget it, then," said Big Dog.

They looked away from the people on the ridge and set off to the west. Once again, Little Dog heard the *cling-clang* of the brass bell around Big Dog's neck with every step he took. After walking for a while, Big Dog began looking back at Little Dog, even keeping his eyes on him several times as if he wanted to make sure Little Dog was still following. Little Dog was keeping close on his tail, but he still kept looking back. Later he turned around and walked backward, keeping his eyes on Little Dog and smiling.

"Why are you walking backward?" asked Little Dog.

"What are you smiling about? Like an idiot," asked Little Dog.

"Guess what I just saw?" said Big Dog.

"Guess what I saw at Uncle Lucky Ox's house when I stole the bucket?" asked Big Dog.

"What?" asked Little Dog.

"Guess," said Big Dog.

"Tell me. What did you see?" asked Little Dog.

"You have to guess," said Big Dog.

"I can't," said Little Dog.

"Guess what I saw Mom doing with Uncle Lucky Ox?" said Big Dog.

"What was she doing?" asked Little Dog.

"Guess. You have to guess," said Big Dog.

"She was cooking for Uncle Lucky Ox. She always goes over and cooks for him," said Little Dog.

"Wrong, wrong," said Big Dog.

"Wrong? Then what?" said Little Dog.

"I'm not going . . ." Suddenly Big Dog fell backward with a clatter. Tripping over a rock, he ended up spread-eagled on his back on the ground. The bucket he was carrying over his shoulder rolled off to one side. Little Dog laughed happily.

"Fuck your mother, Little Doggy. You saw the rock but didn't say anything," said Big Dog.

"Fuck your mother to death, Little Doggy," said Big Dog.

Little Dog just kept on laughing.

Big Dog covered his face with the bucket to see if it had been damaged in the fall, by seeing if he could see any light seeping through. He looked, but saw no light.

"Fuck your mother," Big Dog swore at Little Dog. He wasn't angry; he was swearing for the fun of it. He rubbed his butt as he swore.

They saw a lot of ground squirrels along the way. Some came halfway out of their burrows to look at the two boys, but stayed ready to retreat at any moment. Others stood like rabbits on their hind legs outside their burrows, their forepaws hanging in front of them, following the two boys with their eyes to see what they were up to. Two squirrels were ready to fight on a flat space in front of their burrows. Each looked like it was ready to bite the other; they flew at each other and rolled around. Little Dog picked up a dirt clod and threw it at them. He didn't hit them, but did manage to scare the daylights out of them. They were startled at first and then scampered off as fast as they could down their burrows. The ground squirrels looked fat and well fed.

It was the right time for flushing out ground squirrels to eat. Seeing the squirrels, people who rarely had meat to eat would salivate. But the ancestors of the people of the Wen Clan Caves said that ground squirrels brought a good harvest—the more of them, the better the harvest. Those who flushed out ground squirrels and ate them would be reborn as ground squirrels in their next life. But some people had such a craving that they would sneak off, flush them out, and eat them secretly, away from the village. They were afraid to take them back to the village lest someone find out. Even less did they want that old man whose wrinkled face looked like a mountainside field that had been plowed but not harrowed and whose beard resembled the stubble on graves grazed by sheep to find out. The old man couldn't do anything worthwhile; all he could do was stick his nose in other people's business. Everyone in the Wen Clan Caves feared him; even the Accountant with his flashlight he was always shining at people was a little afraid of him.

Big Dog and Little Dog did not go down into the bed of the West River but stayed above it.

The ground squirrels all lived in dry fields alongside the edge. The walls of the river were steep and high, and it was difficult to pour water there.

The slope beyond the outlet of the river was full of ground squirrel holes. The holes, which all faced south, resembled the hoofprints of horses if one didn't look too closely. Ground squirrels were tricky critters—they spared no effort in digging useless holes with which to fool their enemies. The holes they actually used were all rubbed shiny as they came and went. Every ground squirrel had at least three burrows to live in so as to always keep their enemies confused as to which one they were actually using.

But Big Dog was even trickier than the ground squirrels. In a short time, he had flushed out five of them, all about sixteen centimeters in length. He tied them together with a hemp cord. First he tied the cord around the neck of one, then he looped the cord around its right fore-leg, then tied it to the next squirrel's neck, and so on. The cord was nei-ther too tight nor too loose. It wasn't tight enough to kill them, nor was it loose enough to allow them to escape. At first they were so afraid they wouldn't move. But once their fur had dried out and they had lost their fear somewhat, they would try to escape. But the five squirrels didn't decide on one direction, so they ended up pulling in all directions, with the result that they all struggled but could not get away.

Two girls approached, walking along the edge of West River. They looked about the same age as Little Dog, about seven or eight. They had been picking up potatoes and carried willow baskets. They had heard the wild shouts of Big Dog and Little Dog and had come to see what all the excitement was about.

Seeing the girls watching, the two boys became even more spirited. Big Dog removed the brass bell from his neck and rang it vigorously above the heads of the five squirrels. Frightened, the squirrels all tried to flee. The biggest one of the group shot into a nearby burrow, drag-ging the others behind, knocking some on their backs while banging the heads of the others against the ground. The one that had fled into the burrow only got halfway in, its hind end and tail sticking out. Its tail twitched right and left, and its hind legs clawed the ground. But the other four squirrels had dragged on it and prevented it from get-ting into the burrow.

The boys and girls all laughed loudly.

It was some time before the girl wearing shoes said, "People flush out ground squirrels to eat them. Are you flushing them out to play with?"

Big Dog replied, "You want to eat? Go get some firewood." Hearing this, the two girls set down their baskets and went off to collect some dry firewood.

Big Dog sent Little Dog down to the river to collect some clay in the bucket while he went in search of some stones to pile up to make a stove.

Dry wood was brought and the stove was constructed. But Little Dog had still not returned. He was still down in the riverbed, shouting that he couldn't lift the bucket of clay. The two girls hurried down to the riverbed to help him.

By the time they carried the bucket back, Big Dog had strangled the squirrels with the cord. The eyes of one of the squirrels bulged out and blood trickled from its mouth, blackening its yellow coat. It was the big one. When Big Dog was strangling it, it scratched him. In a rage, Big Dog applied more force and it ended up looking that way. Frightened, the two girls covered their eyes and stepped back.

Big Dog lit the fire and proceeded to cover the squirrels with the clay; they became five lumps of clay. Big Dog put the lumps of yellow clay into the fire to bake. After they turned white and then red, Big Dog removed them from the fire. The clay was hard and resonant when tapped with a stone. He cracked each one and then split them open with a tree branch. The hair and skin of the squirrels were stuck to the clay shell, exposing the white meat. They could all smell the wonderful aroma. He sprinkled salt on the meat after he removed the dry clay.

Afraid of burning his hands, Big Dog pulled out a strip of the white meat with a twig and placed it in his mouth. Exhaling repeatedly as he chewed, he said, "It's good, real good." Little Dog didn't wait for Big Dog to pronounce judgment before he dived in.

The two girls, who had busied themselves helping out, now seemed shy about joining them. The two of them stepped back and stood together, staring at the white clay shells.

"Why aren't you eating? Have some," said Little Dog.

"Eat, eat up," said Big Dog.

Only then did the two girls come over and squat.

After eating, Big Dog said to the two girls, "Let's flush out some more."

The girl wearing shoes replied, "We can't. We have to go pick up potatoes. If we don't, we'll get a beating when we get home."

Big Dog said, "Then we won't eat any if we catch them. You can take them home in place of the potatoes."

"Okay," said the girl wearing shoes.

"Okay," said the barefoot girl.

Big Dog and Little Dog were happy when the two girls said "okay," and became even more spirited. The boys carried the bucket along the bank and were followed by the girls carrying their baskets. They looked as they walked, before finally deciding on where to stop. The hoofprintlike holes in the spot were even more plentiful than in the last place.

Big Dog bent over to look at the holes, and, pointing at one, said, "I'm sure one just went in here."

"Are you sure?" asked the girl wearing shoes.

"I'm sure," replied Big Dog.

"What if there isn't one?" she asked.

"What if there is one?" he replied.

"You tell me," she said.

"Let's bet," he suggested.

"Bet what?" she asked.

"If there is, then I'll kiss you on the lips," he said.

"Well—And if there isn't?" she asked.

"If there isn't, then, then, then you can kiss me on the lips," he said.

"Well—If there isn't, I'll bite you," she said.

"Bite my lips," he said.

"Bite your ear," she countered.

"An ear it is then. You want to bet?" he asked.

"Bet!" said Little Dog.

"You're on," said the barefoot girl.

Lest the ground squirrel get away, Big Dog stood watch at the hole and told the others to go down to the river and get some water. After a while, the three returned, carrying the water and laughing.

So as not to spill any water outside the burrow, Big Dog borrowed one of the girls' trowels and enlarged the hole, shaping it like a funnel. He filled the hole with half a bucket of water. The four of them stood with their eyes glued on the hole. Bubbles broke the surface of the water without stopping. Slowly, the water drained down into the hole. When the funnel was nearly empty, Big Dog poured in some more water. Once more, the bubbles rose. Big Dog said "Soon," and they all spread their hands, ready to pounce. Soon, something rose to the surface. The moment it appeared, Big Dog grabbed it and pulled it out of the hole.

"Ha-ha-ha-ha . . ."

Little Dog and the two girls laughed.

Big Dog was not holding a ground squirrel, but rather an ugly toad. It was covered with muddy water, its legs thrashing about in the air.

Big Dog was furious. He reached back and threw the ugly toad as far as he could.

Having lost the bet, Big Dog and Little Dog offered their ears to the girls. The girl wearing shoes gently nipped Big Dog's ear. The barefoot girl bit Little Dog badly, but she didn't bite his ear. Instead she grabbed his head and bit his left cheek, leaving two rows of tooth marks. Big Dog asked Little Dog if it hurt. Rubbing his face, Little Dog laughed and said, "No, not even a little."

They continued flushing out squirrels.

They flushed out two—one big one and one little one—with the first try. The little one was no bigger than a house rat. Little Dog went after it and pinned it under his undershirt.

After they went for the fourth bucket of water, Big Dog waited for ages for them to return. Finally he shouted for them. Little Dog came up and said the two girls had fallen and broken the bucket and that it was no longer fit to carry water.

"To heck with it. It was stolen anyhow," said Big Dog.

"But we can't flush out ground squirrels now," said Little Dog.

"Sure we can. Fill your pants legs with water," said Big Dog.

"The girls don't have any holes in their pants, so use theirs," said Big Dog.

When they heard the idea, the girls at first disagreed. They said it was shameful to go around bare-assed. Then Little Dog came up with a bright idea, to which the girls agreed. The two girls would wear the two boys' pants while they used theirs, which had no holes, to carry water. Big Dog and Little Dog weren't scared to go bare-assed. They were not ashamed to run back and forth bare-assed.

They had even more fun carrying water in the pants.

Big Dog and the girl who wore shoes carried water in one pair of pants while Little Dog and the barefoot girl carried water in the other pair. The water leaked very quickly from the pants, so they had to be extra fast.

Laughing and shouting, one moment the four of them looked as if a wolf were chasing them; the next moment, with piercing shouts, they looked as if they had been stung by a scorpion. The entire West River was filled with the strange noise they made.

The captured ground squirrels ran in a circle in the leaky bucket.

Ground squirrels can only run, they can't jump. Once they were thrown into the bucket, they never thought of escape. Although they thought it was all over for them, they pressed down on one another, happy only to be on top. A big, fat one was always on top, where it smelled the rear end of one of the others.

"It wants to knock it up," said the girl wearing shoes.

"Yep," said Big Dog.

"What does 'knocking up' mean?" asked Little Dog.

"Knocking out a baby," said the barefoot girl.

"What does 'knocking out a baby' mean?" asked Little Dog.

"That means knocking out a baby," said the barefoot girl.

"What does knocking out a baby mean?" asked Little Dog.

"That means . . ." the barefoot girl looked at Little Dog.

Little Dog quickly looked away.

"Oh, you know, you know. You're just acting dumb and asking me all those questions. Aren't you ashamed? Aren't you ashamed?" said the barefoot girl. When she said "ashamed," she rubbed his face with her index finger.

Little Dog did not avoid her. He opened his mouth as if her were going to laugh, but no sound came out.

Big Dog grabbed the squirrel from the bucket and said, "Fuck your mother. I'm going to strangle you. You won't knock up anyone."

Frightened, the two girls screamed and retreated. Little Dog didn't run away. He helped his brother kill the ground squirrels one by one. All together there were eleven of them.

"What about that one of yours?" asked Big Dog.

"It's here," said Little Dog.

"Has it suffocated?" asked Big Dog.

"No," said Little Dog.

Little Dog reached into his jacket, screamed loudly, and quickly pulled his hand out. The ground squirrel was hanging from his index finger. Its teeth were sunk into his finger and it wouldn't let go. Little Dog shook his hand and cried for his mother. But the more he shook his hand, the tighter the squirrel clung to his finger. Big Dog struck it, but still it wouldn't let go.

Little Dog wailed as if he were fighting for his life. He jumped around, but nothing worked.

The barefoot girl ran over and, holding up Little Dog's hand, with one bite, *kacha,* she crushed the ground squirrel's head. Only then did it release its grip and fall to the ground.

Little Dog stopped crying at once. Big Dog and the girl wearing shoes ceased their turmoil and grew silent.

Everyone was shocked by the barefoot girl's action. Even the toads in the river bottom and the birds in the trees were silenced.

The entire West River was suddenly silent.

"Blood!"

No one knew who shouted "blood." Then the kids grew noisy again.

The skin of Little Dog's index finger had been broken by the ground squirrel, and it was dripping blood.

The barefoot girl grabbed Little Dog and ran. They returned shortly. She had taken ash from the cooking fire and used it to stanch the flow of blood.

"Does it hurt?" asked Big Dog.

"No, not even a little," replied Little Dog.

They began laughing, talking, and fooling around noisily.

The girls' pants were covered with mud. The two boys took the girls' pants down to a pool in the river bottom and washed them. After washing them, they recalled the time of day. Only then did they realize the sun was about to set behind the mountains. They knew they should be getting home.

"Can you come tomorrow?" asked Big Dog.

"Can you?" asked Little Dog.

"Okay," said the girl wearing shoes.

"Okay," said the barefoot girl.

"Take the bucket with you. We stole it. We don't want it. Besides, it's broken," said Big Dog.

The two girls started off toward the west.

They were afraid of getting the bottoms of their pants dirty, so they rolled them up to their knees, exposing four white legs.

The two of them carried the bucket that contained the squirrels.

They also carried the baskets containing the potatoes on their arms.

They talked as they walked. Big Dog and Little Dog couldn't hear what they were saying, but they could see that they were talking.

The boys also saw the large, flat, red sun beside them. Sometimes it was to the left of them, sometimes to the right, sometimes directly in front of them.

Later, they turned south and were lost from sight.

"Can't see them for the ridge. If it weren't for the ridge, we'd still be able to see them," said Little Dog.

"Let's get back," said Big Dog.

Corncob

Most households remain the same over the years without experiencing any big changes. But in the last two years, the Zhu household had changed completely in a number of exciting ways, one after another, all troublesome matters.

First, Old Zhuzhu and Young Zhu decided to share the same woman. The brothers took turns sleeping in the eastern room. You get two weeks, I get two weeks; I get two weeks, you get two weeks. There wasn't a night when the eastern room was quiet and still; Sorghum and Corncob's mom never rested nights.

Then they took the money saved up to pay for a wife before the brothers decided to share the same woman and with it built a new room behind the house. In accordance with the rules of the ancestors, the day the windows and door were hung, one person from each household was invited to their house to loosen their belts and feast on deep-fried cakes. Wen Bao hadn't had such a good meal since being released from jail, and as a result, nearly killed himself eating too much. If someone hadn't gotten him to drink urine to make him throw up, he would have died, bloated with food. Old Guiju brought the urine. Everyone had told him to go and get some urine from the animals; that of a donkey or a horse was okay, but not his own. A man's urine, lacking the right odor, was no good. Old Guiju was worried. How could a donkey or horse be expected to pee on command? But everyone said his urine was no good. What was he to do? In a panic, he suddenly thought of someone and set off to find her. She told him to step outside. He asked what was the matter, for he had seen her pee before. She still insisted that he step outside. He said okay and stepped outside. A short while later, she shouted, "Come in, here's what you wanted." He hurriedly took the urine to Wen Bao, saving his miserable life. Later everyone learned whose urine it was. They asked Wen Bao if it didn't taste better than sugar water. Wen Bao told them to go fuck themselves.

Next, Sorghum, the oldest son of the Zhu household, got a job as a miner up at the coal mine. This was another big, happy event. Everyone knew that with a job, he wouldn't have to worry about getting a woman. The whole thing was arranged by Old Zhao, the cadre who had been sent down to the countryside. After Old Zhao had Sorghum's mother go to West River and sport in the water several times, he arranged the big, happy event. Old Zhao was a good fucking guy with a damned good heart.

The last big, happy event was that the Zhu household spent 300 *yuan* to get Corncob a ghost wife.

Corncob was twenty-seven years old and the second son of Zhuzhu. When he was a month old and the time had come to choose a name for him, his mother had said that the oldest son was named Sorghum, so the youngest should be named Black Soybean: "With these two, we need never fear starving." Zhuzhu said, "Call him Corncob. Look, his little dick is sticking up and looks like a corncob." That's why they named him Corncob.

Corncob's dick really was big and hefty. At fifteen, it could hold up a plowshare. No other young man in the village could do that. Some tried in front of others, some tried in secret, but no one else could do it, only Corncob. Grunt once lost a bet to Corncob on account of this and had to pay with steamed bread of pure oat flour unmixed with sorghum. Grunt normally was not one to be taken advantage of or easily swindled, but this time it was different. When he lost to Corncob, he swore, "Fuck it. Who would have dreamed he could hold it up? Fuck it, he must be a regular Prince Donkey Balls." The unmarried men all laughed at this. They all knew about Prince Donkey Balls. He was a spirit in one of Grunt's stories. The Empress Wu Zetian slept with a different man every night; the following day, she would have him executed, complaining that he was useless. Hundreds, if not thousands, were executed. When the Jade Emperor in Heaven learned about this, he sent Prince Donkey Balls down to sleep with her. In one night, she was satisfied and never wanted or killed another man. Grunt had an endless supply of such off-color tales with which he would regale the unmarried men every night. Listening to the stories, the unmarried men couldn't sit still. They would all rub their asses on the *kang*, as if they had to take a piss and were squirming to hold it in.

To be sure, that organ of his was way beyond the ordinary. Corncob seemed to understand things early, and was different from others. At six, when his parents were doing it at night, he would suddenly strike a match to get a good look at them. For this reason, his mother avoided holding him and sent him to the western room to sleep with his uncle and brother.

At seven, he often went to the brigade's livestock pen, and he also liked to graze the animals with Old Guiju. He went because he wanted to watch the donkeys, mules, cows, and horses pee. He watched the females, not the males. When they peed, he watched how after they'd lifted their tails the pee would gush out the crack in that mound of flesh. After they peed, that mound of flesh would shake several times before the crack would slowly close and disappear, covered by their slowly lowered tails. Unable to see anything, he would have to wait until the next one peed. Corncob hated the tails. If there were no tails, his view of that fleshy area would never be blocked, allowing him a long look, which would be great.

"Uncle Guiju, Uncle Guiju, why do they have tails?" Corncob asked. Old Guiju replied, "It's for the same reason people wear pants—to cover their shame. What's more, if they didn't have tails, they would be at the mercy of the flies and mosquitoes. The itching would be unbearable. The animals have only their tails to swat the shameless flies and mosquitoes."

"Hot! Hot!"

After one of them peed, Corncob would utter an inarticulate, "Hot, hot." Old Guiju could never figure out why the boy got hot so easily.

When he got older, watching animals pee was no longer entirely satisfying; he got the itch to watch women peeing. Unable to watch outside women, he decided to watch his mom. He would watch for when his mom visited the outhouse and estimate when she had dropped her pants and squatted before he would burst in. It would all be so unexpected. At first, his mom figured that they just had to go at the same time, but after several times, she figured out what the little shit was up to. Embarrassed to say anything directly, she did her best to avoid him. She either had to sneak off to the outhouse and not let him know or wait until he went out to play before using the outhouse. Otherwise, she would have to send him out to do something, such as to the courtyard to see if he was needed to help with the stone roller for hulling grain.

When they were out laboring in the fields, Corncob knew what the women were going to do if one of them put down her hoe or sickle or left off working. But he dared not follow them the way he did his mom at home. Instead, he would glance out of the corner of his eye and see where the woman squatted at the foot of the field wall or in the field, and then wait for her to return. After a little while, he would pretend he had to go to the bathroom, leave the group of laborers, and go off to find the spot where the woman had peed. Finding it, he would be overjoyed. He would stoop down and inhale deeply above the spot on the ground made dark and wet by the woman's pee. He would recall what Grunt had said: "When there are no noodles, tofu will do; when there is no pussy, an ass will do." As far as fucking Corncob was concerned, seeing where a woman peed was the next best thing to watching her pee. Fucking Corncob really liked to see where a woman had peed; he really liked to smell a woman's pee. He really did.

Seeing the woman's footprints in the ground, Corncob imagined how she stood there with her legs apart and how she would undo her red or blue waistband and hang it around her neck. Then, after she loosened her pants, they would fall down around her knees, exposing her white ass and thighs. Then she would pee. But if Corncob wasn't in a hurry to watch her pee and wanted her to stand there longer so that he could get a good look at her, then fucking Corncob would imagine how she would lift her underwear or blouse, exposing her white belly, and rub it with her hands. After rubbing her belly, she'd rub her thighs; after rubbing her breasts, she'd rub her back; after rubbing outside, she'd rub inside; after rubbing in front, she'd rub in back. That's the way she'd rub herself. When fucking Corncob no longer felt like watching her rub herself, she'd squat and pee.

Seeing the wet footprints where the woman had done her business, fucking Corncob would imagine how she had peed—whether she had tilted her hips, thrusting out her ass and letting the stream come out from behind, or if she had squatted and her stream of pee had shot out the front. He fucking imagined all of this.

"Hot! Hot!"

At this point, Corncob would have to pronounce "Hot, hot" a few times, after which he would pull out his dick and pee over the exact same spot the woman had just used. He always hoped that the woman had squatted to relieve herself, her pee shooting out from the front, because that's the way most young women did it. Peeing in such a way left a deep, wet furrow in the soil. He could never get enough of such a furrow. He would shove his middle finger into it, slowly penetrating it like an earthworm. Then he would unfasten his own pants, squat, and pee into the furrow to make it even deeper. He really wanted to plant himself in that furrow, that would be good, that would be great.

As time went by, people realized that Corncob liked to look at where women peed and smell their urine. Every time a woman left the group, someone would say, "Go on, go with her." Some women even spoke directly to him and said, "Come along. Come with me." At such times, the skin of his face would crawl and he would blush violently.

People said that fucking Corncob actually had a sense of shame.

Corncob possessed a wicked mind, but lacked the audacity to act upon it. If a woman really had propositioned him, he wouldn't have had the guts to go with her. At night when he dreamed of doing it with women, the one woman he always dreamed about pressed beneath him was his own mother. He dared not dream of other women; if he did, it would be as a voyeur. He would never dream of them pressed beneath him like he dreamed of his mother.

The Zhu household plot was next to Blackie's. One time while Corncob was there digging potatoes, Blackie's son Danwa and his wife Pickup were picking beans. While digging potatoes, Corncob would steal glances at Pickup. He glanced and glanced until she got up and walked to the end of the field and from there down to the bend in the river and out of sight. Seeing Danwa busy picking beans, Corncob slipped off to the end of the field. The field was separated from the bend in the river by a ditch. On the river levee was a large willow tree. From there he could see Pickup, could see her very well. She was a little far off, but he could see her white ass shining in the bright light of the sun. Pickup was not peeing; she was doing something else. She squatted there for ages without standing up. He saw her lift herself a bit, stretch out her hand and feel around for a stone, but without touching the one she could see. She didn't give up; she took two steps forward while still squatting. Corncob found the sight of a white ass moving in such a fashion a lovely and novel view. As he was absorbed in watching the spectacle, someone took hold of his hair. It was Danwa. Danwa yanked his hair and sent him sprawling in the ditch.

"Animal!" said Danwa.

Corncob curled up in the ditch and dared not get up or look at Danwa. He kept his head lowered, his eyes fixed directly ahead.

"You're an animal!" said Danwa.

"You're an animal that eats grass!" said Danwa.

Corncob glanced at Danwa. He looked and immediately lowered his head without saying a word.

"Say it. Say that you're a grass-eating beast. Say it," said Danwa.

"I'm, I'm a grass-eating beast. I'm a donkey, a gray donkey," said Corncob.

"Who's a donkey, a gray donkey?" asked Danwa.

"I am. I'm a grass-eating gray donkey. I'm a grass-eating gray donkey out in the wild," said Corncob.

"Then eat! Eat some grass. Go on, eat!" said Danwa.

Without replying, Corncob reached out and grabbed a handful of grass, shoved it in his mouth, and started chewing. He chewed until green juice was running out the corners of his mouth.

"Swallow it. Why are you just chewing and not swallowing?" asked Danwa.

"Swallow it! Swallow it!"

Corncob stretched his neck and swallowed the green glob. After swallowing, he opened his mouth wide and said "ah," showing Danwa that he had swallowed it all.

"Eat some more, eat some more!" said Danwa.

"But it's bitter. Grass is bitter," said Corncob.

"Have some more. You're shaking your head? You want me to hit you with some stones?" asked Danwa.

"That's enough, that's enough," said Pickup. No one was sure how long Pickup had been there.

Only then did Danwa relent and return to the field to pick black soybeans. Corncob climbed out of the ditch, hacking and spitting, and returned to digging potatoes.

Someone said to Old Zhuzhu, "You should find a wife for Corncob."

"Ai . . ." sighed Old Zhuzhu, shaking her head.

Someone said to Old Zhuzhu's woman, "You better hurry up and find a wife for Corncob."

"Ai . . ." sighed Old Zhuzhu's woman, shaking her head.

There was nothing Corncob's mother and father could do, except sigh and shake their heads.

Corncob really wanted a woman badly. He was in a bad way, especially at night, when he approached the door of the eastern room on bare feet and listened to his mom doing it with his dad or with his uncle. He would get even more worked up. Once he even returned to the western room, mounted his pillow, and humped it.

"Hot! Hot!"

He emitted these "Hot, hots" as he humped his pillow. He woke his dad, who turned away and sighed. Corncob couldn't have cared less. His dad could sigh all he wanted; he would keep making his sounds until he came.

Corncob had learned this from Grunt, who called it "horseback riding." He said that if an unmarried guy didn't learn horseback riding, he ended up with diseased balls and would not be able to get it up, gradually becoming impotent and never being able to get it up again. A man was not considered a man if he couldn't get it up. Fearing they would lose their manhood, the unmarried men took Grunt's advice. As a result, not one of them became impotent and lost his manhood. They were all strong and healthy, and were all very much alive; they had no wish to end like Shepherd Boy hanging by West River.

The villagers all said, "Grunt, you really are the fucking savior of the unmarried men. Dogs and chickens can mate whenever they want, and the unmarried men have their way. Grunt, you really are the fucking savior of the unmarried men."

Learning horseback riding from Grunt was a way to avoid diseased balls. But a pillow is not a woman, and Corncob really wanted a woman. He was in a bad way.

Why can't all the stones on the mountain turn into women? Why can't all the poplars on the southern ridge turn into women? Why can't all the toads in West River and all the lice on the sheep in the grasslands turn into women? If there were more women, getting a wife would be easy and there would be no need to hump a pillow.

A pillow is not a woman. Fucking Corncob really wanted a woman, a fucking woman.

Every two weeks or so after his older brother Sorghum started to work as a miner, the matchmakers appeared at the door. But nothing had worked out because the family couldn't pay the bride price. Corncob knew they were there about his older brother; not one of them was there to act as matchmaker for him. Corncob knew that his older brother would sooner or later get a wife. Once they were married, she'd go to the mine with his older brother. He wouldn't get a share; he had no hopes of being like his uncle, who shared his older brother's wife.

One afternoon, Sorghum returned home, wearing a shiny new uniform issued by the mine. Corncob knew this was because his older brother was supposed to meet a prospective match the next day. While the family was eating that evening, Corncob hurled his steaming bowl to the floor with a crash, startling everyone. They all looked at him.

"I know none of you cares about me!" So saying, he ran to the western room and cried. Sorghum followed and said, "Cob, don't cry. I'm not meeting anyone tomorrow. You can meet her this time. I'm not meeting her; I'm going back to the mine to work tomorrow." Only then did Corncob stop crying.

The following day, Sorghum left his new uniform for Corncob and set off early for the mine.

Fucking Corncob scrubbed his face and neck several times, put on his brother's uniform, and sat at home waiting for the prospective match to arrive. He waited all morning, but no one showed up.

When the girl heard that the one waiting to meet her wasn't the one working at the mine, she refused to meet him. She wanted a breadwinner, not a farmer.

Corncob was angry about having wasted the whole morning itching and waiting for nothing. When he heard that the girl was still at her relative's house in the village, he walked out of the village and waited by the roadside. He waited and waited until they finally showed up. He waited until they passed for quite a distance before swearing at them.

"I fuck your damned ancestors to death!"

"May a donkey fuck you till you're hoarse!"

"Take your two pussy lips and feed them to the cats!"

The girl was accompanied by a man of about forty years of age. How he was related to the girl was unclear. He left the girl and started walking toward Corncob. Seeing how angry the man was, Corncob ran toward the fields in fright.

At home, Corncob was king. He'd fight with his family but not with anyone outside. He ran half a *li* and only stopped and panted when he saw that no one was following.

When he got home, he took off the uniform and threw it in his mother's arms.

"I want to wear a uniform of my own," he said.

"I want to be a worker too," he said.

"Did you hear what I said? I want to be a worker too," he repeated.

His mother, who was sitting on the *kang* stitching a quilt, paid him no mind. The new quilt had big red flowers and a green peacock on a pink background and golden sunflowers blossoming in terraced fields, a scene learned from Dazai. There were also power poles on a dam. The good smell of new cloth was evident. All of this angered Corncob, because he knew it had nothing to do with him. All of this was being prepared for his older brother Sorghum.

"Without a bride you're sewing this for nothing," said Corncob.

"I'll burn it up," said Corncob.

"You think it's easy to get a job as a worker?" asked his mother.

"Old Zhao is working in the Rag Bag Cave," said Corncob.

"Go and see him again," said Corncob.

"Old Zhao isn't your dad or your uncle," replied his mother.

"He's not my dad or my uncle, so why does he sleep with you?" asked Corncob.

Corncob's mother's face flushed red. She bit her lower lip and said nothing.

"You think I didn't know? In the poplar grove by West River," said Corncob.

"We can't let him sleep with you for nothing. If you don't go see him, I will. I'll tell him to get me a job," said Corncob.

"I'll just have to pay him a visit," said Corncob.

Corncob flung open the door and departed. His mother wanted to pursue, but by the time she had gotten off the *kang* and put her shoes on, he was long gone.

Corncob really did go to the Rag Bag Cave in search of Old Zhao and found him right away. Old Zhao was at the empty threshing ground of the village, a rolled newspaper in his hand, giving a talk to members of the commune.

Old Zhao said, "We must prepare for war and for shortages, and serve the people. We must dig deep holes to store up grain and not seek hegemony. A world war will be fought against atomic bombs, which are as small as an egg, but one such atomic bomb can completely destroy our commune. But don't be afraid, because we have guided missiles, which can turn back atomic bombs to the revisionist Soviet Union or imperialist America. All of us are heroes."

"Hope it starts soon; then I can be a soldier, and after being a soldier I can get a job like Leng Da," said Corncob.

Old Zhao's lips moved and then he said, "Seven hundred million people, seven hundred million soldiers, ten thousand miles of mountains and rivers, ten thousand miles of barracks. We will liberate Taiwan and rescue the commune members from the abyss of suffering, and let them lead a wonderful life like ours."

How poor the commune members of Taiwan are, thought Corncob.

So unfortunate living in the abyss of suffering, thought Corncob.

Old Zhao finished speaking and looked in Corncob's direction. The commune members listening to the talk also turned to look at Corncob. Corncob was a little scared. He was about to run away when Old

Zhao recognized him as the son of the beautiful woman from the Wen Clan Caves and walked over to him, smiling.

Corncob said nothing more to Old Zhao than that his mom wanted to talk with him.

Corncob's words raised Old Zhao's hopes. All the women in the Rag Bag Cave were dirty and slovenly—not a single one caught Old Zhao's eye. She was the only woman he was attracted to, this woman who was in her early forties but who looked more like a woman in her early twenties.

Old Zhao was a kindhearted person. Old Zhao knew that the Zhu household was short of money. He nearly shed a tear himself when he saw the tears plainly rolling down Corncob's mother's face.

"Don't cry. Let me think about it," Old Zhao said. "Right, that's it."

Old Zhao tore a page from his small notebook and wrote a few characters. He felt around for his personal seal, which he blew on a couple of times before pressing it to the paper. He said that he and the party secretary of the county brickyard had laid mines together during the war with Japan, and that he would be willing to help. He told her to have Corncob's dad and uncle report there too. He went on to say that temporary work had its good points—it meant a lot of work, but also a lot of money. You were paid for your suffering. If the three of them could stick it out for six months and work their hardest, they could easily earn the money for a bride.

The members of the Zhu household were left speechless by Old Zhao's kindness and didn't know what sort of meal to reciprocate with.

The whole matter infuriated the Accountant because the departure of three able workers would affect the Production Brigade in its attempt to grasp revolution and promote production. Old Zhao said, "You are full of nonsense—they are going to the county brickyard to grasp a greater revolution and promote larger production. Partial and local interests must be given up for the sake of the whole." The Accountant had nothing to say; all he could do was okay their leaving to work elsewhere.

Old Zhuzhu, Young Zhu, and Corncob departed. Kindhearted Old Zhao, worried that Corncob's mother would be afraid to be alone at home, came over from the Rag Bag Cave every day to keep her company. Many afternoons he met her at West River, that nice place, to listen to the sparrows, enjoy the cool breeze, bathe and wash her body and hair in the nice warm pool, and then return to the poplar grove to lie down, lie down, lie down. See how blue the sky is, see how white that cloud is, see how green that tree is, see the sky, cloud, tree, and me in the pupils of your eyes, and, and, and . . .

Less than twenty days after leaving the village, Corncob returned from the brickyard. He'd been dismissed because fucking Corncob was caught secretly watching the female workers pee.

There were at least two hundred woman workers at the brickyard. They lived in ten large work sheds. Corncob had never seen so many women at one time in his entire life. They were all respected and were eighteen to twenty years old. Fucking Corncob just stood there staring like an imbecile. Normally he complained that there were too few women, but here there were too many for him to take in.

Like his father and uncle, the female workers made sun-dried mud bricks. Being young and strong, Corncob carried bricks. No female workers carried bricks. As he carried bricks, he kept his eyes on the brickyard. The kiln was quite a distance from the brickyard, but from their figures, he could distinguish men and women.

In the cafeteria, Corncob always jockeyed to get in line behind a woman worker. If a woman worker cut in front of him in line, he'd act put out, but secretly would be very pleased. If he saw a woman worker coming, he'd hang back a little, leaving a little space in front of himself, and let the girl squeeze in. If she didn't notice, he'd cough a couple of times so she could see that there was a space in front of him where she could squeeze in.

People crowded chaotically around the window to buy food. Corncob would take advantage of the situation to rub his arms against the women's arms. He never dreamed of such a thing in the village. What's more, the women in the village always kept their arms covered with their sleeves as if they were a precious treasure. But the female workers here rolled their sleeves above their elbows. Some even wore short sleeves. Occasionally, when a woman worker lifted her arm, Corncob would catch a glimpse of her black armpit hair. The sight of this black hair made fucking Corncob think of another part of her body. He'd think of the way Grunt described the place: "A hairy ditch where the water runs all year round; a monk comes for a bath, and bumps it with his head and it gushes forth all over the ditch."

Corncob would also look for chances to bump against their breasts. All the female workers had two mounds of soft flesh on their chests. They all had them, some big and some small. Grunt compared the two mounds to bean jelly, but he looked at them more as grave mounds, where he wished to bury himself. If that were the case, how Corncob longed to die. He'd have no regrets.

After five or six days, he grew a little bolder. When everyone was crowded together, he bumped against one of the women workers with that thing in his pants. The woman worker let him bump away until she couldn't stand it any longer before turning around to ask him what the hard thing was. He replied, "It's, it's a flashlight." The woman worker replied, "The CDM should take it away from you." After that, he dared not bump against anyone with his crotch. He did, however, come up with something new. He would press close to the woman worker in front of him and smell her hair. He didn't care if they smelled of sweat, soap, or hair oil, they all smelled good to him. He would inhale deeply. One time, the woman worker tilted her head back suddenly and hit his nose. He cried out in pain. He thought his nose was bleeding, but when he touched it, he found it was not. But it hurt like heck and tears rolled from his eyes. One time in the cafeteria, after he'd gotten his food and was trying to squeeze through, he purposely bumped into a woman worker's breast. Although he was prepared and was carefully carrying his food, one of his steamed buns fell to the floor. The woman worker kept apologizing to him and also took out a meal ticket for him, but he repeatedly refused to take it. He picked up his steamed bread and peeled off the outer surface and ate it. He didn't peel it all that clean, but plopped it in his mouth and chewed it up, grit and all. But he didn't care; he thought it was worth it. Between the offering and refusing, he was able to touch the back of her hand and wrist. It was worth it. Besides touching his mother in his dreams, this was the first time he had actually touched a woman, a young girl. He knew she had to be a virgin. Grunt said that a woman who walked with her legs tightly together was a virgin, while one that walked with her legs slightly apart was someone's wife. This woman worker walked with her legs pressed together.

Fucking Corncob clearly remembered their fifteenth day there. The factory issued their wages and together, among themselves, they had seventy *yuan*. Happily, his father said, "We have to celebrate. Each of us should have a two-*mao* dish and an extra *mantou*." By the time they'd finished eating, it was already dark. Corncob said he was stuffed and wanted to go for a walk. He walked out from the men's sheds and sneaked off to the women's sheds instead. He lay down behind a stack of bricks to look. The windows were too high, so he couldn't see anyone, but he could see three or four clotheslines upon which the women had hung up some small things to dry. Corncob guessed that the clothes must come into direct contact with their flesh. How he wished he could be an article of such clothing. He also wished he could be one of the moths circling the light bulbs. No, not a moth. Moths are too stupid. He'd rather be a fly that could enter the sheds. He would land on one article of clothing, then fly to another one, where he would stick out his hairy tongue and lick the moisture from the clothes. It would be fragrant and sweet; it would taste so good.

Laughter floated from the sheds for the female workers. Amid the laughter, one voice was sharp, urgent and loud. Corncob figured that several girls must be tickling one of their own, forcing her to tell them what she and her sweetheart had done, where he had touched her. The tickled girl refused to say. They tickled her neck, her waist, even her thighs. Corncob also guessed that at that moment they were dressed only in their underwear, and the girl being tickled was on her back on her mattress, her naked arms and legs thrashing about. Fucking Corncob wanted to join in their fun and games. If he did, he wouldn't stop at just tickling. He'd want to strip off her little undies. Anxiously, she would plead for mercy, saying: "Brother Corncob, Brother Corncob, fun is fun, but you can't hold me down and do that." Hearing her, the other girls would laugh.

Corncob would laugh too.

"Ha-ha." Only after laughing aloud to himself did fucking Corncob come to his senses and realize that he was not part of their fun and games, but rather hiding behind a pile of bricks like a thief listening to them. That whole scene was nothing but a product of his imagination.

The sound of splashing water drifted from the female workers' shed. As he was trying to guess what they were washing, a woman worker pushed open the door with her back, carrying a basin of water. *Hua*, she flung the water from the doorway. Water droplets were picked up and carried by the wind. Corncob thought the water had a delectable aroma. It smelled like women. At that moment, Corncob thought of another smell. Fucking Corncob recalled the smell of women's urine. It had been a long time since he had smelled it; he missed the smell.

Corncob had noticed that none of the women took a damned piss in the open; they all had to take care of business in a thing called a women's toilet. He had long since noticed this. He grew anxious because he had no reason to go near the place. He hated that thing called a women's toilet. He also hated the fact that it wasn't linked to the men's toilet. One was by the east wall of the brickyard, one by the west wall, a distance of no less than half a *li*.

Later, Corncob came up with a good solution.

It was on a morning when the kilns had not been fired. Corncob and several other guys jumped the factory wall to go out to the fields and steal some turnips. They returned walking along the wall, planning to enter through the factory gate. They ate the turnips as they walked. While they were walking, Corncob saw and realized that the night-soil pit was actually located outside the wall. With one fucking look, he knew it was the women's toilet.

Water flowed from the toilet through a flume to the night-soil pit. He could also hear the women inside talking.

He took a closer look and saw that there were steps down into the night-soil pit. In the bottom of the pit was a large stone, evidently placed there by the night-soil carter.

The guys with Corncob all complained about the smell and quickly passed by. In no particular hurry, Corncob walked by and took a look, but dared not stop. As he left, he hurled the half turnip in his hand into the pit. The pit buzzed as hundreds of stink bees and thousands of flies took flight in fright.

He had a sudden inspiration. A good fucking idea came to him.

He spent the next few days planning what he was going to do. Finally, early one morning, he sneaked down into the pit and saw what he was hoping to see. The damned thing he imagined was like that of a donkey and a little like that of a sheep. But this was the real thing. He saw it, it was a woman's. He saw it, he fucking saw it.

The first time after he saw one, he fled from the pit and told himself he wouldn't do it again. The next day he saw three and said again he wouldn't do it again.

No more, no more, but he looked again.

No more, no more, but he looked again.

Then one day, as he squatted on the stone in the pit and leaned forward to look, he heard someone shout, "Beat him!" This was followed by several men jumping down from the wall. They were all dressed in faded green army fatigues. They were members of the factory's Committee of the Dictatorship of the Masses.

Fucking Corncob was trussed up tightly and taken to the Committee of the Dictatorship of the Masses office. If the party secretary of the factory hadn't shown up and said he was the nephew of an old revolutionary, he would have met with disaster. After parading him around the factory and struggling against him, they would've sent him to prison to live the good life Wen Bao had described. But he was only beaten when they dragged him back to the Committee of the Dictatorship of the Masses office.

He was dismissed and sent back to the village.

His father and uncle remained at the factory. In order to make more money, they switched from making to carrying bricks.

Corncob returned home. He said he had hurt his back. He said he had fallen while he was carrying bricks and hurt his back. He said the bruises on his face were a result of the fall and the bricks had produced the bruises on his arms. He said he would go back in a couple of days. His mother thought he was telling the truth, so she prepared good food for him. She fixed thin noodles with egg for him and gave him canned pears and apples. Old Zhao had given all these good things to his mother. Old Zhao was neither unkind nor stingy. Every time he visited Corncob's mother for something, he would bring good things. Unable to bring herself to eat them, Corncob's mother put them away. Corncob couldn't care less where it all came from. When he finished eating, he'd go to sleep in the western room. Deciding that he really must have hurt himself, his mother sent for the barefoot doctor. The barefoot doctor had his mother wash his back and then applied three medicinal plasters to his broad back. He gasped and pretended to be in pain. His mother encouraged him to bear the pain. The barefoot doctor also provided him with two kinds of medicine. He was supposed to take two of each pill with warm water after each meal. He complained that they were bitter. When his mother turned her back, he tossed the pills in the stove to cure whatever ills it had.

In a few days, he started going out.

The unmarried men stood around holding their shovels, waiting for the Brigade Leader to shout, "Commune members, to the fields, to the southern ridge to harvest flax" before setting off with him to the fields. Corncob would stoop forward and tell the unmarried men about how he had injured his back carrying bricks and that he was recuperating at home on one *yuan* in disability every day. Jealous, Leng Er snapped, "Fuck your mother. Fuck your mother."

Talking, Corncob would forget what he had said and stand up straight and begin boasting. He told them how he had joined a bunch of hell-raisers in the county town and how he had fooled around with women. He said the county Committee of the Dictatorship of the Masses was on the point of apprehending him when he returned to hide out in the village. Later, he admitted that he hadn't really hurt his back. Chou Bang slapped him unawares several times on his back, but it didn't hurt.

Then he began to elaborate upon how he had spied on the women in the toilet. The unmarried men listened to him and thought he knew what he was talking about and half believed him.

"Come on, let's go and stop a girl on the road," said Corncob. Some of the men shook their heads, some didn't, but not one said a word. He looked at Leng Er, but Leng Er quickly lowered his head and looked at the ground. He cursed them all as useless and said, "I'll go even if you don't. Watch and see if I don't dare." He then set off beyond the village.

Fucking Corncob really did go and hide among the crops and wait for a woman. He was pretty fucking clever. After passing through a village, he hid among the crops and waited until a woman came along. But he really didn't have the nerve to grab her and pin her down. He just came charging out of the field, stamped his feet by the field wall, and shouted, "Stop! Stop where you are." Frightened, the woman dropped her bag and fled. Corncob had to laugh at the way the woman had run for her life; he thought it was pretty interesting.

In the afternoon, he saw another one approaching from a distance. He didn't think shouting alone was enough. He took off his pants and waited for the woman. He waited for the woman to approach before he leaped out and stood in the middle of the road, his legs parted, and shouted, "Look!"

The woman turned and ran, screaming.

He did not pursue, but rather hid again and waited.

It was getting dark. He decided there was no point in waiting longer before putting his pants back on and returning to the village. After dinner, he went to Grunt's place. With nothing to do at night, the unmarried men would gather there for some excitement. Corncob boasted about how he'd had some fun with a couple of women that afternoon. No one believed him. He said, "If you don't believe me, come with me and see. The bag of one of the women is still there in the grass." Leng Er and Lucky Ox said they would go with him. He led them to the place, but there were already people there. They were members of the commune's Committee of the Dictatorship of the Masses, searching the ground with their flashlights. One of them was holding the bag the woman had dropped. The three of them stopped, not daring to advance.

The members of the Committee of the Dictatorship of the Masses shouted to them, asking them what they were doing. Fucking Corncob was so frightened he couldn't speak. Lucky Ox replied from a distance that they were field watchmen. The members of the Committee of the Dictatorship of the Masses asked them no more questions, but would not allow them to approach and told them to be on their way. They had no desire to go on and instead hurried back to the village.

Fucking Corncob became famous.

"Don't spread it around, or the commune Committee of the Dictatorship of the Masses will be here tomorrow for you," said Grunt.

"I'm not afraid of shit," said Corncob.

"Watch your mouth. We'll see how you fucking like it when they've tied you up," said Zits Wu.

"I'm not afraid," said Corncob.

Corncob said he wasn't afraid, but deep down he was. He would tell people to their faces that he wasn't afraid, but when they weren't around, he felt afraid. Recalling how he had been tied up and beaten at the brick factory, he broke into a sweat. He went home and wouldn't show himself outside, much less go out and frighten women.

This time, Corncob was frightened out of his wits. He knew if he was caught, it would mean jail.

Lying on the *kang*, his eyes closed, he could see the members of the Committee of the Dictatorship of the Masses enter in their faded green fatigues, carrying ropes. As someone was speaking outside the gate, he pricked up his ears and listened carefully. He wanted to hear if they were asking directions, asking if this was where Corncob lived.

Three days went by in this fashion. When he saw that nothing had happened, Corncob began to relax a bit. After four or five days more, when no one had come to arrest him, he put everything entirely behind him. Once again he was in the mood to think about women, to think about that group of women of his, one by one.

He thought of the girl at the brick factory whose chest he had bumped against. He guessed that one of the girls he had seen in the toilet had to be her, but which one? He considered each in turn and decided that she was the fourth one. He had seen the fourth one most clearly and had the best impression of her. She was the smiling one. The one he had bumped into was the one who was smiling. No, he had it wrong. The fourth one had to be the one who was tickled by the others in the female workers' shed, the one thrashing around, her arms and legs bare. She was the woman worker he had imagined saying, "Fun is fun, but you can't hold me down and do that."

Then he thought about the two women he had stopped on the road. But regardless of how much he thought about them, he couldn't remember what the two women looked like. He couldn't even remember how old they were. All he knew was that they were women, and that they had both run for their lives, screaming. He also knew that they had what he'd seen in the toilet, what Grunt described as two pieces of meat for the cat.

He thought about Golden Orchid; he thought of Silver Orchid; he thought about Wen Hai's woman who wouldn't take off her pants; he thought about Danwa's woman Pickup as she squatted and moved forward toward the stone, her bare ass showing.

Whoever he thought about, he had to do it with her. He did what Grunt had told them—he put a pillow between his legs and humped it. But in the end, he always ended up feeling that the woman under him was his mother, no one else. By the time he started making his "Hot, hot" sounds, the pillow under him had indeed become a naked woman. That woman was none other than his mother.

Three nights in a row, Corncob humped his pillow and thought about women. Every night it was the same. He felt tired when he was finished. And the pillow always went back to being a pillow and not a woman. His hand always went back to being a hand and not meat for the cat.

Fuck, all he wanted to do was try the real thing. He had seen it, but never tried it. He wanted to taste the meat for the cat and see what it was like. He had seen it, but he hadn't tried it.

Grunt said that when he was a cook in Fu Zuoyi's army, all one needed was money for a good time in a brothel. But no such good places existed any longer. Even if you had money, you couldn't buy it. Corncob had seven *yuan*, five from his brother Sorghum and two he had saved from his food money at the brick factory. In the days Grunt talked about, seven *yuan* would buy seven visits to a brothel. How great. What a luxury.

Widow San had been in a brothel on Sandao Barracks Lane in Datong City. But Widow San had died from jaundice. If she were still alive, he might be able to try his luck with the seven *yuan*, but she was dead. He also heard that Heinu didn't think her cat meat was that big a deal and would let all comers try it. And she didn't ask for money. But Heinu had died in a fire.

Who in the village was like Widow San? Who in the village was as kindhearted as Heinu? He thought about it, but no one came to mind.

Even if you had money, there was no place to spend it.

No place to spend it. Save it.

Spend it on drink.

Then fucking Corncob thought of something else Grunt had said: "Wwhen you're feeling horny, do it with a dog. When you've got money saved up, spend it on drink."

"When you're feeling horny, do it with a dog."

"When you're feeling horny, do it with a dog."

Why hadn't he thought of that before?

"When you're feeling horny, do it with a dog."

He was happy when he thought of this and was suddenly filled with energy. The people in Wen Clan Caves Village were poor and never worried about thieves. The people in Wen Clan Caves Village were poor and couldn't keep a dog. There were no dogs in the village, but there were other things.

There were no dogs in the village, but there were other things.

He set off at once for the livestock pen. Afraid that his mother might hear him open the door and ask where he was going, he slowly opened the side window and quietly slipped into the courtyard. He softly closed the side window and climbed over the western wall.

The door to the livestock pen was ajar; a beam of light cut through the darkness like a knife, cutting the dark courtyard in half.

He pushed open the door. Old Guiju was catching lice, his head pressed close to the coal-oil lamp. A wormwood cord was on the cooking platform. The room was filled with the aroma of burning wormwood.

"You still up, Uncle Guiju?" asked Corncob.

"It's you, Corncob. It's midnight," said Old Guiju.

"I went to the barefoot doctor's for some medicine. I was passing by and saw your light burning."

"I'm old. I don't sleep much."

"I'd be asleep. I like sleeping even better than eating deep-fried cakes."

"I was the same when I was young. The landlord's wife always scolded me."

"Uncle Guiju, I almost forgot to tell you that I heard the barefoot doctor say she was sick."

"Who?"

"Who else? Your landlord's wife."

"You're talking nonsense."

"I'm not kidding."

Seeing Old Guiju become anxious, Corncob was secretly happy. Old Guiju put on his jacket, buttoned it, and then picked up the burning wormwood and blew on it before setting it back on the cooking platform.

Corncob said he thought perhaps he felt lice and took off his pants, showing his bare ass. He turned the crotch of his pants inside out and under the lamp wick searched for lice. Exposed to the light and the cold, the lice burrowed into the seams and hid where Corncob could not find them.

"Sit down for a while. The place is pretty hot; I'm going out for some cool air." Old Guiju departed, leaving Corncob there.

He fucking believed me; he went to her place. He won't be back for an hour and a half, thought Corncob, shutting the door tightly.

He opened the door in the middle wall. Inside were donkeys, horses, and cows. That donkey, that horse, and that cow all had what he was looking for. That fucking good thing.

In what seemed to be a short time to Corncob, Old Guiju returned, pushing open the door. He hurriedly came out through the door in the middle wall while putting on his pants.

Old Guiju said, "You little fuck—you tricked me."

Corncob answered, "Maybe I heard wrong." He left as he finished speaking without looking back. He was limping. The donkey had kicked him in the shin, but his leg wasn't broken. He could still get over the wall into the courtyard and open the side window and climb back into his house.

He took off his pants and struck a match. The place where he had been kicked was swollen. He peeled two medicinal plasters from his back. His mother had managed with difficulty to apply them that very morning, so they were still good. As he pulled them off, he could feel the hair on his back being torn out. He hadn't wanted them originally, but now they would come in handy. He applied the plasters to the place where his leg hurt. They wouldn't stick, so he applied more pressure, but it was no good. He would just have to forget it.

He didn't sleep soundly that night.

First of all, he regretted that he hadn't prepared first. He should have taken a rope to bind the donkey's legs. That way, it couldn't kick or rear up on its hind legs. He'd wasted a lot of energy. He'd not only failed to accomplish what he'd set out to do but also nearly had his leg broken. Next time, he'd take a rope with him. Then he heard the bells of the ox ringing and the mules sneezing. He heard the horses stamping their hoofs, and then he thought he heard the door opening. Then he heard a kind of sound that was a very familiar sound, an unbearably familiar sound.

He opened his eyes. It was getting light. He could make out the red clay brushed on the walls around the *kang*, and on the ground he could see the very white, tall terra-cotta urns. The white porcelain urns looked like several naked women standing there for him.

He heard that sound once more.

He pricked up his ears. The sound was coming from the eastern room.

Had his father or uncle come home at night?

Naked, he quietly entered the main room and stood looking through a crack in the door of the eastern room. He could see the cooking platform, but not the *kang*.

He heard even more distinctly that sound with which he was so familiar.

Quietly he strode through the main room and outside, then stopped to listen by the eastern side window. There was a hole in the hemp paper in the window through which he could see the *kang*. There were two naked bodies lying together on the *kang*. Unconsciously, Corncob stood up straight and clenched his fists. Calming himself, he glued his right eye to the hole in the window for another look.

He could see his mother biting her lower lip with her upper teeth. Her bare legs were straight but spread apart, her elbows against the *kang*; she held something against herself, something like a white urn. Thrusting its big rear end, it resembled a breeding ram.

He knew it wasn't his dad or his uncle. They weren't that white or fat.

He turned and strode back into the main room. Calming himself, he threw open the door to the eastern room and stood there.

He saw that the guy on top of his mother was none other than Old Zhao, the cadre who had been sent down to the countryside.

He saw Old Zhao, the cadre sent down to the countryside, on top of his mother.

Old Zhao was momentarily stunned. Then he quickly knelt to one side and began kowtowing to Corncob.

"Good brother, good brother, good brother . . ." Old Zhao repeated as he kowtowed.

Corncob stood there dumbly without uttering a word. Corncob's mother quickly gathered up Old Zhao's clothes and threw them over him, saying, "You had better leave."

Old Zhao only then came to his senses, stopped kowtowing and saying "good brother," and clutching his clothes, ran away.

Corncob continued to stand there dumbly.

Corncob's mother pulled the blanket to herself and covered her nakedness with it. But she was too late.

Corncob grabbed her, pulled her toward himself, and pinned her down. He was on top on her in a flash.

"Ow," said Corncob's mother, and never uttered another sound. She didn't struggle, scream, or beg for mercy. She simply bit her lower lip with her teeth. She just let Corncob coldly thrust that hard thing between her legs, let her shoulders be held tightly in his strong arms, and let him flail away madly on top of her. She didn't struggle, scream, or beg for mercy. All she did was close her eyes and bite her lip.

Corncob also kept his eyes tightly shut, imagining the woman under him as a whole series of different women. After he'd moaned "Hot, hot" loudly several times, Corncob's mind became clear, and then he realized who it was beneath him. Who it was, who . . .

Corncob climbed off and knelt to one side. The thing between his legs, overbearing at first, throbbed and then began to soften and wilt.

Corncob's mother lay there as if paralyzed, without moving.

Stunned, Corncob couldn't say anything for a while.

"Mom, I didn't mean to do it," he said.

"Mom, I didn't mean to do it. I really didn't," he said.

"Mom, I didn't. Mom, I didn't," he said.

His mother continued to lie there as if paralyzed.

"Oh, Mom, Mom! Oh, oh . . ."

Corncob wept. Corncob hunched over on the *kang* and wept.

"Get out," Corncob's mother said.

"Get out," she said.

Only then did Corncob get off the *kang* and leave.

The whole day, Corncob lay in the western room without moving. He didn't eat or drink, but he didn't feel hungry or thirsty.

After nightfall, he realized he hadn't seen his mother all day. She hadn't come as she always did to ask if he was better and if he had taken his medicine. She hadn't come as usual to ask him what he wanted to eat. He got up and went to the eastern room.

The room was dark. There was a shadow atop the *kang*. He dashed toward the shadow, calling to his mom twice. Hearing no response, he reached out and touched the shadow, only to discover that it wasn't his mother. It was just a blanket. His mother had gotten up and not folded the blanket.

He rushed over to the cooking platform and felt around for the matches. He struck one and saw that his mother was not in the house.

"Damn," he cried. Crying, he ran outside. The first thing he thought of was that crooked tree at West River. He ran there without stopping. His mom was not hanging there. Then he entered the poplar grove at West River. He looked among the poplar trees, but still found no sign of his mother having hanged herself.

The pool in West River was too shallow, so there was no way she could have drowned herself.

Had she thrown herself into a well? He thought about it but decided it was impossible. Wen Clan Caves Village had no tradition of people throwing themselves down wells. They all feared dirtying the well, so they hanged themselves if they wanted to die.

He returned home, struck a match, and checked both the eastern and western rooms. She wasn't back yet. Nor was she in the woodshed.

Then he suddenly thought of the brick factory. He was certain she had gone to the county brick factory to tell his father and uncle what he had done.

It would be a disaster. Other people could be reasoned with, but the two of them would show no mercy.

He had to run away, he thought.

But he needed money to run away. With no money, he would die on the road, he thought.

He knew there was some money left after they'd finished the third room. He searched the house but found nothing.

It was no good without money. A young person begging would get nothing. You could ask, but no one would give.

Then he thought of the Accountant. It had been two years since the fucking Accountant had given them their wages, saying that they owed the brigade for all the grain they'd eaten during the famine. Two years had not been enough to repay it. Everyone in the village had received rations, but some families were already being paid the wages owed them—except his family. Corncob knew why. He knew it was because his mom had not let the Accountant have his way.

"Fuck," he swore a couple of times.

Early the following morning he knocked on the Accountant's door. He knew the Accountant would not be reasonable and give him the money. He stuck a shiny cleaver in his belt. He went with no regard for the consequences.

The Accountant could see that Corncob was disturbed; he was so frightened that he immediately consented to his demands. Over the last two years, one year each work point had been worth 7 *fen*; the following year was a bit better, so each work point was worth 13 *fen*. The total for the two years was 305 *yuan*. The Accountant had originally planned to deduct a little, but seeing Corncob's mood, he didn't dare. Corncob pocketed the money and set off to the north. He was planning to run away beyond the pass.

Leaving the village, he felt there was something wrong with his shoes. He was wearing that bastard Old Zhao's shoes. Fuck, he had been in such a hurry to run that he hadn't taken his shoes. He'd seen the leather shoes and stepped into them. But Corncob had never worn leather shoes. He'd thought they would be great, but hadn't thought that they wouldn't fit right. Throwing them away and going barefoot was not an option—he had to have shoes for a long journey. Also, not having eaten for one day and one night, he was a little hungry. He recalled that there were still some crackers and canned goods at home.

He looked up at the sun and headed back. Entering the house, he decided he ought to take advantage of the light and search for the money again. He knew it was there, he just didn't know where.

He closed the door and windows and began turning everything upside down. As he was searching, he heard something. Someone was shouting and knocking on the door. He looked through a crack in the door. It was his dad. He looked again and saw his uncle and his mother standing there. His uncle had an old blanket on his back and looked like a beggar.

Unable to open the door, Old Zhuzhu thought Corncob was still asleep. He peeked through a hole in the window and saw the urns in the middle of the room, and all the junk from the white wooden trunk scattered all over the *kang*. But there was no sign of Corncob.

Old Zhuzhu struck the door with his fist. Young Zhu and his mother shouted, but no one responded from within.

"Young Zhu, break down the door and see what's going on inside," said Old Zhuzhu.

Young Zhu gave his bedroll to his sister-in-law. He stepped back and steadied himself. Just as he was about to rush the door, *zeng*, a cleaver slid through a crack in the door.

"Who dares?" said Corncob.

"I'll cut up anyone who enters," said Corncob.

The people outside were stunned. No one said a word. None of them had expected to encounter anything like this.

"Crazy fuck," said Old Zhuzhu.

"What's wrong with him?" asked Young Zhu.

Standing behind them, Corncob's mother bit her lip and remained silent.

Inside, they could hear Corncob moving the terra-cotta urns for holding grain and the porcelain ones for pickled vegetables against the door. They couldn't get in through the door. If they tried, they would upset the urns.

Hearing the commotion, the villagers came into the courtyard to see what was going on. The courtyard was half full. They suggested, "Take it easy; talk it over."

"Nephew, talk to us," said Young Zhu.

"Cob, calm down and tell us," said Old Zhuzhu.

"Fuck talking, talk," said Corncob.

"What do you want?" asked Young Zhu.

"What do I want?" said Corncob. "I want a woman."

When the people standing there watching heard this, they burst into laughter. Wen Hai's sons Big Dog and Little Dog were among the crowd. The two of them took the opportunity to raise a rake, and one followed the other saying, "Ha, ha, ha . . . a woman," "Ha, ha, ha . . . a woman." Only after someone scolded them would they be quiet.

"Fuck your ancestors. What the fuck did you do? You are making a fool of yourself," shouted Old Zhuzhu.

"I didn't fucking do anything," said Corncob.

"I made a fool of myself and I didn't. I fucked my mom but I didn't," said Corncob.

The crowd grew silent and stared at Corncob's mother.

Old Zhuzhu and Young Zhu turned and looked at her.

"I told Mom that it wasn't her I fucked. I told Mom. I thought she was a girl from the brick factory," said Corncob.

"I only did it once, no more. I didn't think she was my mom, I thought she was a girl from the brick factory," shouted Corncob.

Corncob's mother suddenly collapsed on the bedroll. Old Zhuzhu slapped her across the face, knocking her to the ground. She covered her face with both hands and wailed.

"Fuck your ancestors, fuck your ancestors," shouted Old Zhuzhu.

Old Zhuzhu was so angry that his hands shook. He swore as he circled the courtyard. The crowd followed, making way for him. Old Zhuzhu looked here and there, searching for something. Finally he wrenched a piece of blue stone from the low wall of the outhouse and dashed toward the cave. He looked as if he were going to hit someone, so everyone quickly got out of his way. He dashed toward the side window to the western room, from where Corncob's voice seemed to be coming, and raised the stone as if to hurl it. But Young Zhu blocked his way. Corncob's mother also screamed and grabbed him around his waist from behind.

"Kill me, I already gave up on living," said Corncob.

Old Zhuzhu shook off Young Zhu and Corncob's mother and sent the stone hurling through the window.

With a crash, the stone made a hole in the window as it hurtled into the house.

"Oh—" came a howl from inside.

"Cob, Cob, Cob, Cob!" Corncob's mother threw herself at the window. Standing on her toes, she looked through the hole in the window. Corncob was curled up on the *kang*, his face covered with blood. Old Zhuzhu thrust the woman away from the window, reached in, and fumbled to unlock it. Suddenly he screamed and collapsed below the window. He was clutching his hand. Young Zhu pulled his hands apart and saw that half of one of his fingers had been hacked off. First he saw the white finger bone, then blood welled and poured from the wound.

"Hurry, hurry!" shouted Corncob's mother. She just kept shouting to hurry but didn't know what to do. Young Zhu ran off to fetch the barefoot doctor. After Old Zhuzhu's wound had been bandaged, Old Zhuzhu's woman told him to look after Corncob too. The barefoot doctor dared not enter the house. He only tossed in a powder to stop bleeding and a bundle of gauze for Corncob to do it himself, but Corncob didn't want it and threw it back through the hole in the window, out into the courtyard.

"I don't want it. I don't want to bandage it," said Corncob.

Old Zhuzhu was in pain. He was covered with sweat and had turned pale. Young Zhu helped him to Caicai's place next door.

Seeing how the excitement had turned into serious trouble, the bystanders got a little scared and lost interest in watching any longer. They were also afraid that Corncob might leap through the window to hack and cut. One by one people left the Zhu courtyard and gathered at the mouths of the alley and the street, poking their heads in and watching. Some people went home and didn't come out again, afraid lest Corncob kill them.

The Accountant wrote something on a piece of paper and dispatched someone with it to the commune Committee of the Dictatorship of the Masses, saying that there were two killers at the Wen Clan Caves, one who had killed his son and one who had killed his father. He asked that they send someone quickly to handle the matter.

But no one came; they said it was family trouble and they could handle the matter themselves. "Bastards," swore the Accountant. No one knew whom he was swearing at—the Committee of the Dictatorship of the Masses, the messenger, or someone else. After swearing, the Accountant chased the pigs into the courtyard and sealed the gate with a wooden club. The Accountant knew that if Corncob tried to kill someone, he would be the first.

All was quiet in the Zhu courtyard. From far off someone's chicken was heard clucking loudly after laying an egg. Some children could also be heard playing in the distance.

Corncob's mother was pressed against the broken window, trying to see within. She couldn't see Corncob. Then she looked through a crack in the door. Corncob wasn't in the main room. Then she tried the eastern room, but he wasn't there either.

Two side windows to the eastern room had been broken ages ago. Whenever someone opened them, they fell off, so they were nailed shut. Corncob's mother figured he was in the western room. She returned to the western room windowsill and, pressing close to the hole, spoke.

"Cob, Cob. Where are you, my child? I'm talking to you," she said.

"They've all left. I'm talking to my baby," she said.

"My Cob, Cob, Cob Cob, Cob Cob!" she called.

Corncob stood up from behind the *kang*. He still held the cleaver in his right hand. His face and neck were covered with dried blood. The red blood had turned purple. His right eye was so swollen that it was scarcely visible. There was a black and blue ring around his eye and a bloody bump, wet and shiny on the brow. The wound had stopped bleeding.

"Come over, Mother will bandage you," said Corncob's mother. She held the gauze that Corncob had thrown back through the hole in the window.

Corncob shook his head. He shook his head and then heaved a sigh.

"Don't shake your head, dear. It'll only make it hurt more," said Corncob's mom.

"Cob, Cob, I didn't tell anyone about that. Why did you have to say it?" she asked.

"They came home because I told them you were very sick. They came home to see you," she said.

"Mom, Mom, Mom," cried Corncob. He pressed against the edge of the *kang* and cried. His shoulders shook as he cried. Corncob's mother stood outside, weeping. She couldn't wipe all her tears away and used the gauze she was holding.

"Cob, Cob. Don't cry, my child. The more you cry, the more your head and brow will hurt," said Corncob's mother.

Corncob cried.

"Oh, Mom," cried Corncob.

Crying, Corncob's mother reached in to unlock the window. She wanted to push the side window open. Corncob heard her and suddenly looked up.

"You can't come in," he said.

"I want to come in and bandage you. You're bleeding again," she replied.

"No, I don't want to," he said.

"You're hurt."

"It doesn't hurt. I'm not afraid of it hurting. I don't even want to live anymore."

Corncob's mom reached in again to unlock the window. Corncob leaped up on the *kang* and stood before the side window.

"Don't unlock it or I'll cut you," he said.

She still tried to unfasten the window, but it was stuck. She turned and pulled. Corncob grabbed his mother's hand with his left hand. She refused to let go of the latch. Corncob was growing desperate. He raised the cleaver and said, "I'll cut you."

"Go ahead. Mother doesn't want to live either," she said.

Corncob didn't cut her. Corncob leaned over and bit his mother on the arm. Feeling the pain, his mother pulled her arm back.

"I want to eat you. I forgot to eat you up that day," he said.

Someone approached. It was Young Zhu.

He could see his sister-in-law holding her arm. He pulled her hand and saw that the skin was broken. He wanted to bandage her arm with the bandages she was holding. She refused. When he tried to snatch them from her, Corncob's mother suddenly threw the medicine and bandages on top of the cave. She decided that she would just suffer her arm to hurt.

The standoff at Old Zhuzhu's house lasted two days and two nights. The person inside didn't come out, and those outside couldn't get in.

"He cut his dad, bit his mom, and did it with his mom too. Nothing like it has ever happened in all the generations of the Wen Clan Caves." The old man whose wrinkled face looked like a mountainside field that had been plowed but not harrowed, and whose beard resembled the stubble left on graves grazed by sheep, scolded Old Zhuzhu.

"And he won't let his parents into the house. Nothing like it has ever happened in all the generations of the Wen Clan Caves," he scolded Old Zhuzhu.

"It would be better to have no son than a son like him," he scolded Old Zhuzhu.

"It would be better not to have him," he scolded Old Zhuzhu.

"What should be done?" asked Old Zhuzhu.

"What should be done? Tie him up and starve him to death; otherwise will he yield?" he scolded Old Zhuzhu.

One morning Corncob heard someone calling his name outside the window, but it wasn't his mother. He listened again and realized it was Sorghum. He thought he was dreaming. He hadn't dreamed of women the last two days. But he had dreamed a good deal about Sorghum. Sorghum this and Sorghum that. He dreamed of Sorghum carrying him on his back and tickling the soles of his feet. He dreamed of Sorghum at New Year's and how when eating dumplings, he squeezed the filling out and gave it to him to eat. He dreamed of Sorghum getting icicles for him at the edge of the well. He dream of Sorghum this and Sorghum that, all his dreams were of Sorghum.

He thought it was a dream.

"Cob. Cob. It's me!" Sorghum called to Corncob from outside.

Corncob knew then what he heard was real.

"Brother, Brother," said Corncob, so overjoyed that he nearly wept. He pressed his lips together and was about to cry, but didn't. He jumped up on the *kang* to open the side window for Sorghum. Behind his brother he saw his mother's brother smiling at him. He had always been close to this uncle.

Half squatting, he unlatched the side window and opened it.

But fucking Corncob never expected that when he let his brother and his uncle into the house that his brother would shout "Fuck you" and throw a handful of ground hot pepper in his eyes. Before he could figure out what was happening, his mother's brother dashed up and pinned him on the *kang*. His father's brother followed immediately through the window and helped to pin him down. They pulled his arms behind his back and tied him up. They tied him tighter than the Committee of the Dictatorship of the Masses had before.

Corncob didn't struggle or shout. He knew there was no point.

He was tied to a plank and his mouth was stuffed full of donkey dung. Then he was taken to the newly excavated room.

No one was yet living in the new room. Sun-dried bricks had been used to seal the main door and windows. In order to put Corncob inside, they removed the bricks that sealed the door and put him in the room, locked the door, and then sealed the room again with the bricks.

Two nights later, the woman of the Zhu household sneaked around back with some food and water. She hadn't finished removing the bricks when Old Zhuzhu and Young Zhu showed up and dragged her away.

Ten days later, Old Zhuzhu paid Grunt and Zits Wu to wash Corncob and had them dress him in Sorghum's new uniform. This washing and dressing were traditions handed down over the generations of the Wen Clan Caves. By washing and dressing the dead, the living made sure the departed soul would not be ridiculed in the underworld. Also, when they were reborn, they would be reborn clean and not suffer. They would be born to be respected.

Later, Grunt and Zits Wu told people that fucking Corncob was still breathing. When they were washing his hand in the basin, it seemed to move in the dirty water, as if he wanted to lift water to his mouth. They said that's what he fucking wanted to do, but couldn't. He didn't have the strength to lift his arm. They also said he couldn't fucking swallow. They felt sorry for him, so they scooped the donkey dung out of his mouth and gave him a cupped handful of dirty water, but he couldn't swallow it. The water just ran out the corners of his mouth.

On the seventeenth day, there was a great deal of commotion at the Zhu household. It was a happy and auspicious day, for they had taken a ghost wife for Corncob.

Corncob's mother's brother had arranged everything for 300 *yuan* in his village. The ghost wife was a virgin girl, who, because she didn't want to marry somebody, had hanged herself from the crooked tree at West River six months earlier. On account of this, the people of Wen Clan Caves were furious and wanted to know "why someone from your village came and hanged herself on our tree; the crooked tree is ours and not yours." But it looked as if things had turned out right. The girl had died in the right place. No doubt about it.

When the girl's coffin was removed from the truck, Corncob's mother wept aloud.

Everyone told her not to cry. "Don't cry, you can't cry on such a happy and auspicious day." Only then did Corncob's mother stop crying.

Everyone said, "Corncob wanted a woman and now he has one. You should smile on such a happy day." Corncob's mother's cheeks twitched. She tried to smile, but couldn't. She almost broke into tears again. She quickly bit her lower lip.